T0146681

GRANT
ME

Em Perna

authorHOUSE®

AuthorHouse™ LLC
1663 Liberty Drive
Bloomington, IN 47403
www.authorhouse.com
Phone: 1-800-839-8640

Published by AuthorHouse 09/18/2014

ISBN: 978-1-4969-4014-8 (sc)
ISBN: 978-1-4969-4012-4 (hc)
ISBN: 978-1-4969-4013-1 (e)

Library of Congress Control Number: 2014916475

This book is dedicated to my dear friend Christie Ricke.
I couldn't have done this without you. Love you girl!

PROLOGUE

The black mask is too close to my face. At least I think it's a mask. Could be any number of things blocking my sight. But it's affecting my equilibrium, as well as my ability to breathe. I can't get air in fast enough through the fabric, causing panic to claw its way up my throat. I need to calm down. Slow breath in, slow puff out. Don't let the panic get to you. I turn my head to the left, hoping that'll allow more air to sneak in the sliver by my chin. Oh, that helped. Relaxing my shoulders I try and piece things together. Nothing so far. Blank. Empty memories. The car I'm riding in turns, and my body, that had been rocking, is almost thrown off the narrow seat. It takes all the strength I have left to keep me from tumbling off. My back settles once we've completed the turn. Where are we? And more importantly, where are we going? My body aches, like it was hit by something. What am I missing?

I can just make out the tiny bit of light at the bottom of my mask, but not enough to see what's just beyond it. Focus. Focus on that light. I try to keep my lids from closing, yet they are heavy, and itching, begging me to let them seal shut. Was I drugged? I close my eyes, and the tiny bit of light is forgotten. I will have to rely on my other senses to snap this puzzle together. My hands are tied behind me, so I run my fingers lightly over what I can find. The soft upholstery under my hands isn't sending me any clues. Just a normal seat. Whoever put me in here didn't feel I needed to use a seatbelt. Another strike against him. A memory flashes quickly through my mind. Dark hair, beautiful greenish eyes. That is all I see before the drug they'd given me is forcing me to sleep again.

EM PERNA

My arms are being pulled, and I'm dumped onto something hard. The ground? Ouch. My ankle twists shooting a pain so severe up my leg that I cry out from it. I'd always thought it was just a metaphor when they say *'seeing stars'*, but look, there they are. White, shining stars, with the black backdrop of the mask. There's a spinning motion and I'm up into the air, being carried. This can't be good. Where are we headed, and why can't I move any of my muscles? It's like I'm paralyzed. My head is hanging backward over an arm, which I'm only slightly happy about, as whoever has me, reeks of body odor. I don't want to add vomiting to my growing list of maladies. Oh, just thinking about it turns my stomach. I really wish I could switch my mind off right now. This is not helping.

I can hear heavy footsteps on the ground, echoing from below my head. The acoustics make it seem like there's a marching band walking through a hall. There is an ominous screech, right next to my freaking ear, and my ears are still buzzing as I'm unceremoniously dumped onto a chair. A really hard chair. I don't have enough cushion back there to be dumped like this, but I think I'll keep that little tidbit to myself. Since my hands are already behind me, I try to subtly rub the injured bone, but before I can move my fingers close enough, they're grabbed, arched upward over the back of the chair, and tied tight to it. Damn. This just keeps getting worse. My muscles are still not cooperating, keeping my head in its downward position.

The hood is ripped, and I mean ripped, hard from my head, taking strands of hair with it as it goes. I'm so happy I can breathe again, that I forgive the hair ripper, and take in my first breath of stale air. Yucky, moldy, wet air. But I can't be picky about it; it *is* air after all. My eyes still aren't working in the dim light, but I can make out shoes in front of me. Brown shoes. What are those? Boat shoes? They look too normal to be related to this creep. My view changes quickly, as my hair is yanked, and my head is thrown back. Ugh, vertigo. I squeeze my eyes shut to ward off the dizziness, but it's replaced with a painful force along my cheek. What. The. Hell. Did this boat-shoe lover just hit me? I don't have time to pout about it, as I'm released from the hair strangle, and my head flies forward again. All I can see are the boat shoes moving away from me. The squeaky door shuts with a final click, and I'm now alone. The footsteps fade down the hall away from me. I'm more terrified than I ever have been in my life. I'm hoping memories will begin to filter back to me, but I'm still a blank slate. Think, think, think! A dripping noise has replaced the silence, now that I have the time to listen. It's louder than my heart beat drumming in my ears. Drip, drip, drip. Water torture. Nice technique. Think. Why am I here? Who has me? Another fleeting vision filters in quickly and is gone again. But this time, I can't hear the dripping anymore, only my heart breaking the rest of the way. Why? Why did he do this to me?

CHAPTER 1

A MONTH BEFORE…

You could never refer to me as your average woman. For starters, I'm what you would call short. Not average. Or below average. Short. I'm 5 feet. Ok…I lied. I'm almost 5 feet, on a good day…in shoes. But for the sake of my ego, I'm going with 5 feet. And as you can imagine, the word *small* could describe pretty much everything about me. *Small* hands, *small* feet, *small* nose, *small* ears, and of course, yup, *small* breasts. Well, smallish. Thankfully I was granted with enough jiggle to make me feel just this side of feminine, and not quite so boyish. My long hair, which I like to refer to as one of my best features, is so blonde it's almost white, and when left out of its tie, rests on my lower back, curling at the ends. Most days, it feels as though a cloud follows me around. Eeyore, I feel your pain. You would think my eyes would pop with my pale skin and white hair but, alas, they are almost as colorless. I've heard them described as 'frosted' or 'icy', neither of which I find very flattering. I'd much rather they stick to one of the multiple choices there are in the good old crayon box. Mind you, I've been told they turn a shade darker with my bevy of moods, so there is that. I've spent too much time dreaming of what my parents may have looked like to give me my unusual coloring. Would they have the same fair skin that hates the sun but loves collecting freckles? Who would I have favored? My mother? Or my father? As I've never met my parents, I guess I'll never know. I gave up that dream a long time ago. I was found when I was just a few weeks old, on the back steps of a church, in a small town in northern Florida. Supposedly, I was so tiny they didn't think

I would make it past the first week. That was my first test for survival, but wouldn't be my last.

Once I was out on my own, I continued to add to my uncommon looks. I know, I know. Why add? But I figure if people are going to stare, let me give them something to look at that's beautiful. First on my list was to add some freaking color to my clean slate. Both my arms are covered with intricate tattoos of things I have loved over the years. On my left arm, I have a unicorn, starting from the top of my shoulder, wrapping around my bicep, ending just above my elbow in blue and green. It's beautiful, and was my first art done when I was barely 18. The three mermaids on my lower arm are my favorite as of yet, looking almost cartoon enough, they resemble some of my favorite anime characters, but not too much, with scales favoring that of a koi fish. They start where the hooves of my black-horned stallion end and are a multitude of reds, oranges, yellows and blues. Yes, color. Color, color, and more color. Their large eyes tell their story, and are exactly what I would have pictured a band of mermaids to look like. If they were real, that is. And I still hold onto a small hope that they are, and they just haven't been discovered yet. On my right arm, I have words written from wrist to shoulder. Some twirling around my arm like angry tornadoes, others interspersed sporadically, and one verse right down the center of my inner forearm. Each with a different meaning, each equally important. And if that weren't enough, my nose is pierced with a tiny diamond that's only visible when the light hits it the right way, and both my nipples have short barbells running through them. Those are my pride and joy, but I'm sad to say, it's been too long since anyone but myself has played with them. Sad fact that.

Today, I'm wishing I had a little more height to my body, as my short toned legs work over time to book it down the back streets of North Miami, while heading home. My hair, braided due to the heat, feels heavy against my back as I continue to take quick peeks over my shoulder every few steps, making sure I'm not being followed. I hate paranoia. You know that feeling? The one that has the hair on your arms standing on end, and your inner warning bells clanging together? Yes, that's the one. I've felt eyes on me since I left, causing me to almost run home.

I turn a corner and lean against the hot concrete building to catch my breath. Breathe, girly. I need to calm down or I'll be giving myself a stroke. I take air in slowly though my nose, slowly out my mouth; my breathing technique uses all of my concentration. Passing out would not be beneficial right now. Willing myself to slow down, I pull my cheap phone from my back pocket and check it for the millionth time. No missed calls or text messages. Phew. Settling my shoulders against the wall for a quick reprieve, I send up a quick prayer that everything is ok, and that all of this is just an overreaction. Wouldn't be the first time, but why am I having this ominous feeling of doom? The traffic is still pretty heavy so my sense of hearing won't help, but that doesn't stop me from holding my breath, to listen to the sounds around me. Leaning forward, I pull my sneaker-clad foot behind me, stretching the tired muscles in my leg, and look up. The sky has already turned to a dark purplish-blue, with the descending sun, making me squint against the streetlights coming to life. I need to get home.

Today has been a long day, with our unscheduled shipment of books, causing me to take this journey at a later time than usual. I glance around one more time at my surroundings, scanning up and down the road, searching for the cause of my distress. Boogieman maybe? Aliens? I've always loved the fact that I have a pretty active imagination, but tonight, I wish I could turn it off from creating nightmares out of every shadow. Shaking out my arms, like I'm preparing for a zombie apocalypse, I make myself walk, not run, down the familiar path.

Using the concrete sidewalk to guide me home, I notice I can just make out the lights to our lot, about fifty yards ahead. Small comfort, but I hold tight to it, and trek on, keeping my vision zeroed in on our home. Usually my walks from work are pretty dull. I work only 2 blocks from our apartment, but tonight this feels infinitely longer.

As I hustle up the barely lit stairs, to the second floor, I make myself look back at the approaching night one last time. The parking lot looks exactly like it always has, with its cracks and craters interspersed throughout. The walkways connecting each section make it appear like a life-size game of shoots and ladders, causing my fellow neighbors to park around the obstacles. I cast a look out at my car, parked under the street lamp and silently promise to bathe her tomorrow. Even in the dim lighting she looks more brown then red. Maybe I'll get lucky and it'll rain overnight. Everything else looks just as it should be I suppose. With an internal shrug of my shoulders, I turn to head inside, when something just past my vehicle catches my eye. My head turns back so fast, that my thick braid smacks the side of my face, landing hard against my breast. It's hard to see, but it looks as if there is a man standing just out of range of the overhead light. If not a man, then that is one *big* woman. He/she has a baseball hat covering their head and dark clothing to help blend into the darkness beyond my car. I contemplate running back down and asking what the hell he/she wants, but think better of it as I take in their size once more. Walking slowly backward up the rest of the stairs, I keep my eyes focused on that spot, and swear I see the whites of their eyes in the distance. It's not unusual for people to be out at this time, so why does this feel so different? The form just stands there unmoving. Goose bumps rise so fast, that I can actually feel the hair growing on top of my head, forcing my hands to reach up and soothe the feeling away. My eyes close with a quick blink and he's gone. What? Who was that? Shaking my head as if to clear it of those thoughts, I curse my creative imagination and head inside.

CHAPTER 2

As I barge through the flimsy door I hear Shelly's loud voice from the living room. "Neva! Come see this."

Yup, that's my name. Perfectly suits my other odd attributes doesn't it? My very first foster family gave me the name for my lack of color, pretty much screwing me out of the chance of ever finding my name on key-chains or those cute license plates, for life. I've just thrown my purse on the entry table, and walked a few steps past our entry, when I see my best friend, holding a piece of paper in the air, while my handsome ten-year old son gives her a look only a preteen boy can pull off to perfection. You know the one that screams embarrassment with a hint of pride thrown in? I walk over to stand next to Shelly and have to look way up to the paper she's waving over her head. "Shell…down here please. How am I supposed to see it?"

"Oh, sorry. I'm just so freakin' proud of him." She moves the paper down closer to my level and practically yells. "He drew this one in like 15 minutes! Isn't it fantastic? It's even better than his last one." Looking back over at Drew, she includes him. "I am so jealous, Drew, seriously. My stick figures look horrible in comparison."

I already know how talented my Drew is, but every time I see one of his drawings, it still takes my breath away. "Oh Drew…this one has to be one of my favorites." I'm not ashamed to admit, my voice shakes just a little. The sheet of loose paper has a medieval dragon drawn in the center, about the size of my hand, with a Celtic cross held in its claw. The fire from his nose curls around the whole dragon, like it's being consumed, and he's shaded in the head to give it a life-like appearance. It's truly fantastic.

He sighs next to me. "Yea, mom. You say that with all of them."

I look back at him, and notice the light blush on each cheekbone. "I'm putting this on the fridge next to the others." As I walk to our small, tidy kitchen, I call over my shoulder, "and I can hear you rolling your eyes at me. But that's just fine and dandy, I love you anyways." Walking back over, I can see he knows what's coming. After kissing his forehead, which is right at my level, I hug him and continue "and for always, bud."

I catch the smile curling one corner of his lips, but I know he'd never admit to it, so I pretend not to see. Shelly comes over to us, hugging from behind, and with her long arms she has no problem getting us both in the hug fest. She waits to comment until we've finished. "I think this piece would look fantastic on your back. But make sure it's closer to your left side so the dragon makes friends with your unicorn and the naked chicks on your arm." She smiles like this is her best idea yet. And I have to say I agree with her.

"I'm on it." I turn to look into the same color eyes as my own. "From now on you are drawing all my art buddy. Now, it's time for you to get to bed. Shell texted me that you finished your homework on the bus, so I'll check it in a few, but tomorrow will come early, and I want you on your A-game for school, so it's nighty-night time for you."

He nods like he expected this. "K. Goodnight mom, night Aunt Shell. I'll see ya in the morning." The last of this was said mid yawn. He leans over slightly to give me a hug. Then turns and hugs Shell, before walking down the hall to his room.

Shelly and I watch him go. Poor kid looks pooped. "That kid is going to be a tall one. He's already taller than you are. I swear he grew two inches over night." She has mischief in her eyes as she continues, "although it's not like being taller than you is hard."

I give her the stink eye, and turn to walk back into the kitchen, while reminding her how cute the nail polish on my middle finger is. "Ha ha. Is that the best you can do? And I'm glad he will have his father's height, God rest his soul, and not mine. In fact I see a lot of Jeremy in him, as he gets older."

Opening our fridge, I fish out the open bottle of California's finest pink wine from the back, then grab the only two wine glasses we own from the cabinet beside me. Removing the cork from it's neck, I fill the two glasses half way for each of us, and throw the empty bottle away, reminding myself to add more wine to my growing shopping list. Taking them over to the couch, I hand Shell her glass first, set mine on the coffee table, and fall back into the cushions with a sigh. With my eyes closed I begin my questions. "So? How was he today? Did he say anything at all? Your one and only text today didn't offer much, and I've been a nervous wreck since then. And before you even attempt asking me if I met any hot men at the bookstore, I am just going to beat you to the punch and say no. Focus, please, and take me out of this misery." I'm dangerously close to pouting.

I watch as she grabs the thick blanket from our couch, and wraps it around her. "You are such a spoilsport." Looking up at the ceiling, she thinks for a second. "Ok fine. I might have asked that a few times. But a girl can hope for her best friend, can't she?"

I don't bother answering. Instead I reach over for my wine and take a sip, while simultaneously removing the sneakers from my tired feet. I realize she'd been quiet while I got comfortable, so I prompt her with a 'move it along' hand gesture. Shelly has been my closest friend since I've been 15-years-old, so I know she'll give it to me straight. She pulls her shoulder length, light brown hair into a low ponytail with the band from her wrist and tucks her long legs onto the couch beside her. She's killing me here. With a serious cast entering her caramel colored eyes, she opens her mouth to lay it out for me, keeping her voice low enough so it's contained to our living room, and not echoed down the hall. "Everything went fine. He was quiet when he got off the bus. But I don't think anyone gave him too hard a time today at school." When I only look at her, she forges ahead. "No really, he smiled when he got off, so I think maybe he made some friends? I stayed far enough back so as not to embarrass him, but I don't think I needed to worry about doing that."

This week, unfortunately, my work schedule has me getting home too late to witness for myself, his new bus situation. It's hard not being there for him as often as I'd like, but if I can't be, I'm content knowing he has Shell in his corner.

My son was diagnosed with ADHD when he started kindergarten. This made learning an extra challenge for him, and kids aren't always the nicest creatures. Our first clue something may be affecting him, was when he was only two years old. We'd noticed certain ticks he seemed to do subconsciously. It began with scratching his fingers, hard enough to bleed, and escalated to licking his hands so much they stayed chapped all day long. The kids in his school didn't understand he couldn't control these urges, and a few kids acted out against him. This is his third school since the first grade because of being bullied. Sure, it started out small. But even small teasing can cause harm to someone that has a hard time fitting in. That year had been our hardest, as I lost my husband, Drew's father, to a random mugging. Maybe his learning disability wouldn't have been such a trial if we weren't mourning his loss. But I'm a true believer everything happens for a reason. Maybe it was to make us stronger people, or maybe it was to bring Shell and I closer together. I might never know the answer to that. It seems you always find who is closest to you during the hardest times, and Shell, being the sister I always considered her to be, stepped right in and kept me from losing the last dregs of my sanity. Plus, I think diverting her attention from her own struggles made it mutually beneficial. Drew's the only person who can truly get Shelly out of her dark thoughts sometimes. Lord knows I try.

"Ok, that's all I can ask for now." I look at my now empty glass and debate if I've had enough. Laying my head back, I look around at our modest apartment. The three-bedroom apartment isn't huge by most standards, but we've made it a home. Even with all our second-hand furniture, and the cream colored walls that we painted on a late night with too much wine, isn't too shabby. The only piece I'd kept from the home we had with Jeremy was our bed. I just couldn't seem to part with it. It's an oak, four-poster, monster of a bed that Goliath could sleep in comfortably, so it takes up three quarters of my room. But I love it too much to part with it. Everything else was just furniture. And if I looked too deeply, I think I sold the rest of the stuff for a new start, plus after losing our main source of income that extra cash was needed. The rental isn't much, but it's ours, and with Shelly sharing the expenses it makes things that much better. Besides, we have each other to come home to and the end of the day.

"Ok," I sigh. I seem to be doing a lot of that tonight. "I'm heading to bed. I'm running errands tomorrow before my shift at the club. Is there anything I can get for you while I'm out? I need to be at A.L. by 7, so I should be done with it all well before Drew gets home."

On the weekdays I work either the morning or afternoon shift at a used bookstore selling all kinds of books, with a full record store in back. Yes, they still sell those. It's owned by a friend of ours, who offered me the job, a month after we lost Jeremy. It doesn't rake in the cash, but it certainly helps with the bills and paying for Drew's medication, since we aren't exactly insured. The Book Club, as it's referred to, has a retro feel to it, and I enjoy working in there. Friday and Saturday nights I work as a bartender, at a night club called 'After Life', till three in the morning. It isn't what I envisioned myself doing with my life at thirty years old, but you do what you have to do. I'm very thankful for Shell, and her willingness to help me out. Her work schedule, as a medical secretary, allows for me to work those afternoon and nights, while knowing Drew is being be looked after by someone I trust.

"No, I'm good for now," she replies. "Although more wine wouldn't hurt. Hey…maybe there will be a hot guy at the club tomorrow night. Fingers crossed for ya."

I give her my best death-stare, which I'm sure she's seen many times before, but it just rolls right off her. As I watch her get up from the couch, I can't help but admire my best friend for her strength, with all the crap she's been put through. She's amazing and I love her so much. You'd never guess by looking at her, all the drama she's been forced to endure. Always first to smile, and last to cry, she gives one hundred percent of herself to those she calls family. We are lucky to have her in our lives. She has one of the biggest hearts of anyone I know, and I realize her wish for me and Drew is to be happy again. She has mentioned on more than one occasion, her hope for me to experience the love I was fortunate to find at such a young age, once more. I'm not as optimistic as she is, when it comes to my love life. And if anyone deserves a happily ever after, it's her. I just wish she felt the same about herself, but for reasons of her past, she chooses to keep things casual with the men she sleeps with, and steers clear of anything long term. One of these days, though, someone is going to sweep her off her feet, and I am going to grab my popcorn and pom poms and enjoy the show. I open my mouth, preparing to say just that, but quickly shut it again before I get myself in trouble by resurrecting that old argument. Instead, I grasp both glasses from our table and head back into the kitchen, leaving her to take care of turning off the lights. After saying goodnight a final time, I check in on a sleeping Drew, and fall heavily into bed. Just as my eyes close with the heaviness of sleep, I remember I never mentioned my crazy walk home. Tomorrow, I promise myself.

CHAPTER 3

The alarm clock had to have been invented by a seriously sadistic human being. The screeching, and honking sounds like car horns on my nightstand. I feel like my eyelids had just closed shut, when the incessant beeping startles me awake. I finally locate the sadistic device, and hit my snooze button for fifteen more minutes of quiet. Lying in bed, with my eyes closed, I listen as Shelly and Drew chat over breakfast in our kitchen. Their bond is special, but I know it must be tough on him not having his father with us anymore. He's never outright said anything, even as a small child after the incident, but how could he not? They were the best of buddies, those short years in his early life. It's times like these that I miss my husband the most. Five years seems so long and yet so short at the same time. How is it possible that that much time has passed already? Rubbing my face, to clear the depressing thoughts, I take in one deep breath and let it go slowly back out through my mouth. I need to break myself out of this funk, so force my body to sit up, and swing my legs out from the warmth of my comforter. It's a struggle, but I get there. Looking down at the piles of clothes on my floor, I face the fact that the room could use a good cleaning. I scrunch my face at the thought. Ugh. I hate to clean. Tomorrow. Procrastination is my key. Finding my hot pink robe that'd been discarded on the floor next to the bed, I throw it over my tank top and underwear and follow my nose to the coffee.

***

After one best friend is caffeinated and headed to work, and one sleepy boy sent off to school, I shower and begin to get ready for my day. My fair complexion has never required any foundation, so my makeup routine is usually the fastest part of getting dressed. Mascara complete, hair braided, I shimmy into my favorite pair of soft jeans, with holes in both the knees, and attach my black braided Lucky belt at my waist. Before grabbing my bra from the drawer, I make sure to tighten the ball on each end of the short barbells though my nipples. Looking down at my right piercing, I make sure it's on extra tight, while checking to see that the gem on the end still shines and sparkles. I love this jewel. It was the last gift Jeremy gave me before he was killed. At the time he gave it to me, the jewel had been set into a gold ring. But a year after he was gone, I had my piercer make it into something I could wear every day. I never wear rings, or even a watch, as I can't stand the feel of anything encompassing my wrists or hands. Not even my wedding ring, which was a sore subject while I was married. That's why I find it so strange that he would buy me something I wouldn't ever wear. I never got the chance to ask him why, as he was taken from us a day later. I look down once more at the blue and white jewel, pat my B boobs for luck, and finish getting dressed with a black tank, which I tuck into the front of my jeans to show off the silver buckle. I find my black ballet flats and slip them onto my feet, then finish off with a light coat of pink lip-gloss and I'm ready for the day.

Ten minutes later I have coffee mug in hand as I head down to my car. Today looks to be another hot one, as the steam ripples above the black asphalt, even as early as it is. Fingers and toes crossed there'll be a good rumble or two later today. My favorite part of living down south is the afternoon thunderstorms. One minute the air is so hot you can taste the humidity, the next you are greeted with my favorite sound. I get such a thrill watching the lightning flash and counting the seconds till the heavy boom that follows. As I pull the hair off my sweaty neck, I look up at the clouds and give it 3 hours, or so, for the show to begin. With luck I should be done with my shopping before the skies open up and I can enjoy it from our porch. Climbing into my 2008 red Honda Civic, I immediately roll the windows down to get the hot air out, turn the key, and smile at my radio. *Alice in Chains* is singing about 'feelin' so small and losin' his soul.' Yup. Today is starting to look to be a good one.

The grocery store is a mad house today. The blistering heat must be sending everyone indoors, and it feels like my corner store is the best place to be. As I stand staring at the hair color selections, I can't help but wish I'd been born a redhead. Or maybe a dark brunette. Shoot, any color would really do to keep my skin from looking so pale. I do this once a month and still I've never colored my hair. But I always dream one day I'll have the guts to try something different. As I put the black hair color box back on the shelf, I feel the hair on the back of my neck rise up. Reaching up, to rub away the goose bumps, I shift slightly to my left and look down the crowded row in search of the cause. Everyone seems to be zoned out in their shopping, but I make another sweep through the mass of busy customers just to make sure. I've never had this persistent sensation of being watched before, and my nerves are on the proverbial knifes edge because of it. Turning my concentration back to my task, I grab the requested bottle of wine, finish grabbing the rest of my goodies, and head to the front of the store. Forty-five dollars and change later, I'm back into the muggy Florida sun once again. Juggling the two full bags on one arm, I'm looking through my cluttered purse in search of my keys when I slam into a wall. Oomph. As I land hard on my backside, the bags and purse fly out of my arms, scattering around me. I look up and blind myself, by looking directly at the bright globe in the sky from my seated position. Seriously, what in *the* hell was that? The seat of my jeans has started to catch fire from the hot ground, but I try to get my bearings before jumping up and beating the nearby wall with my purse. After assessing that yes, I was indeed on the ground in the parking lot, I look up again, and up some more, to the reason for my fall. Nope. No not a wall, but a man. A huge man, by the look of him. So large he may as well *be* a wall. His body shifts to block the sun completely, disguising his features from my vantage point down on the hot asphalt. I watch him bend down to reach for one of the bags closest to his feet, and this new position places him close enough for me to catch a whiff of his cologne. My body moves without me telling it to and I take a subtle sniff to revisit the fragrance, while my brain plays make-believe. I don't know him, or even what his appearance is, but that doesn't stop the sudden urge to lick his neck, only inches from my mouth. He has the most enticing smell. It's like taking a shot of pheromones straight up the nose. The musky fragrance has me fantasizing about hot sweaty sex in the back of a steamy car. Maybe sex in a newer Ford Shelby, with red leather seats, so smooth they cause you to slide against them. Hmmm. I had no idea cologne could smell like that, or why my brain automatically went there, but evidently my imagination wants to have a little fun with his scent. He sets the bags, upright, next to my knees and stands again.

In the corner of my eye, I see a strong tan hand being held out to me, I'm assuming, to help me stand as well. I stare at that hand longer than is necessary. He has big hands, and a thick dark brown watch encompassing his wrist, which causes my own wrist to cringe in sympathy at the offensive gadget. After what feels like forever, I finally take him up on his offer and let him help me off the ground. He pulls me up so fast my head spins, and my hand squeezes his to keep from falling back down again. Vertical once again, and no longer spinning, it becomes apparent why my first thought was that I'd slammed into a wall. Taking in all that is before me, my eyes grow wide at the sight of him. Holy hotness Batman. The man before me is huge. It's not hard to feel small when you are on the bottom side of 5 feet, but this man would make anyone feel small. I'm guessing he has to be at least six and a half feet tall, but I'd definitely need a tape measure to be sure. My eyes are level with a hard stomach covered in a white dress shirt, and his grey suit jacket looks like it was specially made for those broad shoulders. The tiny buttons reflect the light as he moves, keeping my eyes from traveling north like my brain begs me to. Even though he's fully clothed there is no missing the fact that this man is built…everywhere. From his big leather shoes, up along sturdy legs fitting nicely inside grey slacks, and up to his massive arms that pull the material of his jacket. It's a nice combination. I applaud his tailor. Just looking at those arms make things south go a little tingly. Am I purring? I continue up with my visual assessment and finally land on his face. Oh…sure, ok. I'm pretty sure I had been holding my breath, because right then, I suck in an audible gulp of air and let my hungry eyes have their fun with the visual feast. His face is absolutely gorgeous. It's all sharp angles, strong jaw and a prominent nose that suits his face perfectly. But what I'm drawn to are his eyes. As someone whose eyes are remarked upon a lot, I can understand the allure as I gaze into his. They are a stunning shade of hazel, and right now the green is making a big statement. Reluctantly, I leave his eyes to take in the whole picture. His skin has an olive tone to it and I don't think I have ever seen skin so smooth before. This guy is so sexy it's causing my mouth to water. I'm either really thirsty or really horny.

"You ok?" he asks.

His deep voice startles me out of my perusal, making my plummeting thoughts halt mid fall, so it takes me a few agonizing seconds to answer. "Yes, um…sorry about that. I guess I need to watch where I'm walking." I finally get my brain to work correctly, and start to walk around him, but his deep voice stops my legs from continuing any further. "Excuse me, Ma'am?"

I turn back to the rich sound and notice him holding my purse and my bags out to me, in his big hand. Well duh! This *really* hasn't been one of my finest of moments. "Thanks." I reach for my bags, just as the clouds shift, and the ray of sun hints at something under his jacket. With a quick glance down, I notice the gun attached at his waist. Oh,

I hate guns. Like, *loath* guns, with a passion so strong I immediately feel the shiver race up along my spine. I try and keep the creeped-out look off my face, while I take my bags from his hand, then calmly walk over to my car as fast as my little legs will take me, without making it obvious I'm attempting to escape. My hands are shaking so bad it takes three tries to get the key into the lock, before I can get inside and away from him. I understand that many people own guns, know how to use them, and not all of them are scary. But that doesn't mean I want to be around them. As I pull out of the lot, I look back and see the giant, still standing where I left him, with hands on his hips. I have a brief moment to feel bad for my rude behavior. Then it's gone as quick as it came and I am on my way, pulling onto the congested street.

CHAPTER 4

With my shift at the club finally over, I take a minute to lean my elbows against the bar to stretch my aching calves. My poor legs are killing me. Charlene and I have already wiped the bar down and all that's left is to take the bags of trash out to the dumpster and do our last sweep behind the bar. Looking across the club, I see Joey and Michael busy carrying boxes to the side office, so I walk over, grab the trash bags myself and walk to the back door. With bags in each hand, I have to nudge the back door with my butt, making a wide enough space to set the bags down outside, while placing the doorstopper in between the space, keeping the heavy door ajar. The bags seem heavier tonight, making me work for it, but it's also possibly my sore backside from the graceful fall earlier is just making things harder. Yup. I will go with that excuse any day over admitting I need to hit the gym. With that ugly thought in mind, I lift the top, and use all of my strength to fling the bags over the ledge with a crash of empty bottles. When the lid to the trash bin closes with a thudded bang, I think I hear something hit the side of the container. My first thought is that one of the empty bottles got loose and fell out. But as I check the ground, there doesn't seem to be anything around the container. I stand there a moment in a daze. Too little sleep, and too many falls to the ground have taken their toll on me. Not to mention this strange sense of foreboding that's following me around like a dark cloud. My foot kicks out, to knock away a random rock beside me, as I take this quiet minute to my self.

The area behind A.L is usually lit pretty well, but tonight it seems like a B-rated horror movie. Two bulbs must have blown in the overhead fixtures, and the other blinks every few seconds, making it obvious it's next to go, leaving me shrouded in shadows. Leave it to Angelo not to check these things. That man has no business running this club. I feel a sharp pain on my hip accompanying the same sound I'd heard before, and I reach down to grab my stinging side. At first it doesn't register what just happened, keeping me frozen in my spot. But a second later, my fight or flight instinct kicks into overdrive, and I hall ass back to the door. Tired legs forgotten, I make it to the door, kick the wooden stopper out my way and slam it shut behind me. Joey, one of my other bartender buddies, is just turning the corner with his arms full as I fly through the door with a bang. Literally. The enormous box he has balanced on his arm almost gets sent crashing to the floor from my dramatic entry. He manages to set the box down, without it plummeting to earth, and walks over to me slowly. Like I may pass out if he'd walked faster, he takes two steps and stops. "You ok Nev? You look even paler than normal."

I can't get the answer unstuck from my throat. Instead, I raise my hand up from my side to indicate without words that I'm fine, and notice the red staining my fingers. Then it's lights out for me. I have a brief view of his panicked face before darkness takes over.

***

My first thought is how cold I feel. Well, cold and wet. Dammit. I hate being cold and wet. My second thought is directed to whoever is causing me to feel cold and wet, and then what I may do to them if they don't make it stop. Obviously my fall to the floor has convinced my brain I'm suddenly a badass, but I know better so I lock down those thoughts. My eyes attempt opening, but feel too swollen to get any further than a crack. I try and move my arms, but they aren't obeying my silent command to rub the grit away, so I just lie here allowing someone to wipe the intrusive cold over my forehead. After a few irritating swipes I finally get my eyes to open, and stare up at Joey with my head resting on his leg. Sometime while I was out of it, his dirty blonde hair had fallen out of its tie to frame his lean face, ending at his shoulders. All I can see are blue worried eyes. He moves his arm closer to my view and I notice the washcloth held in his hand. Well, that puzzle is solved. I try and act like a big girl, and not gripe about his help, so instead I focus my attention on the rest of the room. Several people I have never seen before are standing around us. I know they are saying something, but for the life of me I can't make it out. I see lips moving, as if they are whispering, but nothing else. This is the quietest I think I've ever heard the club. When Joey speaks it's like a bomb going off.

"Welcome back toots. You scared me there for a moment."

The whispering ceases, waiting for me to say something, but all that I can get out as a reply mimics a cross between a dying whale and a pirate. "Argchst."

Joey's lip curls up on one side, giving me his signature smirk. "Well that makes complete sense." I roll my eyes, then realize that hurts and stop mid roll.

My second attempt at communicating goes a little smoother, but it still sounds like I've gargled salt water. "Did I hit my head?" Reaching up to feel for damage I run my fingers through my hair in search of damage, but can't find anything, before my hand is taken away and placed back by my side.

I get a smile from him before his answer. "You sure tried hard enough. You went down pretty fast." He face turns stern this time, so I break the contact to ignore the burning in my eyes. "Clipped your head on the bench behind you, but I got to you before you made a complete disaster of yourself. Let's leave the bump alone till I can find some ice to put on it, eh? And maybe wait till someone can check you over before you start investigating your head please."

I'm still not looking at him while he says this, but can hear the concern in his voice. My eyes, now that they seem to be working again, look over the mayhem around us. Our boss, Angelo, is standing behind Joey talking to someone and I cringe at the thought of the nasty things he'll no doubt be saying to me when he gets me alone. I shift my attention away from Angelo, and over to the other side of the open door to Charlene, who's peeking around two men in uniform while chewing on her thumb nail. Around her petite face her bright red hair seems to be sticking out like wild snakes wanting to be set free from the clips holding them back. Her worried look triggers me to try and sit up on my own, but Joey holds on tight until I look up at him.

"Just making sure you got this." At my stink eye he lets me go to complete my sit up. That's when I get my first glimpse of the man Angelo is talking to. I'm not sure how I could have missed him, as his presence fills the room to capacity, stealing all the air from my lungs. I stare directly into the hazel eyes of the man I have thought about too many times over the past several hours, and wish for oblivion to take hold of me once more. Oh goodie. Twice in one day this sexy man sees me on the ground. Joey stands first, giving me room to tuck my shaky legs under my butt, then reaches down under my arms to help me stand. My head feels slightly fuzzy, but I stay upright. Giving Joey the go-ahead, he guides me over, with a sturdy hand at my back, to two men waiting to speak to me. It's comfort and support rolled into one. I keep my gait slow to prolong the oncoming encounter and pray my flushed cheeks fade back to pale before we get there. Joey, thankfully, falls back to my pace. Either he thinks my slowness is due to my fall or he's an awesome mind reader and proving to be my *bestest* pal. Checking once more on Char, I give her a small wave telling her I'm good and not to worry. Now I just need to believe it myself.

Walking up to the trio I feel like a six-year-old heading into the principal's office. And with their tall height, and my lack thereof, I probably look that way as well. My man-wall from the grocery store parking lot is dressed exactly how I saw him hours before. Right down to the big watch attached to his wrist. Yeesh. It's the middle of the night. Does the man not sleep?

I purse my lips when the man next to him speaks. "Neva, this is Detective Grant. He's here to ask a few questions when you're up to it." Hmmm, Angelo must be biting his cheek to keep the sarcasm at a minimum in front of the detective and his crew. I glare at the side of his face, daring him to humiliate me even more in front of everyone. I do not need his attitude on top of my craptastic night. He must have eaten his smart cookie today because he just shakes hands with the detective and exits stage left. Good riddance. He and I will not be calling each other besties anytime soon. Sad thing is, I have no idea why he hates me so much or why he doesn't just fire me. But I won't go kicking that particular donkey in the mouth. I need this job to support us and have grown to love my coworkers. They've been added to what I consider to be my funky family, and if I have to put up with a crappy boss, so be it.

Now that I'm standing in front of my mystery wall from the parking lot, I look way up to his handsome face. Yikes. He is still just as tall as I remember. Why couldn't he have shrunk a few inches since I'd last seen him? He practically towers over everyone in the room, especially me. As I get another look at him, this time without the sun hindering my view, I categorize all that I'd missed. His black hair is cut extremely short, almost to his scalp, and he has the sexiest layer of short dark hair along his sharp jaw, above a full mouth. It's a little longer than the normal five o'clock look. Maybe more of a five-thirty or six o'clock shadow. Yum. Looking away from his jaw I glance down and notice, for the second time today, he has his hand stretched out to me and I am just starring. Again. What is it about those hands? They are such big, strong hands. Hands that could pick me up and…wait! Blinking out of my dirty dream I find all eyes on me. I sure hope I kept that last tidbit inside the vault. "Sorry…I think I may have hit my head harder than I thought." I can hear Joey's "mmm hmm" behind me, but I ignore him. I finally put my tiny hand in his large one and politely shake it. It's fascinating to see how beautiful the different colors our hands look when they're intertwined. Like butterscotch and cream. Forcing my attention upward, I make eye contact with the giant.

"Nice to meet you Detective." Oh Lord, help me now. I sound like a cheesy sex phone operator. I just know Joey has that damn smirk on his face, but I'm pretending I meant to sound that way. Ignorance is bliss I say! Hazel eyes to ice blue, the detective stares down at me and I panic for a second thinking he might call me on my voice impersonation, but thankfully someone clears their throat and the moment is broken. Releasing his hand I step back so my neck doesn't have to strain so hard to see him, and look down at the buttons on his shirt. They look gold in our dim back room and I count them, starting at his trim waist, so I don't start talking stupid again.

"Neva Mathews?" I nod and stay silent. "I was called because gun shots were heard behind After Life and once here we were told someone was injured." His voice is just as deep as I remember. "Can you tell us what happened while you were out back?"

I proceed to explain what I had been doing and the sounds I had heard, this time, thankfully, with my normal Neva voice. "At first I thought I heard something hit the side of the trash container when I let the lid drop back down. It wasn't till I felt something on my hip and heard it again that I thought something was wrong." At my comment I am reminded of my hip and look down. Joey is immediately beside me.

"Oh no you don't." Grabbing my hand he squeezes gently before taking my chin and forcing it back up. I *really* appreciate this. I have definitely spent too much time on the ground today. The Detective and the three other men, two sporting Miami PD uniforms and another dressed similar to Detective Grant, move to the side, just as two EMT's walk in carrying a folded stretcher and bags, containing medical supplies to fix me up. It's then the shaking starts. It begins in my toes and works it's way up past my knees and into my queasy stomach. I suddenly have a freaked-out Charlene in my face.

"Breathe honey. All will be fine." What? I *am* fine. What is she talking about? I look up at Detective Grant and catch the look of concern on his face. At least I think that's what it is. His eyebrows are drawn down, creating a V in between his eyes, and they almost appear to be glowing. The look is completely at odds with his tightly coiled body; it has to feel uncomfortable. My head is suddenly pushed from behind, and forced all the way to my knees. Huh….I guess I'm hyperventilating. This is new. Taking as deep a breath as this position allows, my body calms the shaking and the hands holding me down loosen their grip. My first breath that finally reaches my lungs for the first time in seconds, is glorious. I mentally make the decision that sitting is my best option, and my body agrees, as I allow my knees to lower. If I'm gonna land there anyway, I'd like it to be because I chose it this time. Sitting, pretty much exactly where I'd started, I reassure Charlene with a half smile, letting her see this time was planned. "I'm ok." The dizziness passes, and I'm able to raise my head without vomiting on the floor, which I take as a sign of victory. The EMT to my left has already hooked a blood pressure cuff on my arm, while the other is checking the gash on my hip. When did they get closer?

While the men work on me, the room stays eerily silent, almost as if they're waiting for bad news. I'm not sure I like it too much. If there *is* bad news, do I really want all these random folks to witness the fall out? Blessedly, the inspection of my body only takes a few minutes. The gentleman on my left sends me a gentle smile, when he unhooks the cuff from me, and I swear I hear a growl from somewhere above me, echoing in the quiet back room. There are only two men standing close enough to have made the sound, and as I'm ninety percent certain Joey has *never* growled once in his life, that leaves the sexy detective as the source. Interesting. I'm tempted to look up at him to check his expression, but I keep my view on his leather shoes instead. If he's pissed at me, I'm not sure I want to know. He could probably squish me with his thumb; why poke the beast with my curiosity? My vitals and the bump checked, the two EMT's deem me fine as a fiddle. My words, not theirs. It only takes a few more minutes of prodding and they finally leave me, but not before making me promise to let someone know if I start to feel worse, so someone can bring me to the ER. Fat chance, that. There's no way anyone is taking me to the hospital. The last thing I need is to freak out Drew. Not to mention my overprotective best friend.

***

Now fully coherent and one big Band Aid later I am sitting in the main room of the club on a barstool, with Joey and Charlene flanking me on either side. Although I'm the oldest of the three, Joey still acts like my bossy older sibling. If he reminds me to stay seated one more time, I may revoke his best pal card for life. I've worked with him the longest, just over two years, and Char not much less than that. These two mean the world to me. Even when bossy. They make working the nights I'm away from Drew easier to deal with. They've stepped up as surrogate aunt and uncle to Drew, and I can always count on them to keep me laughing, allowing the night to fly by. And a smile on a bartender's face equals many tips in the jar. See? Win-win.

This had never been my dream job. Getting married young we both worked odd jobs to help Jeremy finish school, until it was my turn. Yet my turn never came. We were both surprised when I became pregnant only a few months after the 'I do's'. Not that I have ever regretted the timing, it just made our planning take a different direction. Now, ten years later, I'm slinging drinks to kids with fake ID's part of the time, and slinging books to kids wishing they *had* fake ID's the rest of it. Ah, the life of Neva Mathews.

The club is now empty, except for the few other people I work with, and the four men from the Police station. I am utterly exhausted, and just want to crawl into my bed, maybe have a snuggle or two from my boy. I had braided my hair earlier and stuck it to the top of my head to keep the craziness out of my face, but it's now giving me a worse headache than the newly earned bump. I carefully pull the bobby pins from around the braided bun, and start to unravel the white mass, letting it fall down around my shoulders. Sinking my fingers in to sooth the tightness, I rub my scalp in small circles to get the blood flowing again. Oh, so much better. I sneak a quick peak up at the detective and notice his eyes are centered on my now-free hair. He looks to be concentrating so hard I get a sudden urge to fluff it once or twice to make it worth his while, but resist just in time. I thought I had seen him glancing my way a few times while I was being looked over by the technicians, but could never be totally sure I wasn't in wishful-thinking land. And I'm still wondering about the reason for the growl. At least this time he doesn't seem to be clenching his jaw as tight. I sit on my stool and stare back at him. If he's ok with ogling my hair, the least I can do is return the favor. He really is a sight to see. He's removed the jacket at some point and is standing with strong hands on equally strong hips. A pose I'm beginning to think is his standard alpha pose. One hand is perched right next to his shiny badge and the other just above the gun I'd noticed at the grocery store parking lot. Shifting his eyes, he meets my stare, but quickly turns back to his partner. He's not bad to look at either. If you like that whole blond Viking thing he has going on. And turning my head in Joey's direction, my radar beeps loud and clear that my dear Joey is one of those who do. He catches me looking at him and shrugs before zoning back in on the Viking detective. Atta boy. Rawr.

Turning back to the room, my eyes try hard to stay open, but every blink takes longer to reverse, the action. I am utterly and completely, one hundred and fifty percent, done. In other words, ready to go. I must have said that bit out loud, as Charlene replies to me. "Ok hon, let's get you home. Did you drive this time or did Shelly drop you off tonight? Give me your phone, I'll call her."

"NO!" I must have yelled this time, as everyone turns quickly to look towards my seat. This time, using my inside voice, I try again. "That's ok. It's really late and I don't want to scare her. She'll be scared enough when I explain this to her later. Plus, she'd just have to wake Drew to come and get me and I'd really rather let him stay clueless on this drama, ya know?" I move to slide off my bar stool but I'm not quick enough. Out of thin air, the dark haired detective is at my side with his hand on my arm, keeping my butt on the stool.

"I've got her. I'll make sure she gets home." His eyes are on me, but his comment is directed at Char. She looks at me to make sure I am ok with this, and I gave her a subtle nod and a shrug to let her know it's fine. Riding with him seems like a good plan given bullets were flying at me earlier tonight. I look back into his eyes and a feeling of safety washes over me. Strange, I know. But there it is. For such a big man he's extremely gentle while helping me down off the stool, and his large hand stays at my lower back as I get hugs from the two friends beside me.

On our way to the front door I'm given a business card by Detective Valdez with a direct number that goes through to either himself or Detective Grant. I thank him and try to memorize the number before slipping into my back pocket. I'm busy trying to stay upright, so I miss the hard look Valdez gives his partner over my head. Leaning my tired body against the detective's side sounded perfect in my fuzzy head when I'd thought about it, but now that I'm doing it I'm a little embarrassed at my boldness.

"Time to go." This is growled from a mile above me, causing me to jerk my head up to the sound, confirming he was the one the earlier growl belonged to. I see once more how tight his jaw is clenched. He isn't looking at me but straight ahead to his partner. I want to reach up with my hand and smooth the tension away, but I don't think he'd appreciate that. My grogginess is affecting my common sense. With a final wave I'm pulled in the direction of our exit and one step closer to sleep.

Once outside I notice an enormous black Dodge Ram, parked where we seem to be headed. I take a second to wonder how in *the hell* I'm going to get up in it. When we make it to the passenger side, Grant solves that problem as he opens the my door, looks down at me, then puts his large hands around my waist and picks me up. Before I know it, I'm in my seat, and my seatbelt's buckled. I must have a dazed expression, because I see the left side of his mouth lift slightly like he's trying to smile. I wish I could witness a full-blown smile from him, but it's probably best not to cause my brain any more strenuous activity tonight. That just might bring the dizziness back. After shutting my door he walks around the front, to his side of the truck, but right before he climbs in I see his eyes scan the parking lot with a hand suspiciously lowered over the side his gun. I focus back to my side of the truck to block the thought, and before I can relax my hands from the grip on my belt, we're on the move.

CHAPTER 5

It's quiet in the truck on our journey south. Not an uncomfortable silence. Just quiet. He's kept the radio off, and neither of us has attempted to interrupt the peacefulness. I'd just relaxed enough to feel the sleep pulling me under, when a thought occurs to me and I let out an audible gasp. I see him jerk his head in my direction, before looking back at the road, keeping his mouth in a firm line.

"My car! I left my car. I need my car tomorrow. We have to go back." In all the drama that went down, I'd never answered Charlene when she questioned me whether or not I'd driven to work. We probably walked right by it and I was too focused on the tingles his hand was causing on my back to realize it. He seems to relax at my mini freak-out, and rather than the U-turn I'd been expecting, one of the hands strangling the steering wheel reaches up to rub the back of his neck, before placing it back on the gear shift. "It's fine. I'll have Val drop it off to you at your apartment some time tomorrow. Just give me your keys and it'll be taken care of."

"Val?" I'm probably focusing on the least important part of his speech, but I can't help my curiosity from spilling out first.

"Sorry. My partner. Detective Valdez. He prefers to be called Val by those of us close to him." That makes sense and I'm fine with that. I don't think I'd want someone I'd never met driving my car. Petty? Yes. But I need that car. Ok, this mollifies my anxiety enough to sink back into the seat. The truck feels like it's moving in slow motion now, with its monotonous movements lulling me into a lethargic state. Every time I blink my lids stick together, begging me to keep them shut. Now that the adrenaline is wearing off, my body is reminding me how tired I am. I need to keep talking or he'll be witnessing a sleeping Nev.

"Thank you." I don't know if he understands I'm thanking him for helping me return my car, or for the safety I feel for when he's near. Either way I never get the chance to find out. Right before I slip into dreamland I hear him ask me a question.

"Neva? Do you have idea why the Carlos gang would be trying to hurt you?" I wish I had the energy to answer.

***

This time when I wake, it isn't due to my alarm. Thanking God for small mercies, I stretch my arms over my head and immediately feel all the aches from the day before. My back is sore, giving me the sense that my falls to Earth were as bone-jarring as I'd originally thought. I can only imagine how ridiculous I'd looked yesterday in front of the detective. That's when I realize I have no memory of how I got to bed. My last cognitive thought from the night before is freaking out about my car. My eyes fly open and I sit straight up in bed, groaning from the stiff movement. With my hair covering half my face, I immediately see I'm not alone to witness my miserable state. Shelly sits in my corner reading chair, with a magazine on her lap, filing her nails. The look on her face says she's an extremely pissed off best friend. I think I shall keep quiet until I can determine what I've done to cause that look. I don't have to wait long.

"Well...I can guess what your answer would be if I asked about meeting any hot men last night." This is said while still focusing on her nails. I cringe internally and have a brief moment to worry about Drew until I hear a bowl being dropped into the kitchen sink. She must not have informed him about last night or he'd be in here as well. "Hmmmm," is all that makes it past my dry throat.

"Would you like to tell me why I was woken in the wee hours of the morning by sleeping beauty and her hulking detective?" Before I can open my mouth for a comeback she moves along. "I mean, it's pretty hot to be carried to bed like a princess, especially if it's by her detective knight in armor, that appears suspiciously similar to Armani." As she waits for my response, I get one perfectly plucked eyebrow arched up her forehead. "You plan on answering me? Or do you plan to just sit there with dried drool on your chin? I'll assume the drool is remnants from the deep sleep you've been in, and not from gazing at your knight, before dozing off. Or maybe it's both?"

I absently wipe my face before answering. Hmmm, how best to drop this bomb? "Well, after work last night I may, or may not, have been shot at."

"WHAT??!! What are you talking about? And why didn't you call me when this happened?" Ok, maybe I should have eased into that statement.

I hold both my hands up in front of me. "Shhh. Do you want Drew to hear you? I'm fine. I'm actually not sure why I was shot at. That's why Detective Grant was bringing me home. He and three other officers came to the club and questioned us after it happened, and he offered to bring me home. Seriously, I was fine and I didn't want to wake you for something I was planning on telling you when I got home." I throw her a sheepish expression. "Except, I guess I passed out on our way here. Did you say he carried me? Oh, by the way, do you know if my car made it back?"

"Yes, your keys are on the hook in the kitchen." Her look of concern is quickly replaced by a sarcastic one. "And yes to being carried. It was like 'damsels in distress gone wild' in here." She goes mute, while she rolls the information I dropped on her around in in her mind. I can practically hear the hamster wheel turning from here. Part of it, I know, is stemmed from worry. The other more scary part is taking her brain on a lascivious trip south. I need to keep the hamsters moving in a northern direction. When she looks back up at me, I can see the tears that had formed while she'd been thinking, in the corner of her eyes, and I instantly feel bad for doubting her. She discreetly sniffs, then blows out a quick breath of air.

Disposing of her nail file, she folds her arms across her chest. "K. Drew slept through all the craziness, so I just told him you overslept. But you know he'll be worried since you never sleep through Saturday morning breakfast." I do know this. But I'm relieved he hasn't been made aware of his mom's frightening night. I have an urge to run out my door and hug him, but right as I'm about to move, the phone rings. Before I can get my legs untangled from the sheet, I hear Drew answer the phone in the kitchen.

"Mom! Phone!"

"Coming!" I finally free my legs and stand next the bed. I wobble slightly as the blood moves back into my feet, and that's when I notice I'm still dressed in my work uniform, sans shoes. Convenient for my walk to the phone, I guess. Not so convenient if Drew happens to notice. I'm counting on the fact he only pays attention to the things he wants to. I'll have to change before my hug. I hold a finger up at Shelly, to indicate we'll finish this when I return, and hop over the clean pile of clothes beside my bed, to grab my robe from the hook by my tiny bathroom. And yes, I see the messed up logic of clean clothes on the floor versus robe on my hook, but I have more important things to worry about today. As I walk past our couch, Drew gives me a quick wave before turning his attention back to the TV. I blow a kiss back at him and answer the phone. "Hello?"

The deep voice that replies causes my heart to beat faster. "Yes ma'am. This is Detective Grant. I'm calling to see if you might have time to come in today, to the station. I have just a few more questions I wanted to ask you last night before…well before you fell asleep." I smile at his uncomfortable pause. I bet he doesn't have women passing out in his car everyday. My smile drops from my lips and an uncomfortable pinch settles low in my gut. At least I hope he doesn't.

I bite my lip to keep from shouting *yes*. "Um sure. Let me get myself put together and I'd be happy to. By the way, can you tell your partner I said thank you for getting my car back to me?"

"Sure will. Does an hour sound fair?" He asks.

I can't keep the butterflies from their whirlwind at the thought of seeing him today. It's not like I haven't seen a sexy man before, even if I fib to Shelly about the ones I do. White lies are mandatory, for those questions, or she'd be hounding me for info daily. So why do I feel like a teenager with my first crush again? "Yes thanks, I'll see you soon." I'm still holding the phone, with the smile on my face, when I feel Shelly grab it from my hand and place it back on the counter. I hear her whisper close to my ear. "Well, well, well…I think someone is smitten." I don't reply to her. I need to analyze these new feelings before I say it out loud. But, I'm pretty sure she's right.

As I walk to my car I have to mentally keep my hands from fidgeting with my pink baby doll top. I have it paired with my dark wash bootleg jeans, fresh from the dryer, which helps to make my ass seem curvier that it really is. And more importantly, I'm wearing my knock-off, Kate Spade ankle boots that add three inches to my height. It isn't much, but it's a step up in the right direction. I'd be lying if I said I haven't dressed a little nicer than I normally would to see a certain tall detective. As I get closer to my car, I notice a recognizable black Ram parked in the spot behind mine. And leaning against the front bumper, dressed this time in a dark brown suit, white shirt with two buttons undone, and mirrored shades, is none other than Detective Grant himself. Since I have shades on myself, I let my eyes travel over him slowly, and am greeted with a brief view of a gold chain and something resembling a locket, hanging at the base of his neck. He straightens his stance and walks in silence to my side of the car. I had opened my mouth to ask why he wasn't waiting at the station for me to arrive, but before I'm able to speak, he gently takes my arm and guides me to the passenger side of his truck. My head is still buzzing from the sight of him, so it doesn't immediately register what he's up to until he lifted me, once again, into his truck with my seatbelt buckled like you would a toddler. Without moving his body he turns his head in my direction, which now places him only an inch or two from me, and stares directly at me. I keep my eyes averted to hide my excitement, in fear of being too obvious. But can't help my uneven breathing from being noticed, as I stare at his full mouth, which starts to move. "You're riding with me." He says this like a decree and there's no choice in the matter. I should be pissed by that alpha move, but, I check my emotions…nope. Not pissed. Definitely not the emotion shining though my subconscious. I keep my face blank from all thoughts and clear my throat. He stares a heartbeat longer, then backs out and closes my door with a solid click.

This time our ride is filled with the quiet murmur of a sports talk host on his radio. I'm not sure if he feels the same sexual tension I'm experiencing, or if I'm alone in this, but it's rapidly getting out of hand on my end. Yet, even if he does feel the same, am I really ready for it?

My body has forgotten was it's like to feel this way. Lost in thought, I don't realize we've parked till there's a hand on my arm telling me we've arrived.

***

The police station is exactly how I pictured one would look like. Beige carpet lines the floor and a matching ugly bland color on the walls. We walk through the main room, housing several neatly scattered desks that apparently belong to the few people either sitting or standing beside them. Some are on phones, or typing away at their computers. That's all I'm allowed to see before Grant leads me down the long corridor and into a corner office. Opening the door for me, he allows me to walk in first, giving me a few seconds to look over his office while he speaks with someone out in the hall. The room isn't as large as I would have expected a detective's office to be. Although, my only frame of reference is TV shows. For all I know it could be a huge room compared to some others. His desk sits center stage in a dark cherry wood, with a matching bookcase to the side. It's screams that a *man* sits in here. He has a black laptop open on top but nothing else beside it. No knick-knacks, paperweights, or any pictures are displayed to ease my curiosity. I know I'm running out of time, so I avert my attention sideways and am once again disappointed with his lack of keepsakes. Very little adorns the walls except for two plaques that I'm unable read from my spot at the door. I don't hear him enter until the door latches shut and he's taking my elbow to guide me to one of the chairs in front of his desk. My thank you is stiff, but I soften it by throwing a half smile over at him as he rounds his desk to take the big chair on the opposite side of his big desk. After taking a folder from a drawer he places it unopened in front of his clasped hands and brings his eyes up. Hesitating a moment before speaking, he looks back down at the folder in front of him and reaches for something in his suit jacket, so I take the time to look back over at the wall to my left. Squinting to get a better look at the plaques, I vaguely make out his name before he speaks.

"Have you ever heard the name Bartolo Aracelia Carlos before?" When I spin my head back in his direction my eyes automatically settle on what he must have dug from his pocket. Perched on his nose is a pair of gold reading glasses. Wow. They give him an air of sophistication, but there is no hiding the sexiness behind the glass. I am so stunned by how sexy this is that I don't remember his question.

"I'm sorry...what?" He looks down at his notes and I swear I see his lip turn up in the corner, sending those damn butterflies back into the vortex I call my stomach. I want to smile back, but he removes the glasses and levels me with a hard look. The butterflies stop and start again, but for a different reason this time. I'm disconcerted by the seriousness on his face. I hope I can take what he's about to say.

"The name Bartolo Aracelia Carlos. Have you ever heard that name before?"

Nothing's coming to mind and it must show clearly on my face, but I still shake my head *no* to clarify. He sighs and sets his elbows atop the folder on his desk and steeples his fingers over his discarded glasses. The last time I was this bizarre combination of scared and excited, I was giving birth to Drew. I'm praying this isn't as painful. I want to prompt him, but I sit motionless as he prepares himself to lay it all out for me. After a moment he begins to talk. And what he says rocks my world.

CHAPTER 6

"**I** believe your late husband may have been involved in an underground crime ring. We have knowledge that Jeremy Mathews was in possession of something stolen from a powerful group located in South America." Nothing he's saying is making sense. Jeremy? *My* Jeremy? He must be mistaken. I give him a look he can't mistake for anything other than disbelief, but that doesn't stop him from continuing his crazy talk. "Do you by any chance know what your husband was working on before he was killed on March 15, 2009?"

My lips are dry, but with effort, I get them to work. "Uh, yes?" I don't mean for that to come out as a question, but stop from correcting myself. This guy must have his facts screwed up. "He was a history teacher at the local high school in Miami Springs where we lived at the time. As far as I know that was what paid the bills." Was that sarcasm in my voice? He lets it slide but his eyes flash a warning when they look back at me.

"I can understand this is tough news to hear…"

"Oh! You think just maybe?" I don't care that I've cut him off. This is getting ridiculous. I'm not sure where he's headed with this but he needs to stop talking. He's patient with his response but it isn't helping me dial down my agitation.

"Yes, I can understand the feeling of betrayal by someone you are close to." He lets that statement hang in the air a moment before moving ahead. This time when he speaks, his words come out slow, as if I were having trouble before understanding him. "I only asked if you knew because we think that this organization may be targeting you for a reason. Do you have any information that you think may be relevant?

Or maybe something of value that your husband may have shown you?" He pauses, but I just stare at him in shock. His eye twitches as if he's become uncomfortable. Join the club, buddy. "I'm sorry to ask this but was your husband ever violent with you?"

I suck in a breath to hold the tears in. If I move right now, they will fall, and the last thing I want is for him to see me cry. I think he's still talking, but nothing of what he said after his last question is sinking into my confused brain. I'm up out of my chair and out through his office door before he has a chance to stand. I hear my name being called as I rush into the ladies room but ignore it as I run into the first stall I find, closest to the bathroom entrance. Shutting and locking the stall, I lean back against the door and try to stop the tears streaming from my eyes. Nothing can stop them now; they just keep dropping onto my shirt. What is he saying? There is no way Jeremy could have been involved in this, let alone be *violent* towards myself or Drew. Damn him and his intrusive questions. Sure, it's easy to forget the flaws of someone gone for so long, but wouldn't I remember something this big? Not to mention there is no way I would ever allow Drew to be around something or *someone* that could hurt him? Especially not his father. I have no doubt of the love he had for us.

I must have been sitting here for a long time, running everything in my mind over and over, when I hear the squeak of the door. I quietly dry my tears and blow my nose, then turn to leave my hiding spot. It takes me a few tries to open the stall door, but I walk out with my head held high, preparing to put myself back together, and step next to the sink. I glance up at my reflection, to check my face for water damage, but instead see Grant leaning against the wall behind me. Thick arms crossed at his chest, his jaw hard as stone, and his big body tense. His eyes dart over my obviously blotchy face and once more I see the muscles in his jaw compress. The man moves so fast I flinch. Suddenly

I am lifted in his strong arms. I feel a moment of weightlessness before it's gone and I'm starring at his handsome face. My mind and heart are mad at him, but that doesn't stop my legs from searching for some way to anchor my flying body, and hooking my ankles behind his back. My arms, which had been holding his thick biceps during my flight, grip tight just as his mouth slams down on my own. This is not a tender kiss. It's a kiss filled with so many warring emotions. Anger, for things said. Passion, from the pull of our bodies, and the craving we have for each other. Hate, at myself for succumbing to his demand. How can I give him a piece of myself after what he's said, regardless of his intentions in asking that question?

My back is pushed against the hard surface behind me but his hands are there to take the brunt of the aggressive push. It's a hostile meeting of lips, sucking and biting. My mouth seems to have a mind of it's own, and opens to let his tongue slide inside. He moves a hand up in my hair to anchor my head to the side and I bite his lip in reprimand and praise. I'm not sure if I'm trying to win this battle, or surrender to it.

With my hands, I pull his face closer, to offer him all that I have, while trying to push away from him simultaneously. Our struggle for control is all consuming, and feels like I've waited a lifetime to be here, in his arms. My hands leave his face to travel down to his broad shoulders that tighten as I explore. He has so much muscle it could take weeks to find the end to them. I'm not aware I've been grinding my pelvis against him, until he reciprocates with his own, eliciting a tortured groan, that I not only hear but also feel. I gasp loudly and break the kiss, allowing room for his mouth to travel along my throat. Oh, Lord have mercy, his lips suck at the base of my neck, clenching my core. I'm so ready for him to take me there. His short beard grazes and tickles, causing my fingers to tighten against his neck in response to the feelings flaring through me. I need more. More of this. More of him. I hear a whisper of his name and realize it's come from me, right before there's a sudden bang against my back. I don't know who is more surprised by this. Me, for giving in, when I know I should have kicked him out as soon as I saw him. Or him, for making out in the little girls room. He drops my legs and sets me down to step away from me. With us now standing several feet apart, our breathing seems to be in sync and the sound echoes off the tile. I look at his collar, unable to meet his eyes with my own, and I stare at the chain around his neck, barely visible through the opening of his shirt. The bang startles me once more and I spin around at the sound bracing my hands to open the door, but Grant beats me to it by reaching around me and unlocking the door. It dawns on me that I just made out in the police stations bathroom like some horny crazy person. Or more correctly, a 30-year-old horny woman. As soon as the door opens I try to make a quick get away, but Grant's faster. Of course he is. He takes my shoulders and steers me around a very confused elderly woman who appears like she's torn between giving us a piece of her mind or taking care of what she came to do. Nature wins the battle, and she disappears inside, without much fanfare, leaving us standing in the hallway all alone. He braces his legs apart and crosses his arms as if preparing to go into battle. I wish I had a step stool to stand on, so I wouldn't feel this small next to him. Funny, how I didn't mind his height while he held me up in his arms. I need to derail that train, and fast, before I attack him here in the hall.

"Will you come back to my office so we can try this again?" He pauses as he realizes how that sounds, and I see his eyes shut tight, shaking his head. As he runs his hand at the top of his short hair, I can't help but notice how the shirtsleeves tighten around his thick bicep. "That's...not what I meant."

I can't stop a smile from forming on my face at his obvious discomfort. Yes, I'm still miffed at him, but it's a relief to see him show a human side instead of his hard-assery self – the only side he's allowed me to see so far. And then it hits me what he *is* asking, and the smile's wiped clean off my face. On one hand, I just want to go back home and drown my night in cheap wine and one of Shelly's famous chocolate cakes while veg'ing in front of mindless television. But on the other hand, I want answers, even if they are hard to hear. Answers only *he* has. And if I'm being honest, I have to admit, a part of me is disappointed that he meant *talk* and not reenact what we just experienced only moments before. Damn my hormones. My body is still humming like a finely tuned race car, and my heart feels like it may fly out of my chest, but I play it off by crossing my arms and directing my eyes upward. I'm sure my fair complexion is making it quite obvious how aroused I am because…that was *some* kiss. I think he knew what my answer was going to be before I did, because he doesn't wait for it, just turns to walk back to his office. Sighing, I follow a step behind, and finally seem to find my voice, which sounds a little breathless when I answer. "Ok, yes. Let's pick my brain shall we. And I'd like you to explain why you'd ask if my husband, the same husband who showed both myself and our son nothing but love and support, would be violent towards me." We progress down the hall, back to his office, and stop by the door that is still ajar from our exit. I wait for him to let me enter but he stops my movement by bending at the waist and raising his arms to cage in my body against the wall. Seriously, I'm getting used to this position. The hall is empty, thank God, but he still lowers his voice as not to share his words beyond his man-made cocoon.

"Seeing as my tongue was just in your mouth you should know my name is Jason. Jason Grant." He stops and bends further, so his face is the only thing visible. I can still see the desire there in his eyes, but something else has taken a front seat. He opens his mouth, like he's planning to go on with more, but instead straightens up to his full height and opens the door, holding his arm out for me to precede him.

CHAPTER 7

JASON

As I sit behind my desk, I can't help but stare at the woman in front me. It's something I've done numerous times from afar, but is so much sweeter now that I've had the pleasure of tasting her. With her head angled down, the cloud of her silky white hair flows around her, making her appear like a porcelain doll. Her small fingers move quickly while she types away on her phone. I remember all too well what those fingers feel like gripping the back of my neck and I flex mine in response. What is it about this frail human that has captivated my interest, beyond what I need to gain from her? In all of my 36 years I have never, not once, felt this way. It's only been days since she crashed into my life and it already feels like a lifetime. I've watched her many times over a good portion of the past year, without her knowledge, but having this woman within my reach is a completely different struggle. There was a time when I could look at her part in this case clinically, but the more I dig into her daily life, the more I hunger for her attention. My chest gets tight every time I see her, however this protectiveness at the thought of her being hurt is new, and I'm not exactly sure how to handle it. Especially when I'm the instigator. Am I really such an asshole, that I needed to see her reaction when asked if her late husband was abusive?

I've never considered myself an overly aggressive man, as my size usually speaks for itself. Not to mention that there's been enough violence in my life that I'm normally able to rein in my demons without being outwardly combative. At least most of the time. In my line of work it takes patience rather than barbaric actions to get me to my end goal. So why now?

She tosses her phone back into the huge contraption I presume is a purse and looks back up at me. I notice she won't meet my eyes and part of me is thankful, while the other unfamiliar part of me wants to force her eyes up to mine. They are big, compared to the rest of her features, and radiate intensity. Which speaks volumes about her nature. When she speaks, her voice is guarded. Normally, I feel pride in my intimidating presence, but today I need her on board with me, and what we plan to do, so I relax my features to help assure her I mean no harm. I need to make sure she sees me as a friend, not a foe.

"Sorry. Was just checking in." She says.

I nod to her comment like I'm supposed to. I know from my research that she lives with a close friend, and her ten-year-old son, and has been widowed for a little over five years. Out of foster care at eighteen and married a month after, to her late husband. I also know why this group is looking for her, although divulging that information now won't benefit my mission. I understand all too well what these men we're dealing with are like first hand. They are not people I want around Neva or her family, even if it is a risk I'm prepared to take. Nevertheless I can't in good conscience offer up a kid to these freaks, leaving me with no other option than the one we've concocted. I wait till she's settled to speak. "That's fine. I wanted to talk to you anyway about providing a safeguard to your son and friend while we figure out what we're dealing with." I've surprised her I can see. She will realize soon enough that everything I do serves a purpose. I never claimed to play god, but I always strive to gain as much information as the man upstairs.

"Oh, I see. Yes, thank you. They are very important to me." She pauses a moment. "Wait… you really think there's a chance someone would go after them? I'm just not understanding this. My husband has been gone for 5 years. Why now?"

I won't divulge the truth to her, but I will give her as much as I can in the meantime. "This organization has many names. *De Pista*, *El Todopoderoso*, *Una Regala*. But those who are closest to its inhabitance refer to it as "*El Carlos*" which is basically an underground gang run by some powerful people. I say underground meaning they only surface when they feel like it, and when they do, hell looks nice in comparison." I lean back in my chair and absently reach for the chain I have permanently around my neck. Some days the memories are harder to ignore. Especially when one name in particular is brought up. I release it and set my hands back against the armrests.

"So, you're saying that my husband had something of theirs and just now they're wanting it back?" She asks doubtfully.

No. That's not all I'm saying. Unfortunately that's all she's obtaining from me until the right time presents itself. She casts her eyes downward, deep in thought for a moment, before she gasps, making her pale eyes cloud over and darken. These unfamiliar feelings make my gut go tight and I clench my hands into fists. My patience is running a thin line as I wait for her to speak and ease my vexation.

CHAPTER 8

NEVA

A memory as clear as day begins to play out like it's happening now rather than years before. A night that has been too painful to recall. It has made it's way to the forefront of my mind and it takes every bit of my strength not to reach for my chest where I can feel my heart breaking all over again. I try and stop it by rubbing the palm of my hands along my temples, but it forces it's way through my mind like a bullet. It starts with soft words; legs and arms entangled, mouths searching, moaning, moving, and heat. I breathe through it and allow the memory to continue from there. It's painful in its intensity. Complex, beautiful and heartbreaking all at once.

I lay on my stomach with my hands tucked under my pillow. My head is turned so my view of Jeremy is only slightly blocked by the hair that I haven't bothered to move out of my eyes. But even with my eyes closed I would be able to picture his perfect body in my mind. Our cream colored sheets barely cover his hips and his hard chest is still moving up and down as fast as my own. The smile he gives me is full of male pride, but I won't tease him this time, as it's definitely deserved. My eyes glide down over the dips and valleys of taut muscle and land at the tiny white scar from his youth on his lower abdomen. On shaky arms I push my body closer to kiss it at the same time his arm, above his head, moves down to stroke my hair. I lean my forehead down and can feel every quick breath his body makes and the shudder from my kiss.

"Te querré para siempre. Tu eres mi vida."

I smile at his beautiful declaration of love and trail my finger lightly against the line of dark hair leading downward. His stomach tightens as he begins to sit up and lays my body back onto the pillows. I get a fantastic view of his back as it rises from our bed and I only have to turn my head slightly to continue my inspection as he walks to the sliding doors of the closet. Closing my eyes I reach over and pull the blanket we had thrown to the side over my chilled body, enjoying the relaxed feeling that only a powerful orgasm can produce. The bed dips down on my right and once again the goose bumps on my arms raise as the blanket is lowered just below my chest. I don't open my eyes but I can feel his stare on my body as strong as his hands had been earlier. My hand closest to him is dragged out of its warm sheath and his lips kiss each finger until I feel a cool band being slipped on my middle finger. My hand curls into a ball and I look up to see a blue and white stone more beautiful than I can put into words enveloping my finger. It has the same iridescent look of an opal, but this stone has a glimmer inside that seems to go on forever. The pure brilliance of it seems almost magical and it's hard to look away from. I hold my hand out and notice the gem is set into the gold band instead of being bracketed like most rings I've seen. My hand has already started to tingle; as beautiful as this ring is, I want to take it off and make the feeling stop. My eyes are questioning when they move away from my hand to the navy blue eyes of my husband, but the look on his face stops all movement of my body and the questions on my tongue.

"You know I love you and Drew." His voice is so low I have to strain to hear him. "You will both always be the center of my universe."

I start to feel nauseous and don't understand why. I move to sit up but Jeremy puts both hands on my shoulders and leans down till his lips are barely touching mine. The pupils of his eyes go huge right before he kisses me. Our love making that night was all consuming. I was never more thankful our child slept so soundly and that loud noises rarely woke him. I knew I would have bruises on my hips and thighs tomorrow from how passionately our bodies

*moved as one and how tight he held me to him. Before falling asleep he tucked
my limp body against his and kissed the back of my head.*

"I'm going to fix this Nev. I swear it."

*I was unable to make sense of this as unconsciousness pulled me under. He
gifted me one more kiss the next morning after I got Drew ready for school.
From the doorway of our home Drew and I watched him walk to his car. That
was the last time I would watch him from our door.*

I blink and I'm not standing in the doorway of our home anymore.
My throat closes so tight I put my hands up, to rub where it hurts. I can
tell my cheeks are wet, and I look up through my tears at the hazel eyes
in front of me, not the navy blue of my memories. Remembering that
night has me feeling such shame for what I had just done with Grant.
Rationally, my brain knows Jeremy is gone, and has been for a long
time. But telling myself that now, while his memory is still so fresh,
won't keep the horrendous feeling from seeping into my veins. And on
the tail end of it, is how I felt earlier while this *detective* tried to slander
my husband's reputation. The guilt and anger hit me so strong I want to
bend over and empty what little I had eaten earlier, but I swallow and
breathe slowly in and out through my nose to let it pass.

My shaking hand starts to reach for the stone I know is under my
shirt. Not wanting to make it obvious I'm hiding something, I settle
my hand beside me on the chair instead. I suddenly want to run as far
and as fast as I can. I know he is waiting for me to speak, but I can't get
the words to form on my dry lips. Could it be? Could this stone, the
same stone I've carried with me for years, be what all of this is about?
I can't do this right now. If I admit this out loud it will solidify that
I was married to someone I never really knew. I can't do that. Not to
Jeremy's memory, or to me. It's just all too much. I clear my throat and
then immediately start coughing from my notably dry throat. Like I've

swallowed sandpaper. Grant stands quickly and bends to retrieve a small water bottle from his mini refrigerator, set next to his bookcase. I've never been so thankful for a first sip of water. After several slow drinks from the bottle I place it, now empty, back on his desk.

"Thank you. But I think that is all I can handle today. I need to go home." I say.

I can only imagine the amount of questions he wants to ask, but his only response is to nod, open the drawer, put the open file back into it and take out a red binder before locking it and pocketing the key. He rips a loose sheet of paper from the binder and begins to scribble for several agonizing seconds. Folding the paper in half, then halved again, he walks around to stand next to my chair, and squats his large body next to me, so we are more equal in height. I watch his big hand as he places it under my chin and turns my head in his direction. With a knowing gaze, he waits till he has my attention, then slips the square into my hand and closes my fingers around it.

"This is my personal information. Different from the card Val gave to you for emergencies. This number will send you directly to me. If I'm not near my cell phone at home, it will alert me through my house phone. Day or night. If there is *anything* I can do for you I want my number to be the first you call. If you feel threatened in any way, or remember something that might help, I want my number to be the first you call." His look is so hot it feels like my soul is being branded. "If there is *anything* you *need*, I want my number to be the first that you call. Am I making myself clear? Anything, anytime."

My head bobs in a yes motion, but the words that I say put a look of hurt on his face and I loathe to see it. "I'm sorry, but this is just too much to deal with right now. But I appreciate the offer." I haven't for one second forgotten what kissing this man feels like. But with muted anger still simmering from his questions, plus the memory I relived only moments ago, there is ice water on my libido and my heart is closed for anything more. Adding to the perplexity of feelings is an immense feeling of loss for this man. Like he was mine for a moment and now he's been ripped from me. I'm not sure how to process this, so I tuck it away for later and stand to leave.

My heart races as we walk out of his office. None of our limbs are touching, yet we move as one out into the hall as if connected by an invisible cable. We take the same path as when we'd arrived and I watch the passing of the bathroom door from my peripheral. We make it past without my cheeks flushing, just as Grant's partner turns the corner, with fire in his eyes, intercepting us before we can enter the main room. We halt just feet from him and I shiver at the sheer malevolence burning inside his brown irises. His height rivals that of Grant's, giving the impression I'm standing between two large statues. Grant uses his fallback stance; hands at hips, and challenges Valdez with a grunted *"What?"* I don't want to be around when these two let loose, so I continue to head to where I remember the doors to be, where freedom awaits me. The tension is thick as I pass, but I make it by them unscathed and around to my destination in no time.

I opt to stand just inside the station doors instead of braving the walk to his truck on my own, but I wish I could run home and skip the impending awkward ride. I don't have to wait long before Grant's stepping up beside me. I want to ask if he's ok. His expression is a mix of murder and hurt. I put my hand against his hard forearm and look up about to offer, what…hope? I'm sorry? But I don't get the chance as my hand is taken off and he walks past me through the door. I don't know what I was expecting, but his shut out was not it. Straightening my shoulders, I raise my chin, and follow in his wake. Fine. Lesson learned.

Even in his funk mood, he's still the gentleman, opening my door and helping lift me inside. If only that were enough to soothe the sting of his rejection. We're wedged between two cop cars, making his reach not as efficient as his last attempt, and this time I'm able to buckle my own seatbelt. I smirk at my small victory, admittedly a slightly juvenile response. We ride home in silence, which I'm part glad, part sad about, and just as we pull over the speed bumps marking the entrance of the apartment, he clears his throat. Phew. My ears have been ringing from the noiseless cab. I refuse to turn my head in his direction, proving I can give Shell a run for her money in the stubborn department.

"Here we are. I'm sorry today has been difficult." Understatement, but I keep that to myself. "Remember to call if you need anything. And…" I wait for more. I should just hop out and leave him to his thoughts, but I sit still like a good little girl and wait. "And if you think of anything, I need you to call me. Please." That *please* is added almost as an afterthought. I check the clock on the dash and realize I only have an hour to get myself ready for my afternoon shift, so I cut him off with a quick *ok* and hop out the truck. I know he waits for me to safely arrive at my door by the reflection of his truck in the window I pass. I never turn to look back, just make my way inside, all the while attempting to sever the invisible cable tying us together.

Our apartment is thankfully empty when I close and lock the door. I don't think I could handle the Shelly inquisition right now. I need time to process the last hour or two before I can put it into words. Sliding my butt down along the door, I land hard on my bruised backside, not really feeling anything but hurt and sadness. I wish I had a time machine to go back to when I was unaware of the information I'd received today. I'd pay some big bucks for it. With nothing I can do to change it, I crawl back to standing to prepare for my shift. They say what doesn't kill you makes you stronger, but unfortunately I would make a shitty superhero.

CHAPTER 9

A week flies by with not a sound from Mr. Jason Grant, but it hasn't kept my day dreaming from spinning on a constant replay of the short time I'd spent with him. The anger at his questions is still there, followed closely behind by my desire to see him, but I've kept myself busy to ignore both. There also haven't been any more close encounters with the men supposedly behind the shooting. I've spoken with Detective Valdez twice, with no more answers from him than I'd had before.

This span of time back in my normal routine has given me a chance to think, then think again, about the memory I had and what Jeremy was trying to tell me. So many questions still run through me in a continuous loop. The most annoying question to stir from all this is: is my childhood love responsible for finding a possible connection to a new man? I want to rip that question from my subconscious and light a match to it. Why would I go there? It took me two days to confide in Shell after the morning spent at his office. I still feel bad I couldn't instantly spit out what had been said, but I needed to make sense of it on my own first. After work that night I gave myself permission to have a pain-filled night alone in my room to cry, and came to the realization that no matter what Jeremy was involved in, or mistakes he'd made, I will never regret my time with him or the love we shared. Do I still have a sense of duplicity? Of course I do. Can't help that fact. I guess that won't go away until there's a reason for the decisions he'd made, which may never happen. It takes another full hour with my thoughts to be content with my choice to keep moving forward and focus on the future, not the past. Nothing can change it anyway.

***

I'm standing on our counter when Drew and Shell walk through our apartment door. I might have laughed at the look of surprise on their faces, but I still feel a tad guilty for my actions. I wave at them, then turn back to the cabinets pretending I'm up here looking for something high on the top shelf, while surreptitiously checking to make sure the tiny package I've placed above our cabinets isn't visible. Reaching beside me I open the cabinet and grab the first thing I see. That'll work. Unneeded glass in hand, I sit down on the counter and jump the rest of the way onto the ground. Never one to leave an opportunity open, I can hear Shelly cracking jokes with Drew.

"I'd have paid good money to see your mom's climb up there. Bet that was quite a show."

Rolling my eyes at her snark, my response has a dry tone. "When did you become such a comedian?" I need to keep myself busy, or I'll start to question my actions. Or worse, spill the beans. I can just picture her reaction. Nope. Stay strong here Nev. I fill the glass with water, because I might as well use it, and turn to face her. Then find myself emptying the dishwasher.

Shelly leans over to grab a plate, then goes about making a snack while she talks. "Oh, my dear pocket sized friend, …I've only been telling you how awesomely funny I am for, like, ever." She receives a dishtowel snap as my reply. I know I'm short. I mean, hello, I need a friggin' booster seat at the movie theater, but we've been slinging friendly insults at each other for so long, it just seems natural to carry on like this.

Drew walks back around the corner, from his room, with a new sketchpad and pencil case, saving me from having to respond. He slumps down into the seat at our table. He's been a little somber since they've arrived. I walk over and lift the front of his hair away from his face to get a good look into his eyes. Eyes that are so focused on the table I'm surprised there isn't a hole burned straight through the surface. I keep my voice low. "You ok? Did you guys have fun?" Still not meeting my eyes, he takes a pencil out and begins to make long strokes on the page.

"Yea mom, fine." At his tone my eyes fly to Shelly's and her confused expression mirrors my own. In response, I receive a one-shoulder shrug from her just as there is a knock at our door. Shifting my attention back to Drew while Shelly answers the door, I lean down to kiss the top of his head. It's hard not to worry about him. But from what I've been told, he's thriving in school. I'm praying this is just a preteen mood change.

"Oh Snow White… your prince has come a calling." I make a face directed to her back, at the off-key sing-song voice of one of her Disney Princesses. Well, at least I think that's what she'd been attempting. Or it was a horrible dolphin imitation? It's a toss up. She steps to the side and I see Jason filling our doorway. The man can rock a suit. But the man in jeans and a long sleeved Henley? There aren't words to describe it. The sleeves of his dark green shirt are pulled up, showing thick forearms with the material across his chest pulled snug, leaving a seriously impressive image. The mirrored shades I'd seen before are tucked up at the collar of his shirt. Gah! Shell is still talking, I think, but all I hear is my own breathing. My fingers tingle, pleading with me to reach out and touch him, and my heart feels lighter with him standing here. It only takes a few more moments to realize it's because I've missed him. Is there a law somewhere that states you shouldn't miss someone this much, if you barely know him? But I did, I do. It feels natural to have him in our living space. Ugh, I think I need my head examined.

"…and don't even think to try to name me one of your dwarves." Shelly says.

"I'm not sure there's a dwarf in Snow White named shopaholic." This is spoken by the newly smart-mouthed kid behind me. It surprises me so much that before I know it, both Shell and I are full out laughing. Poor Drew doesn't know what to do with us, just rolls his baby ice-blues and carries on with his artwork. Not that I blame him. We can be a handful on a good day.

With a hand on her hip, Shell levels him with a look. "HEY! My awesome shopping tendencies just bought you a new sketch pad mister." Her attempt at acting offended is ruined by the huge smile on her face and the laughter tears still evident under her eyes. She looks at me and I raise my eyebrow and blow her a kiss. She *is* pretty awesome. Even if I'd have picked a different fake dwarf name, like Smartass.

Wiping at my own conspicuous tears, I focus back on the man candy and see him smiling at my son. I stop mid laugh at the familiar sensation of butterflies swirling in my stomach. No one seems to notice my reaction, which I'm grateful for, as it gives me time to get my act together, and also check my hiding spot back in the kitchen. With a glance up, I can just make out the corner of the box above the cabinet. Dammit. I'm sure no one will ever notice it's there. But it still causes my heart to palpitate at the thought of it being discovered. There are a few moments of silence before I do the polite thing and make introductions. "I guess you already met Shelly a few weeks ago." She offers him a full out curtsy, including the grip of her imaginary skirt. "So I'll just introduce my son. Jason, this is Drew. Drew, this is Detective Grant." I know my mistake before the last word leaves my mouth.

"You're a Detective?" I hold my breath while I prepare to be bombarded with questions as to why he's here, but all I hear is "COOL! Can I see your badge?" My heart skips and starts again, while I watch Drew leap off the couch to stand before Jason. Jason crouches down to one knee in front of Drew, so he can look straight ahead, and answers his question. "Sorry bud, I'm not working tonight." At Drew's disappointment he adds a compromise. "But how about I swing by later this week and I'll show it to you then, if that's ok with your mom?"

He's practically levitating. "Deal... Can I see your gun too?"

Shell sees my look and steps in for me. "Hey now buddy, don't push it. Your mom can only handle you growing up so fast a little a time." The exaggerated wink in my direction is so far from subtle I'm sure the neighbors see it. "Ok Drew…I know we just got back, but how does a quick walk over to Mel's sound? Give your mom a few minutes to talk to your new friend?" That's perfect. Melanie is the elderly neighbor we've been helping since her husband passed a few months ago. She loves the company. Especially Drew's. Those two are kindred spirits.

After a promise from Drew to tell her I said hi, plus another more reluctant promise not to eat too many of her cookies, I send them on their way. Locking the door behind them, I turn to find Jason at our bookshelf holding the picture of Drew and I last spring at the roller skating palace. He's running his knuckles across the glass with a look I can't decipher from the angle of his face. Not wanting to interrupt, but needing to say something, I ask the first thing that pops into my brain. "Would you like something to drink?"

Setting the frame back he clears his throat. "No, but thank you. I just came by to check on how you were doing. Val says he spoke with you this week, but I wanted to check for myself." He finally faces me and I nervously grab my hair, pulling it over one shoulder. It's tame today, even with the awful humidity. I think he wants a response from me.

"Oh. I'm good. No more scary bullets." I try and relax my arms while I mention the last part, but it's not an easy feat.

Nodding, he puts his hands into his pockets and rocks back on his heels. "Good. That's good." I have no idea what to say now. I glance in the kitchen wishing he'd given me the green light to make him a drink, so at least I could keep my hands busy. I snap back to attention when I see him walking to the door. Wait? That's it? He can't just leave. I'm not ready for him to go. There is so much I want to say, and yet I just stand here, watching while he pulls his key ring from his pocket. He pauses long enough for my hope to rise. "Are you working at the club on Friday?" When I answer with a quick yes he looks at me and then heads out the door. I'm standing in the apartment alone and confused. What was that all about?

CHAPTER 10

Thursday finds me working the early shift at the bookstore. Matt, my adorable geeky book buddy, is working with me today. I've already moved all the sci-fi novels to the back of the store making room for the new romance selection being delivered this afternoon, but I still need to organize the discount section and set up the coffee pot so it's ready. He was supposed to be quick with our bagel run next door, but I haven't seen him since he left fifteen minutes ago. I'd heard the bell over the door ring five of those minutes ago, so I know he has to be back. Where the hell is he and why isn't he back here swooping in to save me from lugging this thing to the front? The ladder I'm carrying is heavier than I am, so picking it up is a no-go. Maybe I can just try dragging it behind me? Ugh. I seriously need to work out my arms, but that's mean I have to work out the rest of me too. Yea, no thanks. I shudder at the thought. I've been blessed with a high metabolism that keeps me slim, but I know I could improve more than one area of my body. I give one more stab at moving the ladder, but the stupid thing won't budge. This is ridiculous.

"Hey Matt? Where are you? I need you to bring this up to the front for me." I'm about to just lay the dang thing down in the middle of the aisle and make him get it himself, when I hear a snort and look up to see Matt watching me perform my morning workout.

"Just enjoying the show Tinker Bell." Grr. I want to grab all that thick dark hair and shake him. But I'd have to be able to reach him to do that. I look at the ladder and consider my options. Well, that's out.

"What is it with you and Shell and your Disney references? I swear if you break out in song I'm walking right out that door and you'll be forced to set up the section with all the hot men on the covers by yourself." That gets his attention and the ladder is gracefully removed from my arms. Huh. He makes it looks so easy. I revisit my quest for gym application. Nope, still not motivated enough. Why bother when I can just enjoy watching Matt lug it for me. His lean muscles are displayed as he moves. Nice.

"Lizzie and I just watched Tinker Bell last night. It's on the brain. One week in Orlando and it's all she wants to watch. I'm so out of my league with these girly things. She's going to wake up one day and realize what a lug she has for a father. I tried to put the game on last night and she lost her mind. You'd have thought I was ripping the legs off her dolls. So, Tinker Bell won that round."

I laugh at his dramatic tirade. Picturing him watching that movie is just too cute. "Nonsense, You are an amazing father. But please make my day brighter, and tell me you let her dress you up to watch it. I see bows and tulle in your future." He and Lizzie just got back from their vacation yesterday, and I've been dying to hear how much she loved it. Liz is his sweet 3-year-old daughter. Matt's a single parent just like I am. Only difference is Liz's mother has never been in the picture. Well, she was there for her birth, but not much longer. I'm still not 100% on that whole story. But I admire Matt for taking charge and never looking back. Shell and I take Liz once a month for 'girl time' and Matt reciprocates with Drew to give him 'boy time'. I'm not sure what all that entails, but as long as they're not putting dollar bills in a stripper's thong while chugging beer, I'm okay with it. I shudder. Please God, give me a few more years till he's interested the opposite sex.

It's really too bad Matt and I aren't attracted to each other. He and Lizzie both mean the world to me. But as I've experienced true love, I won't settle for anything less. And neither should Matt. I have full confidence his soul mate is just around the corner. Lost in thought I slam face first into Matt's back. When did he stop? "Oompf. Sorry."

"I was wrong. Tinker Bell has more grace than you do. If there were a clumsy princess you'd fit perfectly. You could have your own ride at Disney World and everything. Including neck braces and knee-pads. Speaking of graceful princesses, your partner in crime informed me of the mess you seem to have landed in. You okay? And is there anything I can do?"

"You mean my wicked step-sister? Why is she going behind my back and blabbing my drama? Besides, it's nothing. I'm sure it was all a misunderstanding." Yep, that's what I said.

"She just cares about you and wanted to give me a heads up in case you landed in more trouble. Not to mention the fact that we happen to be friends. I've been waiting for you to share since we got here, but since we have approximately…" He cranes his neck to look at the clock hanging by the coffee machine, "…four and a half minutes to eat the bagels I picked up before the herd of book lovers descend on us, you need to start talking fast."

We walk over and grab two bar stools, set up for the costumers, and dig in. I love carbs. Especially carbs with gooey cream cheese. Frickin' delicious. In between bites I fill him in on the theatrics of the past week and get a few stories about Liz riding *Dumbo* and *Winnie the Pooh*. We continue chatting while he unlocks the door and I turn the sign around to notify all the book hoarders we're open for business. Normally the afternoon is the busiest, so I sit back at the counter to finish drinking my coffee while the store is still quiet. Matt has just walked back up from depositing the ladder in storage, when I see the *look* telling me he wants more info. He's not happy that's all I can give him. Which makes two of us in the grumpty dumpty department. Great. Their childishness is rubbing off on me.

Leaning over the counter in front of me, he offers the other half of his bagel. He knows me so well. "So, you're saying this detective is hot."

My hot coffee is swallowed too fast and I start coughing it back up. With my eyes watering, from the sting of my freshly burned throat, it takes too much effort to glare at him. I stick with denial. "I never said that. In fact how is it, that out of everything I just told you, that's your first question? How about, 'how's your hip Neva?' or better yet 'how's your head Neva?" I throw my bottom lip out and try my hardest to look pathetic. If that doesn't work I may have to bring out the big guns and make my bottom lip quiver just right. Dagnabbit I can tell it's not working. A shrug will have to do then. I pour the rest of my coffee out in the sink and settle my non-injured hip along the drawer, waiting for his answer. Inside I'm pouting. Not because he hasn't asked if I'm all right, but that I'm so transparent where Jason is concerned. Obviously I need to work on my poker face.

"First of all, I can see you're fine. You have one of the hardest heads I know. Plus I'm sure Shell would have spread the word if you were seriously hurt. And no. I'm in no way down playing what you went through. I just already knew you were ok and wanted to get to the good stuff." I keep my face blank and smooth, giving nothing away. "Fine. Shell may have mentioned a, and I quote here, 'sexy beast carrying his beauty' through your apartment that night. But your red face kinda gave it away anyways." Cursing my fair skin, it takes me a second to come up with something believable.

"Ok. I admit the man is nice to look at. But there are tons of those out in the wild. So what." I can feel my face getting redder. This is not going the way I planned it.

Hi eyes narrow. "Hmmm. There's something you're not telling me. I'm afraid to question you more about it though. Your face looks to be ripe for the picking, my tomato friend. But teasing you aside, you know I just want you to be happy. It'd be nice to see you interested in someone you care about, and vice versa. Drew would be happy too."

I take a step closer to him, preparing for battle. I can't believe he said that. "What? You've been talking to Drew about me and my love life?" At his look I sigh and correct myself. "Fine. *Lack* of love life. Whatever, Captain Literal. I'm perfectly happy right now. There is no need to add a man to make me happier." Ugh. The lies keep piling up. The time I spent crying alone in my room showed me I need to put the past where it belongs and look ahead at what life has to offer. And I thought I had done that. So why am I still doubting? "There may have been a kiss. Or two. Or maybe it was just one really long kiss with breaks and a halftime show. Not sure at this point. But yes, if I have to admit it, I find the man attractive and could see myself climbing that mountain like a monkey climbs a tree. Not that I've put much thought into it. I'm just saying." I look down at the coffee mug I'm strangling. Maybe if I stare long enough, and not look back up to his knowing face, it might fill back up all on it's own for me. Or at the very least show me my future. That'd work too.

"I love you Nev, like the little sister you were meant to be. And I always will. Your happiness means a lot to me. That's all I was saying. And it's not anything in particular Drew has said. I just know how that boy thinks. You are his world. And whatever it is, whether it's finding love again or something else, he just wants you to be happy. You deserve it."

Big fat tears collect in the corner of my eyes. My voice is quiet when I answer back. "K. Love you too."

"Ok, mushiness is put away now. Let's get these books sorted. I need something to replace the disturbing image of your kissing and half time show. There are some things I don't need to know. Ever. Oh and by the way, I've decided I'll drive you home today. I know you like to walk most days but I'm going for the better safe than sorry method."

I don't argue, just nod with a smile, and move over to him, then throw my arms around his waist in a huge hug. "Got it. Let's get to work. I'll even let you go work out back and organize the records, since I know that gets your precious geeky side glowing."

He practically skips away from me. Well, more of a manly swagger, but the goofy smile he shows, says it all. "Deal."

Hours later, after work, I close the door to Matt's car and wave once more through the glass, before heading up our walkway. I'm betting he'll wait till he sees I am inside to head over and pick up Liz. I make it to our landing and lean against the railing, overlooking the parking lot below. Sure enough I was right. Seeing me upstairs, he backs his black Mazda CX out of the spot, and pulls onto Lyons Road. I stand for a minute listening to the quiet rumble of thunder I can here in the distance. I can't help but think about the last time I stood here, feeling my skin crawl, looking out into the dark. But for now, it's bright and the slight breeze from the impending storm causes the palm trees to move like they're dancing to the tune of a drum. I turn from the view and walk over to our door. Looking down I spot an envelope, face down in front of the outdoor rug. Figuring Shelly must have dropped it from our mail I snatch it up and shove it into my purse.

Stepping inside I hear a deep, recognizable voice followed by another much higher tone of voice. Huh? I spy Shelly sitting on the kitchen counter, legs swinging like she's five, her finger to her lips. Double huh? I place my bag as quietly as I can, on the table and then super sleuth it over to Shell. Both Jason and Drew have their backs to me at our kitchen table, with an open backpack between them. I look back over to Shell, preparing to ask what's going on, but I must not have been as quiet as I'd thought. My normally quiet child has been replaced with someone much louder.

"MOM. Look! Mr. Grant brought his badge for me to see and then he said I could hold it. But Aunt Shell said I needed to finish up my homework first, then Mr. Grant wanted to know what homework I was doin'. So I said, uck, math and then he said he'd help me. I'm done. Isn't that cool? Can I see your badge now Mr. Grant?" I couldn't pin point a time in which he actually took a breath during that spiel.

"Cool." I reply. My eyes connect with Jason's and I can't describe the emotion about to claw out of me. Gratitude? Happiness? Lust? Maybe all of the above? Why is this affecting me so much? It's not like Drew isn't around other males. Or me either for that matter. Joey and Matt are a big part of our lives. So what it is about seeing these two together that has my heart melting? Whatever it is, it's pretty powerful. I stare at Jason, waiting for him to tell me what's going on. This is the second time he's shown up here. Not that I'm complaining. I shift my attention to Shell, searching for a clue, but she's either giving us privacy or she's playing dumb. She's looking down at her iPad completely ignoring my stare. "Hey Shell? I sent you a new Tom Hiddleston pin today while at work."

"AH. Seriously?" She starts swiping her iPad, probably switching from a game to check her boards.

I pucker my lips at my fib and fess up. "Nope. Just wanted your attention."

"That's just mean Nev." Playing the part of clueless brunette, she pretends to only now notice the two others in the room. "Oh, are you boys done with homework already? Isn't it sweet Nev? Jason was helping Drew with his math homework." I have to give it to her. She's pretty convincing. Now to ferret out the *why.*

"You're right. That's very sweet. Jason? Can I see you in the kitchen a moment? And Drew. Proud of you Buddy. I'll come check on it in just a second, okay?" I don't give anyone a chance to respond, as I just walk around Shelly's swinging legs, and into our tiny kitchen. As privacy goes, this is not the best solution. But as my other options are out, it'll have to do. I'm not taking him into my bedroom that's for sure. Temptation, you are *such* a shrew. Well…not like I'd jump his bones with Drew here, but seriously, why risk it? I hear him tell Drew "great job" to his temporary student, before he comes to stand before me. I'm about to inquire about todays visit, but he beats me to the punch.

"Hey. I'd apologize for barging in on your family, but I originally came over to see if you'd like to have dinner with me tonight. I admit I should have called first. I made a hasty decision and found myself already here. Next thing I know, I'm offering my math skill services." He leans his long body against the counter behind him and pauses to look down at the floor. I feel a mixture of excited, flattered and confused. There needs to be a word created for those combined emotions. Exflatercon? Whatever. I need to focus on the important stuff here. I decide to be blunt.

"Does the dinner invite have to do with that gang and the information you need from me? I mean, is there more I need to know?" I will feel so embarrassed if I misread his intentions, even if only to myself. It's been so long since I've done this courting thing, I'm just not caught up on how to handle a crush. He looks to be debating how to answer. Why is this so difficult? It either is, or it isn't. He finally raises his head to look back towards the entrance of the living room. Is it Shelly? Would he rather ask her?

"He reminds me of someone I used to know." Okay, not Shell. I am too happy about this. "Listen, I know I should have asked before coming, and I…like I said…I was originally planning on inviting you to dinner. But would it be out of place if I asked both you *and* Drew to dinner?" His vulnerability is killing me, causing my eyes to sting. It's my turn to glance towards the living room. I am completely blown away. Totally and completely unexpected. Holy Moses, this was not *at all* how I envisioned this conversation playing out. It only takes a second to come to my verdict. If. And that is an 'if' with a capital 'I'. *If* this man is someone I plan on seeing, shouldn't I make sure he's compatible with my son before I jump the gun?

"Ok, let me talk to Drew and get changed. Was there anywhere you had in mind?" I ask.

He answers so fast I wonder if he'd been expecting my response. A second reminder that I need to work on my transparency issues. "If it's ok with you I was thinking we could leave it up to Drew." That was a great answer and I smile to let him know I agree.

"Sounds good. I'll go now and talk to him." I'm back around the corner and almost land face to chest into Shell. I can see the guilt practically pouring out of her, causing me to lean closer and whisper to her. "Hmmm. Peeping-Tom much Shell? Yeesh, you're worse than the ten-year-old. Is he back in his room?" Out of the corner of my eye, I see Jason looking down at his phone. He roves his eyes back and forth reading, and then looks back up at us.

"If you'll excuse me a moment, I need to take this call." To me he adds, "If I'm not back by the time you're ready, I'll just be out in the hall waiting for you." He says no more, just turns and squeezes between our bodies. We both watch his back retreat, while he grabs his keys off the same table as my purse. Well, my eyes may have diverted lower for a brief second, but that's all. My sigh is loud in the quiet apartment. I get an elbow in my side redirecting my focus again.

"Drool alert, drool alert. Beep, beep, beep." I don't even bother trying to deny it. There *is* drool. The way he swaggered out has me eager to follow him and watch more.

"Yes, I sent him back, since it's not like you were whispering." I have to dredge my mind up - its sunk to the gutter, and remember what we'd been talking about. "We were all of four feet from you guys while y'all talked. I had to eavesdrop. And don't give me that look. How else was I to keep a look out if Drew tried sneaking back in here? Plus, when have you ever not told me something? I'd only be finding out later anyway, and this way I can give you my opinion."

"Good point." At the light in her eyes, I clarify. "About Drew, not the eavesdropping. I need to ask him if he wants to go to dinner and if so, it's up to him where we go. Am I doing the right thing here? We barely know Jason. I don't want this to end up hurting Drew."

Placing her freshly manicured fingers on top of my shoulders, she cocks her head to the side. "If you were parading men in and out every few days, I might say that could affect Drew. But honey, it's been *five years*. I know you. If you didn't like him you'd never be considering this. Take it slow and see where this can go. I think it's nice he wants to include Drew. That says a lot about him; you know this too. He understands you come as a package deal."

Relief... relief is all I feel right now. I'm so lucky to have her. "Thank you. That helped a lot. I'm gonna go talk to Drew. Can you let Jason know if he comes back in, that I'll be right out?" I wrap my arms around Shelly's skinny waist, as she affirms me she will, then make my way down the hall to the dungeon Drew calls his bedroom.

CHAPTER 11

I stand just outside his door, preparing myself for the state of his room. "Hey Bud?" Biting the bullet, I knock quick and enter the dungeon. As much as I'd like to say I'm one of those moms that makes her kid keep his room spotless, I was just never made that way. Unfortunately untidiness has been inherited and I never know what I may walk in to. Sure enough I see my favorite little man lying on his bed filled with school books, clothes and a random Minecraft pickaxe. Scooting over a few books I sit on the edge of the bed, while grabbing the pickaxe, then bend slightly so I can make eye contact.

"Hey… you ok?" I try and keep the mood light since I don't want to bombard him with too much while something is obviously bothering him. I opt for playfulness, to get a smile out of him, and pretend to chop on his math book with the axe. Something I've seen him do numerous times on my computer, but with wood or cobblestone. I stop when I notice I'm getting the opposite response I'd hoped for. He takes it out of my hand and shakes his head while setting it next to his bed. I let out a laugh at our role reversal.

I'm relieved when his response is cheerful. "Yea mom. Aunt Shell said I needed to wait for you. Mr. Grant showed me some cool stuff for figuring out my math homework. He made it super easy. Although I kinda wanted to chop my math book too before he showed me. Can he stay for dinner? I never got to see his badge. I think he should stay for dinner."

"Ok, slow down for just a second." I can't help it. This kid puts a smile on my face daily. "That's why I came in here. Would you want to go out to dinner? Just you, me, and Detective Grant?"

"YES! Can we go to our favorite place? I think he'd like it too. He told me he's half Italian so I bet he'd like it." If he had a tail, it'd be wagging. He's just so excited. That makes two of us. My metaphorical tail has been extremely busy since I got home.

When I respond, I try to calm my own excitement so as not to give myself away. "That's a great idea. Why don't you change from your school clothes and meet us out there. And try to pick something clean." I look around and offer some advice. "Maybe something you're not sitting on."

"Gotcha." He starts to jump off the bed, but cuts off mid leap and tackles me. He gives the best hugs. "I love you mamma bear."

"I love you too baby bear. I'll see ya in five."

***

Back in my room I throw my purse on the bed and run to my tiny closet. Hmmm. What to wear for a maybe/kinda date thing. I strip down to my bra and underwear and check myself in the mirror. Hair still up from work. Leaving it. It's too hot for it down. Cute pink lace push-up bra and matching thong. Eh... No one but me will see it tonight, but I love how I feel wearing it, so I'm leaving that too. I check back in my closet and see my tight jean capris with the folded cuff and jeweled pockets. Squeezing those on, I search for a cute top to complete it. Hmm. Maybe something to cover up my arms? I've never been embarrassed by my tattoos. They are a part of me and I'm not ashamed of them. But tonight, I think I'm going to accentuate my other attributes for a change. It really is too muggy to wear long sleeves, but I have a sheer black top that will still be cool, and soften my look. Black tank under it and I'm ready to go. One thing about not wearing jewelry is that it's one less step I need to worry about. Black ballet flats finish it off, and now to switch my bag.

Grabbing my purse off the bed, I turn it upside down, dumping its contents all over. The white envelope lays on top the mess I've created, having fallen face up. The chill-bumps on my arms are instant, rising to a high level, and my breathing is choppy. In a fine red ink - someone had taken the time to write in calligraphy - is my name. Just my name. With shaky fingers I pick it up and then take a minute to breathe through my panic. Why is this freaking me out so much? For all I know it could be an invitation of some sort and I'm losing my cool in here. Ok. Just do it. I close my eyes, because that helps, and rip the top off. Pulling the single loose paper from the sleeve I start to open the page. I want to scream but I don't. Screaming will only scare them. I need to stay calm and put this away to evaluate later.

No, I need to start thinking about this rationally. Ok, I know I need to tell Jason. But how to do this without letting Shelly and Drew know? Breathe. Slow in. Slow out. I look down, one more time, at the red script and can feel the tears building up. That just won't do. Puffy eyes are like waving a red flag in front of Shell's face at the same time screaming *something's wrong here.* I'm coming to realize I may be in more trouble than I'd originally thought. I'm sorely tempted to take a match and burn this. Forget I ever saw these words. But, I resist by setting the paper back inside the mangled envelope, then stuffing it back inside my empty purse and shoving it under my bed. There. That'll have to do for now. Out of sight, out of mind. One more quick peek at my reflection and I bravely walk out my bedroom door. I can tell the smile on my face is forced so I look down and focus on the tan carpet to keep my eyes from giving me away.

"Okie dokie y'all. I'm all set. Who's ready for some Italian? Shell, you'll be okay tonight?" I notice she gives me a funny look. Well, no wonder. That was a stupid question. One I'm wondering why I even asked. Gah! Whoever said there are no stupid questions is just plain stupid. That's my story and I'm sticking it to her. Or whatever. I'm not sure that was even right. And now I'm arguing with myself. Deep breath. I need to get a grip here. Once more, slow in, slow out. A tad better; I only want to throw up a little now. My eyes connect with hazel, and I feel rooted to my spot on the floor. I'm convinced those eyes see right through me. Right at that moment, I feel my heart stutter in my chest, making me forget my breathing exercises. I may need to demonstrate those exercises to Jason, as he doesn't seem to be breathing himself all too well. I break from his impenetrable stare to control myself and switch to Drew. Thankfully he's oblivious to his crazy mom and her hormonal fits. The piece of crumpled paper that hits my face snaps me out of my moment. "Ouch?"

"Oh please… that so did not hurt. And as much fun as this… well… whatever you'd want to call…uh…" Shelly waves her hand between Jason and I. "…*this*. You guys should get going if you want to make it before they get slammed."

"Oh. Yea." Clearing my throat I start to move towards the door. "You ready Drew?" Without an actual answer he just starts moving, so I take that as a yes. Jason follows behind us and grabs the handle to open the door for he and I to move through first. Looking up at him over my shoulder, I'm reminded of how tall he is. I should have worn shoes with a heel. Not that it'd help much, but at least I wouldn't feel so small compared to him.

Shelly yells from behind us, sending us off with her assent. "You kids have fun and don't stay out too late. J, my man, make sure to get them home at a reasonable hour, would ya? They have work and school tomorrow." She waves one more time and closes our door. J? One afternoon with him and she already has a nickname? His body is at an imposing standstill as he waits for her to finish, not offering more then a tilt of his head. I focus with one step in front of the other while repeating my silent mantra. I can do this. I can do this. As I loop my arm though Drew's, we start our descent for the parking lot and away we go.

CHAPTER 12

JASON

The ride to the restaurant is filled with Neva and her son talking in hushed tones to each other. If I were paying attention, and not brooding, I may feel comfortable stepping in to their conversation. But my mind keeps replaying the moment Neva walked out of her bedroom, when I was met with her barely restrained panic, pouring off her in waves. I'm trying to figure out what had changed in the 15 minutes I was away on the phone. Was I too forward to ask them to dinner? My phone call to Val had already made me on edge, I don't need this complication in my life, but I'm so intoxicated by this beautiful woman that my reasoning has taken a hike to areas off limits. I need to stay focused on my goal, as Val repeatedly reminds me. I laughed as he stated that the look on my face, when I mention Neva, has clued him in to the fact that my feelings are more involved than they should be. I say '*fuck that*' I'm a grown ass man and can deal with this. I switch gears, to take us smoothly through a yellowish stoplight, and relax back into my seat to angle my peripheral view better. That see-through shirt has my mind wishing for things I know should be forbidden. It reveals just enough to hint at creamy skin, kissed with colorful tattoos my hands ache to explore. I bet she has no idea how provocative she looks.

Shifting my eyes upward, I connect with the innocent eyes in my backseat. I hate the guilt condemning me. In the short time I've spent with him I can already tell he's a good kid. The struggle he's bound to brings back such strong memories, I can almost touch them. If I'm to continue on this track I need to keep a lengthy distance. One that I

73

have been programmed to keep and have no doubt I'm capable of. Even if it's becoming a battle all of my own making. The urge to turn this truck around and shield them from any future threats, has me grabbed in a vice grip.

We finally pull into the filled parking lot and find a spot big enough to fit my truck. With it's tail end facing the curb, I'm satisfied we're capable of evacuating in a hurry if the need arises. Dropping them off at the door would be the correct thing to do, I'm sure. But I'm not letting these two out of my sight tonight, even for a minute. There's too much at stake, and I'm not willing to risk it.

That uncomfortable feeling in my gut is back, as I force my hands let go of the wheel before exposing my discomfort. I watch as Neva puts a hand out for the handle, but I grab her arm, probably tighter than I should, and stop her forward movement. It pisses me off that she isn't used to someone taking care of her. It may seem trite in the big picture, but as a man, it feels wrong not opening the door for her. Her warm skin is like silk under my fingers. "Wait." The impact of my order is harsher than intended, but has the desired response, as she lets her hand release the handle.

Opening my door first, I scan the lot and run my sight through every license plate I see. The good thing about a memory like mine is having no need to write anything down, unless I want to. Two cars over I see the black Audi A4 and shake my head. If that motherfucker acknowledges her while we are in here, God help him. I flex my hands, while mentally berating myself for automatically reaching for the hidden knife in my boot. This night just keeps getting longer. I take my time walking around to the other side of my vehicle to adjust my plan for tonight and I thank whoever's listening that she obeyed my command to stay in with the door shut. Opening both doors simultaneously, I reach for Neva's tiny hand and allow her to step down. I seem to always forget our height differences until she's before me, since her presence suggests someone much larger. Walking to the door takes a lifetime and I am not too ashamed to admit I'm relieved once we've cleared the double doors. Scanning the tables visible from my viewpoint I don't see my target immediately. Shaking off the impulsive desire to find him, I wait for our turn to be seated.

The hostess returns to her podium throwing a lewd look on her face in my direction. She has the body I usually find attractive, and is taller than the woman next to me by at least six inches. But there's nothing there to hold my interest. A month ago I'd have taken her up on that offer. Sorry doll, not this time. I offer her a smirk and place my hand at Neva's back to silently inform her I'm not interested. When she tries to seat us to the left of the restaurant, I make a polite suggestion that a booth may be more comfortable, and we are guided to the opposite direction. With my back to the kitchen, I make sure to keep my appearance relaxed and indifferent while scanning the nearby tables. I haven't seen him yet, but I know he'll come crawling out from somewhere, like the roach he is.

"Mr. Grant, you said like Italian. Is this ok? My favorite is the chicken parm. You should try that." Drew says.

The innocent question pulls me from my search. Glancing back at my unopened menu, I quietly agree that works for me and bid him a smile. Neva seems to be studying her menu like she'll be quizzed on it later, in alphabetical order. I get the sense she's nervous, but is it me? Or did she notice the car we walked by earlier as well? The slight vibration of our table tells me her leg is bouncing to a fast rhythm. At that moment, the vibration ceases, as our waiter fills the glasses with water, and sets warm bread in between us. I considered having a piece, but it looks like it may be devoured by the growing boy across from me, so keep I my hands propped next to the menu and out of his way.

As several seconds pass, I wait for a pair of ice blue eyes to lift, hoping she'll send me a clue about the cause of her apprehension, but before I'm granted the opportunity, movement to my left catches my attention. And there he is. I zero in on the man. He's dressed in an expensive suit, black hair slicked back, and beady, penetrating eyes roaming over his neighboring tables. I detect the exact moment recognition sets in and I have no problem returning his hard glare. He transfers his glare to the back of the head, barely visible above the booth, and the glare turns to knowing sneer. I growl under my breath, one I hope is only audible to my own ears. This bastard may be her boss, but he and I both know it's only for show. The wicked smile he throws my way, I assume, is to intimidate me, but as I have a good 30 pounds on him, not to mention a shit load of information, so I feel confident when I ignore it. I really need to get him out of here before causing a scene I do not need right now.

I look back to my dinner companions and witness Neva stroking the back of Drew's hair, speaking softly. I swallow hard at the envy that collides, head on, with my raging insides. I'm standing beside our booth before my brain has a chance to play catch-up and am looming over the smaller man, who dares to walk closer to our table. He doesn't even look up at me, just curls his lips, disguising his sneer into a smile, barely hiding the poison he's desperate to spread. I can't wait for my turn at beating him senseless. My blood boils with how near he is to someone I consider *mine*.

"Ah, my lovely snow princessa." Her head snaps up to his statement and I stand still as stone behind him, scarcely able to keep my hands from snapping his neck. It's a close call. "What a lovely surprise. And you brought your handsome son to dinner with you this evening." With a quick glance back at me he extends a hand back. "And what interesting company you keep."

Neva's hand stays on the back of Drew's spine and she inches her body closer to him. That a-girl. At least she senses the danger in front of her. Even if she's pegged me wrong, I feel better knowing she can discern this kind of trouble, for I'm a whole different breed of dangerous. I move closer to Angelo so that only a centimeter separates our bodies. As I'm a head taller, I can look over him and watch their reactions. One small sign of distress, from either of them, and he's gone. Normally I keep my distance with others, but I need this closeness to hide the blade I have positioned at his kidney. I manage to retain eye contact with Drew, hopefully conveying through a calming sentiment, that he and I will take care of his mom. Him with a calming hand, and me with a sharp dagger. The blade does its job; I sense the muscles in his back tighten in front of me. I want to demand this idiota move away from our table, but instead simply push the knife in far enough to break the skin. This is my favorite hunting dagger, tapered to a razor-sharp edge, which allows me to slice through his brown jacket, directly to the body beneath, without much force. I watch his hands fly up on their own, as he rocks forward away from my threat. I can smell the anxiety pouring off of him, and I want to laugh in his face. My second favorite scent is that of fear. My first, well, it smells suspiciously like the woman before us. I lean down and whisper "leave" into his ear, then calmly straighten to my full height once again, using it to my advantage.

Without another word, he nods his head and stumbles away from our space, eating up the distance back to his confused dinner partner. By the looks of her, she's getting a rude awakening as to the crony she chose to spend the evening with. I wish I could feel sorry for her, but my concern is directed elsewhere. Neva and Drew watch his retreating back, which gives me time to stow the knife inside my front pocket. I hear the sigh emitting from below me at the table as I slide back into my seat and grab ahold of the clenched hand that had gone to her own knife during our interlude. Granted, it was a dinner knife, but it made my heart happy to watch the defending of her cub. Her eyelids close and shoulders relax but mine stay the same. I'm proud of her, a sentiment I don't give out lightly. She has a fire inside her that's rewarding to witness.

"You okay mom?" The quiet question does its job, and Neva stops the wobble of her chin by hugging him.

She fidgets, as I'd observed her doing earlier. It's become a conspicuous tell when she's uneasy, but she hides it well from her son. "I'm okay Bud. Sorry about that guys. My boss hasn't ever seen me outside of work before. It was just weird for both of us." With shaking digits, her eyes revert back to her menu, as if she hadn't memorized it once we were seated. "Did we pick what we want for dinner yet? I think I'll be going for the spaghetti. It may not be original but it's great comfort food."

After I motion for our waiter's attention, he slowly makes his way back over to our table. Not many were aware of the menace only feet from their meals, but our server must have been close enough to sense it. With our meal ordered, we all sit back and attempt to resume the enjoyable dinner we'd originally planned. At the signal from my phone, I excuse myself to take care of business, but don't move far. I keep myself standing close enough to have the table in my sight, in case they need me. The phone call is just as I'd predicted. Same story, different words. And even though my response isn't what he wants to hear, he takes great pleasure in my recount of the scene earlier, with our adversary. In this we are in accord. I wait just long enough for him to finish with his relay of information then head back to our table. Conversation picks up once I'm back, and I discover what a smart kid Drew is. Something I'd suspected from the first moment we'd been introduced. It's humbling to watch the interaction between the mother and son. He has a shy quality to his speech, but once he starts enjoying himself, he shows his brilliant mind and respectful manner. Without conscience thought, my fingers wrap around the locket at the base of my throat, and pull hard enough for the sensation to send an acute pinch at the back of my neck, bringing me out my rumination. I remind myself this is why I'm here right now. Even if the reminder is turning hollow and the fine lines are blurring at the edge.

"…but it's ok. I like this school. They have a Lego team and my friend Geoff is on it too. Next week we are making space ships and I can't wait!"

After seconds pass with silence, I decide to interject with something that had been eating at my curiosity. "That sounds like a lot of fun. May I ask why there have been so many schools?" My inquiry is met with more silence. I'm afraid this question may have been too personal. Thankfully Neva answers, but I can tell she's wary on how to proceed.

"Not all kids have an easy go of it with learning. And some kids need an extra push to get where they need to go." She looks over at Drew and he encourages her that it's fine to move on with him as the topic. "Drew has an extreme case of ADHD. He was diagnosed a little over five years ago. I'm sure there are many boys and girls that have the same condition but I can only speak from our experience. When he was three we noticed him doing several things almost uncontrollably. At the time, as he is my only child, I thought these were normal kid things and tried to stop him from doing them. Just like you would when a child tries to touch something hot. You teach them 'no' and move on to your next learning obstacle. But these 'tics', as his psychiatrist referred to them, would not stop and continued into kindergarten. Most kids his age had already gone through a year or more of preschool, but we just couldn't afford it at the time so kindergarten was his first exposure to school. Thankfully his teacher was amazing and recognized immediately what he was going through. Many months of testing later and we learned what he was experiencing had a name. Unfortunately..." She stops to glance over at Drew. "...well, some of the kids didn't understand what he was going through and acted against him."

When her eyes connect once more with mine I'm hit with such sadness. It makes me want to reach for her, over the obstacle between us, but I choose to keep my distance. My heart wants to soften towards this angelic woman, yet I must remind myself, again, to stay strong. But the longer I spend with her, the more I want from her. Not just her mind and body, but her heart as well. These are dangerous thoughts to have, but I ache all the same.

"Anyway, he's gone to three schools now in five years for being bullied. I really hate that term. But that's the easiest way to explain it. With his second school we were still adjusting his medication, but the damage was already done. He's such a brave young man and I couldn't be more proud. If it weren't for the parent/teacher meeting I might still be in the dark about his struggles with his peers at school. So far, this new school seems to be doing great for him. As you heard there are a ton of programs that are geared towards kids that need that extra, uh, oomph ...I guess you could say. Am I explaining it okay Drew? This is your story so I won't go on if I'm making you feel bad."

"It's fine mom. Can I get ice cream? And can I borrow your pen? I've found all the words in my puzzle but I want to cross them off."

Reaching inside her bag she stops cold then relaxes and fishes out a pen. Her eyes dart quickly to me and away again in fast movements.

She places a serene look on her face and passes over the writing utensil to him. "Yup, here ya go. And when you're finished I'd love some new art work please."

The rest of our meal goes back to more benign topics and the admiring of his depiction of underwater fish Drew has drawn on the corner of his kid's menu. When it's time to go I can't tell whether I'm happy the dinner is over, or feeling another unfamiliar emotion, which can only be construed as bereft. As the server brings the check I hand my card over without looking over the final price.

"Wait." I turn back to Neva and watch her holding cash out to his retreating back. She glances back at me with a look of shock. "What are you doing? I was going to pay for Drew and I. Here." Handing the money over the table, her look of shock morphs to a hopeful one that I'll take it from her. I'm once again reminded that she hasn't had anyone to treat her appropriately. I plan to remedy that, starting now.

"No. I asked you both to dinner tonight, therefore the dinner is paid by me. My payment was your company and your conversation. Please put that away and use it for yourselves." I reply.

"I can't let you do that. I'm sorry, but I make my own way." She's still waving the money in front of her. I take it out of her hand, fold it in half and reach for her purse. She's not fast enough to stop me from moving the bag to my side of the table, and slipping her money back into the zippered pocket.

When I'm finished with my task, I make sure to connect my eyes with hers for her to heed my sincerity. "I commend you for your willingness to make your own way. I won't hold you back from that. But on this... in this, I will not yield. It is my treat. Let me do this for you. Admittedly, I am not an easy man to get to know, I live on a cops salary, and I do not have much to offer anyone, beside myself. But spoiling you like you deserve to be treated? That I can do." She dips her chin in acceptance and relaxes back next to Drew. Both look over to me with the same expression of gratitude. I hadn't taken the time to notice how similar their features are to each other until now. Their eyes are the same luminous shade and size. In fact, except for their hair color, there's little that doesn't match. Right at this moment those eyes are filling with tears. I swallow hard.

"Thank you. For dinner, for your company as well." She nudges next to her and widens her eyes at Drew, prompting another offer of thanks.

"It's my pleasure." And it is. I've enjoyed our evening together. By the time I've signed my name on the receipt, they have moved to stand and are collecting their belongings for us to head out. It's a natural reaction to place my hand against Neva's back on our way to the door; it feels *nice* having her close to me. No, *nice* doesn't begin to describe the feeling when she's near. The black Audi is gone when we walk out, which is what I'd expected, allowing me to concentrate on getting my charges to the car without added drama.

When we arrive back at their home, we discover that Drew has fallen asleep, propped against the back window. One glance at her face and I see the wheels spinning, trying to play out how she's going to get him upstairs. I don't know why it bothers me that she doesn't automatically turn to me, but it does. "I'll carry him up for you, if that's alright." The boy has already reached his mother in height so there is no way, unless she wakes him, she will accomplish this on her own.

"Thanks…. again." She says.

As she leads the way up the stairs, I take the rear, with a limp boy held in my arms. After she unlocks her door, and points the way to his room, it's a quiet walk down their hall. The boy is a solid mass in my arms, but I make it without his awareness. I slip out of his room to give him and his mother privacy, but not before familiarizing myself with the parts of the apartment I haven't seen yet. The hall is filled with large picture frames holding a multitude of pictures. I stop at the frame furthest from his room. Reaching up I softly trace the outline, without transferring my prints to the glass, of the portrait. Neva has a smile on her face, one I've yet to be fortunate enough to witness, and her hair is down disappearing below the frame. Her delicate face is flawless. She is truly bewitching.

The door down the hall latches and I turn to the pictures tangible form. Without cognitive thought, I trace the contours of her face just I had her image behind it's glass barrier. She leans into my embrace as I'd hoped. "I should leave you to your night." I don't want to leave. The door to her room is open, giving me ideas on how we can spend it together. But I know that is dangerous. I have to bend down quite a ways to touch my lips to hers, but the prize is worth the journey. I make sure the kiss is hard enough to *feel* her, but not enough to send the message that I'm staying. She blinks slowly when I release her and I have to steady her, with my hand, when her body leans further than she expected it to. With no more to be done tonight, I make myself walk away and back out into the night. There is too much at stake to succumb to my desires. At least not tonight.

CHAPTER 13

NEVA

After the eventful day I had yesterday, it feels good to have some time to myself. This morning has me sitting on our small back porch, coffee mug in my hand, enjoying the sounds of my city coming to life. Our patio has just enough cover to block the early morning rays from landing on me, but as I'm still dressed for bed I've added a light blanket to wrap around me, to spare the neighbors the view of my white legs. Sipping slowly, as not to burn my tongue, I run through my morning so far. Drew was in high spirits this morning as, in his words, he had an "awesome time last night" and practically ran down to the bus.

I haven't seen Shell since we left for dinner, but the note taped to my door tells me that whichever hook-up she visited last night turned into an all-nighter. Hopefully I'll get a rundown of her night when she makes it home from work this afternoon. I love her, but I can't help but worry for her just as strongly. Tonight is my first Friday night away from the club in over a month. Fridays are the big money-making nights and Angelo likes to rotate every couple of Fridays to the weekday workers. Which works well for me, as it gives me something to look forward to. Tonight Matt is taking both Drew and Liz to Chuck E Cheese and a sleepover. This will give Shelly and me a much needed girl's night and, I'm hoping, some girly bonding time.

Looking down over the lot below, it reminds me of our walk back up from dinner, and watching Jason carry my son in his arms. His actions confuse me. In fact, I'm confused on so many things it's hard for me to sort it all through my sleepy mind. Was it a date? I wanted it to be a date, even if we were joined by Drew. Parts of the evening I thought I saw genuine interest on his part. I *know* I saw it for Drew. And the kiss? Even if it was just a graze of his lips, it was still a memorable kiss. And why would I answer with so much detail when it comes to Drew's troubles with school? I don't think I've ever felt more comfortable discussing something usually so hard to think about, let alone *talk* about. I *hate* talking about Drew and his issues. Not that I'm ashamed of him. A small part of me feels like it's my fault and I could have prevented it. But that's not the reason for usually keeping my trap shut. It's hard to know he's dealt with these things alone, while I'm miles away at work or home. Why add insult to injury by repeatedly pointing out the things he struggles with?

If I'm being honest with myself, I have to acknowledge how great it felt to watch Drew open up to Jason. And likewise, how great Jason was working with Drew. It was scary how fast Jason picked out the correct words in the puzzle after Drew crossed through the ones he'd already found. But more than that, it was the kindness he showed my son that made my heart do the happy dance. I was able to see past the sexy exterior of him to the softness underneath it. And I needed to see that softness after the testosterone battle earlier on in the evening. Who the *hell* does Angelo think he is coming over and making a scene? Oh, he might not have raised his voice, or even called much attention to our booth, but I know good and well he was up to something. At work is one thing. But when I'm off the clock and not answering to him? I. DO. NOT. THINK. SO. I couldn't hear what Jason said to him, but I caught the look on Angelo's face when he said it. It wasn't exactly fear, but it was a close second. And as I probably had that same look on my face, more than once last night, I know what to look for. My biggest clue was the shaking of the hands he raised before walking away. I will never understand his hatred of me. And I can't find it in me to care. So long as he doesn't bring it around Drew. Call me all the names you want while it's just me and, go ahead, treat me like trash, but leave my family out of it.

Realizing my cup is empty I remove the blanket to stand. As I rise up, I head back through the sliding doors to refill my cup when I hear a knock at the door. I wrap my blanket toga style around my barely clothed body and ask who it is. After waiting a solid minute, I stretch my feet as tall as they can go and reach for the peephole too high for my short stature. Hmm, that's strange. Seeing no one on the other side, I open our door and peek out through the crack the chain has afforded me. I close my eyes to shut out the vision of the unwanted envelope placed on our doormat in the exact same spot as before. Crouching down I reach my hand out and snag it fast, then slam the door shut, while snapping the lock in place and running full speed to my room.

I'm out of breath. Completely out of breath. So much so, I have to sit at the corner of my mattress and fight off a wave of dizziness. Please, not another one. Ripping back the glued flap I don't take the time to chicken out. What I see has my knee bouncing, and a headache pushing it's way up my skull. This letter is almost identical in script, but this time the words don't make any sense. Not that the first letter explained a whole lot, but I at least grasped the concept of the warning. I refold it and lay in on top of my comforter. Decision made, I head out of my room.

Coming back from the kitchen, armed with Ziploc bag, I gently place the new and old envelopes inside and grab the folded paper given to me by Jason, with his personal number. Stupid, stupid me. I should have made time last night to talk to him about the first one, but never had a chance without little ears listening in. There may have been time on the way home, but I can't change it now. Actually, I'd completely forgotten about it once we'd left for dinner. It wasn't until I reached for my pen that I was forced to remember. It's time I told someone before this gets worse.

***

I've never been so thankful I need a padded bra than right now. If I were wearing something less padded, I think my nipples might cut straight through my shirt. It's freezing in this small room. I look up at the air vent pointed directly at me. Well, that explains a lot. Sliding the chair over, I rub my arms to alleviate the chill bumps. Once I'd called Jason, I was informed an undercover police cruiser would be escorting me to the station. Within 10 minutes I had thrown on clothes and texted Shell to give her a heads up on my new program for the morning. Now I'm here, in a small room alone, and freezing my tiny butt off. I had just managed to control the shaking from nerves, when it started all over again from the freezing. Is this part of an interrogation tactic? Do they teach meat locker interrogation in detective school? It's working. I'd spill my guts right now for a pair of socks and a hat. The only thing missing from my cell/torture chamber is the two-way mirror you always see on crime shows. Blowing hot air into my hands, I have my eyes closed enjoying the quick respite from frost-bite, when I feel a warm hand on my shoulder. I must not have been stuck to my chair like I'd assumed. If it weren't for the hand holding me down, I may have vaulted Olympic-style over the table I'm sitting at from fright. I see Detective Valdez move opposite the table I'm at, so I know the hand doesn't belong to him. But he is the one to speak first. This is the most informal I've seen him. Dark wash jeans and a white, collared polo shirt. His short blonde hair is still styled in his usual pompous way, but he's let his facial hair grow out. He's morphed into a rugged, golf-playing Viking. Interesting.

"Neva. We've run the envelopes for fingerprints. But unfortunately I'm not very hopeful we'll find anything useful." The hand on my shoulder moves to cup the back of my neck and gently squeezes it. I turn my face as much as his hand allows, and get a glimpse of an extremely stern-looking Jason. His hard face is directed at his partner, giving me a side view. But there is no mistaking that he looks *pissed*. I turn back as Valdez continues, obviously ignoring Jason's look. "You told me on the phone this letter today was one of two you've received? When was the first delivered?" He holds a hand up stopping my question. "I know you can't tell me what time it was put in front of your door. I'm looking for the time you noticed it was there. We have someone looking into the surveillance tapes at your apartment complex, but as they are usually only pointed at the parking lot and entrances to stairwells, it may be difficult to get something. But that doesn't mean we won't find anything."

"Um… the first was when Matt brought me home from work, at around maybe 4:30? But I didn't open it until about an hour later. I know I should have said something when it happened. But with dinner plans I guess it slipped my mind." The hand on my neck drops giving me mobility of my neck and a clearer view of its owner. The partners are communicating silently. One still pissed, and the other unreadable. I'm not liking this feeling. And I'm not talking about my iced toes or my chattering teeth. I'd very much like to be included in this silent discussion. I'd clap my hands to get their attention but my hands might break off. Finally recollecting they have a third person, not invited to their man-party, they look back at me.

"I'm going to leave you with Jason to go over any more information you can give us. Meanwhile, I'll be right outside. Try to recall if there is anything you think would help." When he's a foot from the door he turns back to us. "And Neva? If you can think of anything, anything at all that your husband may have shared with you before his death, I suggest you let us know." With that sweet warning he's gone.

88

Jason moves to the spot his partner had just vacated, and removes his jacket, laying it across the back of the chair. I block out the sight of his gun strapped on his hip and focus my eyes upward. I can't say he's any less pissed than when we were a trio, but his face isn't as pinched with just the two of us. Maybe if I apologize, he'll lose the rest of his stress.

"I'm sorry. I should have made time to tell you last night. I honestly wasn't even thinking about it once we left. Then, when I did remember, I had Drew next to me and he doesn't need to know about this. He idolizes the memory of his father. He may have been young when his father passed, but they had a close bond that will always stick with him. I don't want this getting back to him and taint what little remembrance he has." I stop talking as he stares down at me. It's almost as if he's looking right through me. I guess my apology didn't help. I want to say more, but don't know what to do at this point. Finally, after what feels like an eternity, he pulls the chair around and positions it next to mine. After taking his seat, he leans forward to rest his arms on his knees. His face is close enough for me to touch. My fingers curl in want from it.

"Neva, we need to know what we are looking for here so we can help you. Do you grasp what these letters are telling you?"

Forcing my eyes away from his beard I try an explain myself. "I can understand the first one. *'We are watching you'* is pretty self-explanatory. At least the action is. Not the *who*. But the second? *He who watches you may be the creator of your demise?* Um…no. Who's 'he'? And are they inferring I'm next to die?" I blow a quick breath through my lips and glance down at my shaking fingers. My voice seems so small when I ask. "Why?" Okay, so if what I'm thinking this has to do with is the cause, then I really should tell him. But can I do it? I look back up and my train of thought freezes. He has such a handsome face. I run my eyes over it looking for flaws but find none. Even his nose is straight.

My hand reaches up like a magnet drawn to it's mate and I run my fingers lightly over the coarse hair against his jaw, just like I'd wanted to from the moment he sat down. His mouth flattens in a hard line, so my finger closest traces the edge of his bottom lip to smooth it. Without conscious thought I move my face closer and blow softly before pressing my lips to his, as he'd done to me last night. At first I'm shocked by my own behavior and my eyes fly to his. The fire in the hazel depths fuels my own, causing a battle for dominance as the kiss consumes us. I lose the battle almost immediately. Big hands grab me around my waist and pull me right off my chair and into his lap. My earlier chill is wiped clean from my mind as my body lays snug against his warm one, and my breasts are pressed close to his chest. My hand reaches up, to hold myself steady, and curls against the base of his neck. I'm hot. Or maybe on fire. I can't seem to get close enough as he devours my mouth with his own. My lips are ripped from his as he grips my hair, and the slight pain on my skull only adds to my madness.

The peppering of kisses on my throat, in-between the harsher sucking against my neck, keeps me guessing as to where he'll take me next. I know where I want to go, and I grind myself against his erection to plead my case. He drags his lips upward along the column of my sensitive neck, then nibbling at my chin, and finally to my lips once more, where he bites my bottom lip. The sensation causes me to tighten my knees on his outer thighs. It feels too good. If he stops I may internally combust. He still has my hair in his fist and maneuvers my face to angle it better, like I'm a doll for him to play with. His other hand pulls at the barbell and I moan into his mouth. I'm suddenly dumped from his lap into the chair I'd been sitting in, and watch as Jason bends to lean over the metal table. Hands that had just been on me are now flat atop the hard surface. Breathing hard, he doesn't raise his head to speak with whoever entered the room during our moment of insanity.

"What?" He says in a biting tone.

Wiping my mouth, I look back toward the door and notice a man I've never met before. If I had to guess I'd say he's almost as tall as Jason, maybe two or three inches shorter, yet his body is more of what you'd see on a swimmer. He has dark hair, but with lighter waves running through it, making it appear soft and it looks to be in need of a serious trim. The front lies just over his left eye that is cloaked behind a pair of black-rimmed glasses. The dark brown irises focus through the glass on me, then quickly dart over to Jason. I can swear I see a blush on his cheeks. I let out a small smile for him to hopefully erase the memory of what he walked in on. When he talks, he doesn't look at either one of us, just focuses on the far wall behind us.

"Uh…Val says he needs you to see something. I'm gonna just head back out. Sorry to interrupt." And 'poof' he's gone. I turn away from the door and notice I'm eye level with a pretty serious erection. I bet that hurts. I know I do. The ache has me shifting in my chair reaching for some sort of friction. There's a tingle that has spread throughout my body. My scalp, my lips, everywhere. I watch him straighten his back and walk around the metal table, putting distance once again between us. Can I blame him? Absolutely. I did just throw my over-eager self at him. I can't even remember what we'd been talking about to begin with. It kinda seems inconsequential now.

It's actually turns me on more when I hear the deep timber of his voice. *So* not helping. "If you'll excuse me. I…" His eyes slice right through me. I can see what he's trying to say and the hurt I feel takes me by surprise, while also dampening my hormonal frenzy. I duck my head down to shelter the moisture that blurs my vision, right before I snatch my purse from the back of my uncomfortable chair. No sense in staying where I'm unwanted.

"It's fine. I need to get going anyway." I'm up and stalking to the exit, that I barely make out through the fog, with my purse flung over my shoulder.

"Wait!" I stiffen at his harsh command, while concentrating on the door. Argh, I'm only steps away from freedom. I should just keep walking. But the longer I stand here, waiting, the more I want to turn around. Nothing more is said. It's just him, this living, breathing silence and me. What is he waiting for? Can't he see I'm desperately trying to keep it together here? I wish he'd just end my misery and let me leave with the tiny amount of dignity I have left.

And then all hope vanishes with his next words, and my heart plummets. "This can't happen again. I'm sorry. I thought it was what I wanted. I'm just,…I'm sorry, Neva. I truly wish I could. I'll make sure someone follows you home." His voice sounds strained. But that could still be left over from the disrupted kiss. I promised myself I'd never give my heart away again. It's just too easy to get stripped from you. But the moment I slammed into the tall detective, my heart decided for me. I'm appalled at my behavior. I had thought that after our dinner date we were on the same page. Apparently I was seeing things that weren't there. I choose, at this moment, to walk through the door, and away from him, without offering up a reply. My leather-soled shoes echo on the wall as I pass the main room, then out to my car. If asked, I couldn't describe a single person that has walked by me. My mind is too focused on getting out of here.

I stare down at the key in my hand while sitting in my hot car. Going home sounds utterly depressing. It'll be several more hours till Shelly gets home and I can't sit in our apartment alone replaying the last hour of my life. Turning the ignition, I set the A/C to as cold as possible, and pull out of the lot. I feel like yelling at the thought of leaving, but what's the point. Waste of perfectly good air, if you ask me. Instead I drive as if someone's chasing me, but as I look in the rearview mirror I can safely say there isn't anyone following me. Not yet anyway. He probably doesn't want to waste anyone's time. Now I'm being petulant. Throw in a foot stomp, with my bottom lip puckered out, and I'll have sufficiently reverted back to my childhood.

Turning the corner, my car steers itself down a familiar path, one I could drive down blindfolded because I've been here so many times. Crossing through the gated entrance, the large trees covering the drive cast shadows blocking out the sun, giving an appearance matching the numbness of my soul. Dark and dreary, with tons of shadows, but if you look hard enough, the sun is just beyond it. I need to focus on the sun behind the clouds, and not the crappy shadows.

It's been exactly three weeks since I've taken this drive. Almost the exact amount of time since I met *him*. Getting out of my car, I walk the pathway marked by small plants. The walk up the slope takes more time than it usually would, due to my slow pace. Cresting the small hill I sit down in my spot and look at the grave. The dead flowers from my last visit are scattered on top, most likely from the previous thunderstorm. I feel bad that my hands are empty of something to replace them with. In fact, I can't think of a time I've visited and not brought something. Sometimes it flowers, but mostly I bring our son to visit, giving Drew private moments to talk to his father.

I trace his name engraved into the stone, starting at the cursive J and ending with the Y. I push on to complete his name, first, middle, and last, then settle my hand back into my lap. It was never supposed to be this way. We had our whole life planned. I swipe at the tear that's escaped down my cheek with the back of my hand then confide in the one who used to be my best friend.

"Hey." My voice sounds like I've swallowed glass. "So…you know I love you. I'm just having a really hard time right now, learning things I never knew about you. Where did you find that ring? And why did you give it to me? I have crazy people after me now. I'm pissed at you, but still miss you. I wish you were here just so I could yell at you then make up with you. Did you give it to me for a reason? I just don't get it."

As I ramble, my hands stay busy by ripping small weeds from the earth beside me. "And why now after five years, are they, or he, trying to get it back?" Rubbing my sore eyes I lie down next to his grave, giving up my landscaping. If I continue, the grass will be bare. Plus I need my mind clear to finish what I'm about to say. When I start again, it comes out as a whispered tone, like I'm telling this huge secret. "I've met someone. And for a brief instant I thought there was this connection. I'm sorry I'm bringing this to you. This is probably the last thing you want to hear from me. But you've always been my best friend, since you, Shelly, and me were kids and you helped us in that horrible algebra class. Up until you left us, I always came to you for everything. Even when Brad Johansson asked me to prom. I thought you were going to flip your lid." I laugh to myself. "But I'm glad he did or you never would have gotten your butt in gear to ask me out. *Scared* of me you said. HA. I'm not scary." My sigh is loud to my ears. "*I* am scared though. I'm scared of never being loved again. I'm scared of these men who want the last memory I have of you. I'm scared I just threw myself at a man who I need to help me, and he may not want to now. I'm scared that my selfishness, not wanting to give up that jewel, will blow back on Shelly and Drew. I'm scared of feeling lonely when I'm not really alone. Guh…I sound pathetic. And I miss you. I want you to know that no matter what length of time passes you will always be with me. But someday I hope to find someone. Never to replace you, but to feel loved again and give my love in return. And I want you to be okay with it. Silly as it sounds."

I move to sit up and see a shadow move behind me. I'm still concentrating on the words I've just spoken from the heart, not really worried I may have been overheard. Turning my head, I can just make out what seems to be a man hidden by the trees. I can't discern anything more as the loud crack startles me to duck my head. I feel the shards of marble stinging my hands and face, most likely leaving cuts along my skin, but I don't stay seated for long to find out for sure. I'm up and over the headstone running fast away from the threat. I may be short, but my little legs can run fast when needed. I don't hear any more gunshots until I make it to the line of pine trees and slam my back against its thick trunk. What…what? This can't be real.

Another gunshot, causing my ears to ring, has me falling to my knees on the hard earth. I make a split decision, checking around me, then sprinting full speed to the next cluster of trees about ten feet away. My legs move like they're coated in molasses, but I know I'm moving faster than it feels. Oh! I must not be, as the next shot he takes hits closer to his target and I cry out falling face down, punishing my hands against loose sticks and rocks. My leg burns but if I look down I will most definitely lose consciousness, so that's not an option right now. I'll have to deal with it later. I have quite an extensive list in my later column.

I peek through my hair that's fallen from its bun, disrupting my view of all but directly in front of me. Moving my knees up to make a run for it, I am suddenly slammed down into the ground once again, this time cutting my face in the process. I struggle to move him off me, but his weight is much greater than mine and my body is easily pinned beneath him. Something hard is poked into my lower back and I freeze my struggling. Okay, okay, I get it. I just need to breathe. He presses closer to me and breathing becomes difficult with my chest compressed against the earth. This is not how I want to die. The mask covering his face brushes my shoulder, making my body involuntarily move away, but he immobilizes me by knocking something hard against the back of my head. Fuck…that really hurt. In a heavily accented murmur he asks me a question. It takes two more times and another shake of my limp body for the words to register. "Where is it? This can be over, if you just give us what we are looking for."

Like I've pushed a magic button, his weight is gone, and I'm alone with only my bruised and battered frame. I know I should move. Just get up and run. Even as I hear scuffling somewhere behind me, I still don't move, and nothing my brain is telling me to do is working. I try bringing my legs up to curl into a ball, when a pair of large black boots and the bottom of dark slacks make their way into my line of sight. Hands move over my arms first, making a path down my back and stop at my legs. I'm gently rolled onto my back and I get my first sight of whom I'm dealing with. Jason is kneeling next to me staring down at my legs. It's hard to see behind the mirrored shades, covering his upper face, but the grim regard is plain to see in the way his frowning mouth turns down in the corners. The relief I feel is instant. There's no wonder, or questioning. The reason he's here is immaterial to me. I'm just so happy to be alive and here with him. I blink and the next instant I'm gazing at a naked chest, as he rips off his shirt and tears it in two. That is a seriously sexy chest. My eyes connect first with the chain around his neck. This is the first time I've seen it unhindered. It's beautiful. The locket is in the shape of an oval with a cross etched into the front, and shines as it swings with his movements. Moving down with just my eyes, I'm met with hard pecs absent of any hair, leading down to a chiseled abdomen. The muscles covering his stomach are so defined I can easily count all six of them. They move and tighten as he bends over me. I'm completely immersed in my visual molestation, so it takes the hard pinch at my thigh to snap me back to reality. "Ouch."

"Sorry. You've got a pretty deep cut on your leg. I'm attempting to cut off the blood flow and stop it from bleeding too badly. Does your head hurt?"

I hadn't even thought about my head. "I'm not sure. I feel kinda numb right now. Does it look bad?" He studies my leg, not giving my face the attention I was hoping for. I will judge his reaction to help clue me in on my level of panic required. "I need you to look at me please. I don't want to freak out here and I'm getting dangerously close to losing it. If you could just let me know it's ok. Please." That catches his full attention and he takes the glasses off to look at me.

"You'll be okay. A little banged up, but okay." Sunglasses back in their resting spot on his nose, he puts his attention back to my bleeding leg. The shock is wearing off and I'm starting to feel the pain. It's not as bad as it probably should be yet it's still uncomfortable. Reaching under my body he lifts me into his arms like he's plucked a feather off the ground, instead of a hundred plus pound body. Strong arms surround me and once again the relief settles me. My limbs are dead weight and my head lulls back against him for support, giving me swimmy head. I don't think I should feel like this. My words come out sounding as if I've drunk myself silly. "Why do I feel strange?"

"I'm taking you to a doctor friend of mine. I think keeping a low profile right now is best. He'll take a look-see at your injuries and decide if you need to head to the emergency room. I'm sure he's seen worse, and your dizziness may just be stress related, but I want to be sure. He shouldn't have any trouble fixing you up, if you need it. Do I need to call your roommate to inform her you won't be home to get Drew?" He asks.

"Mm. No? My... Matt-t-t-t. MMmmatt. Has him. Hmm. I feel like I'm flying. We are up so high." I feel too weird to be able to tell if he's lying to me or not. But it makes sense that this is due to stress.

"Neva. I need you to keep talking to me. I'm afraid you've lost quite a bit of blood from your leg wound. Unless there's somewhere you're hurt worse, that I haven't seen? How does your head feel?"

The rambled questions aren't making sense. I'm stuck on my Matt comment and worry how to let Drew know I'm ok. "Neva!" My eyes snap back open. I didn't know I'd closed them. Hmm. He has the most bitable jaw. I'd love a chance to kiss him again. He sighs like he heard me. Guh… I hope I didn't say that out loud. And wait, he made it seem this was stress related. Did he say I was bleeding?

My seatbelt is snapped into place and the door closes loudly, making my head throb. Through the slits of my lids I watch a still-naked chest lean across me to grab something out of the glove box. That's motivation to stay awake right there, in olive-colored hard flesh. Yum. Why is the car vibrating? I'm propped against the door, so I'm able to keep him in my sights, while he talks on his phone. He has the phone pressed to his ear and he's talking in soft tones, too low for me to hear, and starts the car. Is it me who's vibrating then? Shouldn't it be the car that does that? The feeling started before the car did.

As he finishes the call, he places the phone down and his warm hand on top of my knee. He must have heard me, or he's superman, because he has no problem correcting my assumption that the vibration is not from the car. "I believe you're shaking due to shock. It'll be okay." He takes his eyes off the road long enough for me to worry, but he allows me to see the fear he's holding back when he does. "Do you hear me? I will make this better." I believe him, but the feeling of my cold and icy hands are distracting me again. I just want to take a quick nap and I'm sure to bounce back to normal. Right? The last thing I'm aware of is an extremely warm hand grabbing mine before I fall asleep.

CHAPTER 14

"... S hould be fine. I gave her a strong sedative last night for pain. She should be waking soon."

"Ok. I just don't get it. Why are people shooting at her? This is the second time this has happened. What aren't y'all telling me?" The first voice I'd heard doesn't sound familiar, but the second has me trying to sit up, except my body seems to want to stay warm under this blanket. "Shell…" I don't think she heard me so I try it again. This time I use more force. "Shelly…" I feel the bed dip next to me, and a hand smoothing my hair, like I do to Drew when I'm comforting him.

"Hey sexy, how you feeling?"

I crack my eyes open but shut them to ward off the bright light. "Light." I hope she gets my meaning because anything more right now doesn't sound too promising. The lights behind my eyelids dim to a preferable level and I attempt to open them a second time. The first thing I detect is a worried best friend hovering above me. "Stop chewing your lip. I'm not dead am I? Wait! Where's Drew? Is he ok?" I'm trying not to panic.

She pats my hand freed during my second attempt at sitting up. "He's fine. Matt has him and is keeping him occupied. I stopped there before coming here. No need to worry. He and Lizzie are helping with yard work. Better him than me. I told Drew you had an accident but not to freak out. He's braver than we give him credit for. He made sure you were okay then went to help Liz put away her toys. That kid is gold, I tell ya."

"Must be the influence of his amazing Aunt." I try to smile but it doesn't quite come off as I'd hoped if the grimace on her face is anything to go by. "So, tell me. How long have I been here? And where is *here,* exactly?" I catch sight of a wall clock that reads 7:52 and my curiosity gets the better of me. "Is that PM or AM?"

"First, you are at the house of a friend of Jason's. I was never fully introduced, as it was crazy when I arrived, so I can't give you a name. This mystery friend's house is in Sunrise, to give you a geographical picture. Thankfully it only took me thirty minutes with traffic to get here. But enough of my issues! I guess he had to sedate you last night due to the handful of wounds you are now sporting. Nice black eye by the way. Can you tell everyone I kicked your ass? I could use the street cred." She pauses to look at the ceiling in thought. "Although, I'm not sure how good that'd make me appear seeing as you fit in my pocket. But I digress…"

"Please don't make me laugh. I think I'll wet the bed." I snort through my response.

"Oh! I never thought of that. It's been almost 24 hours. Let's get you up so you can pop a squat and then I'll finish. I'm sure Jason wants to come check on you too. Do you need me to help sit you up?"

Just the thought of moving right now has me pausing. "Maybe. Nothing hurts too bad at the moment but things may change when I'm on the move." She reaches under me guiding me to sit upright. The pinch in my left leg smarts when I move it, and my face pounds to the beat of my pulse, making this an unpleasant experience. Oiy. This does not feel good at all. I always knew sit-ups were evil. Nature is *really* making herself a nuisance, so I need to suck it up and get a move on. Standing takes it's time but I hobble ungracefully to the bathroom with

Shelly's support. It doesn't help that I'm swimming in these borrowed pants. "Whose clothes are these? They're huge."

"They're Jason's workout clothes. You look ridiculous, but it was kind of sweet to find you wearing his clothes when I arrived. It's like a new idea for 'pinky friends'. I'll buy y'all shirts that match and you can tie your pinkies together with string." At my look of doubt she adds. "Don't worry, I'll make it work for you guys."

"Please shut up and walk faster. I may just pee right here and tell them you did it." I joke.

This speeds us up, thank God. "Walking faster now. Boy, are you cranky when you don't feel well. I should have remembered that from flu season two years ago. I thought about smothering you in your sleep more than once then. But as I'm the best of the besties, I refrained. You're welcome." She lets go of me to enter, thankfully alone, to take care of my needs. I'm done in no time, clean my hands and open the door. Walking back out, Shell is right outside to help me return to the bed I've been borrowing.

My breathing stops at the sight of Jason reclining in the chair, one leg resting on his knee, and rocking a charcoal grey suit. Let's not forget the gold rim reading glasses that cause my knees to go weak. Lord, help me. If I weren't in so much pain I'd crawl over to him then climb in his lap and replace the folder he has laying there. I try to keep my voice low when asking Shell what type of pain meds the mystery friend gave me, but the curl of his lip tells me I wasn't successful keeping that question to just us girls.

I wasn't really asking for an answer. More of a general question about my lightheadedness. But leave it to Shelly, she answers it anyway.

"No idea chick, but I'm asking him for a refill in injection form so I can just knock you out when you piss me off."

"Ha-ha. I'm firing you as my best friend. Where's the sympathy?" I smirk up at her. It feels good to keep things light.

"It's here somewhere. I'm sure this hulk in my chair has enough for the both of us. I'll just stand here and look pretty." Speaking of the hulk, he stands tall as we move closer, sets the folder in the chair, then acts as though he's not sure how to help. Shelly solves his dilemma by snapping her fingers and points from me to the bed. "Sir Knight, help me move this damsel into her sleeping chamber." They both maneuver me slowly and I sink into the soft mattress. It's sad that I could use another nap so soon. Shell is tucking the covers around me as if I'm five and story time is next on my agenda.

"Enough Shell." I soften that harsh statement by squeezing her hand, informing her it's alright. "I think I'm snug as a bug now. Can someone *please* tell me what's going on? I remember everything up until the car ride. Well, I remember bits and pieces of the car ride, but after that is a blank slate." It's Jason who answers.

"When I got you, your leg was bleeding enough that I needed to apply pressure and I was confident stitches were needed. Once we arrived, Carmine - that's whose house we are in - gave you something to relax you, so he could examine you. You have several small cuts on your hands and knees, all superficial. Nothing a little antibiotic ointment won't cure. And the soreness on your face is from the beating it took, I assume during a fall, and is bruised. It may take a few days for the swelling to subside and the bruises to fade. I'm told you also have two quarter size bruises on your lower back. If I had to guess from what he explained to me, it would appear that you had a *Beretta* shoved against you. It also matches the casing we found last night, and the wound on your leg. And before you look down to check, you only needed stitching glue to seal it once it stopped bleeding. Got your outer thigh and thankfully was just a graze, but enough to bleed pretty well. We have our best men searching for the perp. He took off before I made it to you and I chose to check on you instead of chasing him. I regret that." The last part is said as almost an afterthought.

He looks away from us and the urge to comfort him takes a strong hold of me. "You know it's not your fault you let him get away right?" His face angles back around, but his face remains vacant. "Thank you. I appreciate you being there." Shelly uses the break in speaking to ask her own question.

"Not to devalue your awesome cop skills, but why *were* you there? That's some superhero timing." Blunt as always, is my gal. But I'm glad she asked and not me. He opens his mouth and closes it. The door behind him opens, and a man, I'm guessing our mystery friend, walks in. He has kind eyes the shade of cinnamon, and when standing next to Jason, the top of his head reaches just below is shoulder. He's an attractive man, if you go for the lanky older men in lab coats type. He gently shoos my two information gurus out of the room and it's now just him and I. I guess I'll be hearing the rest of what I'd missed later.

The examination by Dr. Carmine is quick and somewhat painless. I still don't have his last name, so for now I'll be referring to him as *Dr. Carmine.* Just feels too weird calling him by his given name when we are still strangers. Well, strangers that just shared personal information and naked body parts. He's very kind though. Only peeked at the exposed skin that was necessary. My leg appears to hurt worse than it really is. And yay me! I stayed conscious the whole time, only light dizziness, but I call that a success. Looks like I'll be adding another tiny scar to my white leg. The scratch at my hip has just started to heal. Now I get to start the process all over again.

After he steps out Shelly walks back in and resumes her spot next to me. "This is some big drama for little 'ole you. Let's play a game. You tell me what the *hell* is going on, and I'll share what I know about the delectable duo out there." She points to the door while finishing her sentence.

"You think the doctor is delectable?" I mean, ok. I guess I can see it. She just usually goes for a different type.

"What? No. Well, he's cute, I guess, if you go for that type. And I assure you I don't. I'm as tall as he is and I could never wear my classy hooker heels next to him. I was referring to Jason and his partner. They are out there in some sort of he-man, pissed-alpha stand off. I could hear growling and grunting but not much else. What'd you do? They aren't fighting over who gets to keep you are they? You're not turning kinky and going ménage chic on me are you? Oh! If you do, can I watch? Just for informational purposes, of course."

"Of course my naughty best friend, if that were the case then you could watch." I laugh at her face turned wicked. "But no. I am in no way attracted Detective Valdez. The last time I saw him he sent me a pretty big warning. I don't think crossing him is in my best interest, nor do I think he has the hots for me." I think on it for a second. "When I was at the station, they seemed to be mad at each other then too. Which reminds me, I need to explain why I was there in the first place. Get comfy, and please get your naughty mind away from threesomes. That is *so* not happening."

***

Shelly still hasn't said anything. I'd finished my speech minutes ago. The emotions pouring off her keep changing, and I'm trying to nail down which one I'm more nervous about. Finally, after what feels like a year has passed, she puts me out of my misery.

"So you're saying that a group of…" She puts her hands up to make quotation marks with her fingers "crazy people are after you for something Jeremy may, or may not, have told you, shown you, given you, whatever? Do I have that right? And do you know what it is?" At my sheepish expression she gasps. "You do! What? And why aren't you just handing it over to the delectable duo now? My God Nev! This could all be over right now."

"I know that. And I've thought about it a million times, once I put the pieces together. But Shell, it was the last thing Jeremy gave me. I know it sounds stupid, but I can't part with it. Or I thought I couldn't. I was trying to figure out a way to save that memory and get these nut jobs to leave me alone. I don't know. Saying that out loud sounds crazy. What should I do?"

"Hmm… ok. Let's talk about *what* it is and maybe we can decide *what* to do. First things first, I think telling Jason is your best bet here. He can keep you safe and maybe warm your bed while he's there."

I don't like the face she's showing me. It's known as her mischief expression. Plus, she's crazy. "You're crazy. And if you want to talk crazy, I already made the mistake of throwing myself at him. He let me know that I wasn't on the menu. And that's fine. Really." If I say it enough it has to be true. Right?

"I don't believe you. There is no way that man out there doesn't want to nibble his way from appetizer to dessert with you. He almost didn't let me enter your room. Like I was a threat to you and he was the sexy guard protecting his queen. I swear, that man wants you." Her dreamy expression has me cringing. "It's all very romantic if you think about it. Y'all would make some beautiful babies together. And just think how cute Drew would be as an older brother. And they'd come equipped with an amazing Aunt ready for some spoiling." She just keeps getting more excited. I try an interrupt her as she continues to get way ahead of herself, but she just talks right over me. "I picture a beach wedding at sunset. With just your close friends. We'll blow bubbles as you walk back down the aisle instead of throwing rice, less messy, and we can have the reception under a tent nearby."

When I realize she's finished with her game of make-believe, and I won't get cut off again, I speak slow as to let her know I'm serious. "I think you've jumped the gun just a tad. There are no wedding bells or babies crying anywhere in my future. I've gone that road and lost my heart in the process. I can't do that again. I'll admit I'd enjoy the companionship. And to feel that all-consuming love again would be something I'd cherish. But it's just not in the cards Shell." Especially when I'd just been reminded that feelings aren't always reciprocated. But I leave that out.

"Party pooper. I have it planned and it's beautiful. But fine, my dream will have to wait for now." She pouts.

"You could have that dream yourself and I'd be cheering you on. You need to set loose the hookup parade and find your *one*. I know what you went through was traumatic." I throw my hand up to stop her from her snark. I'm treading dangerous territory here, but it needs to be said. "All I'm saying is that it would have changed anyone. But you're in a better place now, and this time it could be great." I see her physically shutting down on me while I talk.

"Whatever. Let's focus on your drama and leave mine in the past where it belongs. Now, let's come up with a plan to help you, your Majesty." I decide to leave it alone, for now. But I give her a look to say it'll be revisited soon.

Our planning session is interrupted by a stern-faced detective entering the room. And not the one I'd been secretly hoping for. By facial expression alone, I can see this is not going to be a happy chat. Shelly exits by letting me know she'll head over to Matt's to check on Drew again, and see if he can take him another night, hopefully keeping him out of harm's way. I don't like being away from him right now, but the thought of him being brought into this mess outweighs my desire to have him close. I'll make it up to him when I've fixed this. His safety comes first, always.

Valdez enters the room no further inside than the door. Just leans his solid mass against it once Shell closes it behind her. Why am I so nervous? It's not like I've done anything wrong. Well, *technically*, not yet. I'm still trying to compartmentalize the right and wrong columns I've devised with Shell, for keeping my hidden jewelry a secret. For now at least. And if anyone is going to know, it'll be Jason I tell first. Not his grumpy partner.

"I need you to leave Jason alone." Uh…what? "Whatever you think is happening between you two needs to end. Now." I can't keep the shock off my face. "Oh, I see. You thought you were special." He freakin' laughs. *Laughs* at me. He's starting to piss me off. But that tiny hope I still had floating in the back of my subconscious has been effectively smashed into pieces. Not that is was a huge hope. But I'd be lying to myself if I said it wasn't there. "You are one of many he likes to play with. If you were smart, you'd hand over the item you're hiding and walk away without looking back. He has his own agenda when it comes to what we're looking for. Forget you ever met Jason. Save yourself the embarrassment now and go back to your boring life." He takes a step away from the door, giving me the impression he's trying to appear intimidating. It's working. "And Neva, don't think you can play this game and win. It would be a stupid idea to try." With those dire words he turns and walks out the door. Well, that solves my problem of what to do. There is no way I'm giving that bastard anything. Even if its to save my own hide. I'll figure out a way to fix this on my own, thank you very much.

***

With strict instructions on how to care for my leg, and a strong antibiotic and prescription in hand, Dr. Carmine allows me to head home. Jason has been quiet on our drive and I don't have the energy to change that. I'm mad at him. A-freaking-gain. Was he only around to get what he needed for his own end game? And I was just a means to that end? I cannot forgive him if he used Drew to get there. He's innocent in all this. I don't bring men in my life for a reason. I should have followed that plan with Jason as well. I'll have to break the news to Drew that his buddy won't be coming around anymore. He may have made it plain as day he doesn't want me on a personal level, minus the kissing and groping sessions, but he made future plans with an impressionable boy who truly admires him. That won't work if he's only using us.

Twenty minutes of strained silence later, we pull into a spot a few feet away from our stairwell. I look up at our living room window, and see the lights are out. Either Shelly is not home yet, or she's gone to bed already. I slump back. Ugh. That lonely feeling is creeping back in. Jason is quietly waiting for my exit, but I seem to be stuck to my seat, wallowing in my own pity party. I want to show him my best impersonation of a two-year-olds temper tantrum before I walk away. It's a close call, but I hold it in. Barely. I take in a calming breath, and let it out slowly, then make my head turn in his direction. I had been prepared to exit with a polite *'thanks, it was nice knowing ya'* but keep silent as I observe the white knuckles punishing his steering wheel. Fine. He can be mad too. I don't care at this point.

I want to tune him out while he speaks, but I don't. "If there was a way to make this work, I'd move Heaven and Earth to do it." His attention transfers to my side of the truck, but I'm still giving him the cold shoulder. "You are very special to me Neva. I'll do whatever I can to keep you and Drew safe. If you decide you want someone else to help you, I'll send you the name of the man I'd trust with my life. And if you find what I'm looking for, I'd appreciate it if I'm the first one you call."

There's that word again. *'Special'*. Yeah, I'm not buying it this time. And I won't call him out on his mistake in the words he unintentionally used. He said *I'm,* like this is personal for him. I'm too busy pouting to care. Besides, I think I'm done with his game. Just wish it didn't hurt so freaking much.

CHAPTER 15

Tonight has me covering Trixie's Wednesday night shift at the club. I don't usually work on weeknights, but her sister is having her first baby and she wanted to be there. So here I am, decked out in my club-working attire, working a shift that I wasn't expecting to do. It's hotter than balls in here tonight, making my black tank top stick to my skin, and I'm questioning, for the twentieth time, why I picked jeans to wear before I left. But as I actually *wanted* tips tonight, I figured I'd show less of my pale skin. A few extra bucks in the bank will be worth my discomfort. I promise myself a bowl of ice cream as a treat for later.

As I was getting myself ready for tonight, I couldn't believe how the beginning of this week has blown by. After I got home from Dr. Carmine's on Sunday? I found Shelly nestled on our couch, waiting for me to arrive. I didn't want to admit it, but hearing that Jason had taken the time to update Shelly on when I was coming home made me feel all mushy on the insides. Later that night, which was well past her bedtime, we decided to have a family meeting on the following day, once Drew was home. Between the two of us, because Drew didn't need to know the nitty-gritty, we decided it was best to contact our apartment supervisor and inquire about a security system. And with Shelly flirting her way through that conversation, they were in and out late yesterday afternoon. Our apartment, not Shelly. Shell also convinced me to take a gun class and shooting lessons, again not shared with Drew. He'd have wanted to join us if he was aware that plan, while I'm not looking forward to it in the least. But after much threatening and begging, I reluctantly agreed with her. I did make her compromise though. She'll join a women's defense class with me, as well, and if I can't handle using a gun we'll drop it and stick to just self-defense. We've also chosen to drive Drew to and from school each day. He was not a happy kid at the thought of losing time with his new friends, but just like his mom, he pouted his way through his agreement like a pro. It helps that an unmarked police car has been noticed following us wherever we go.

My mind has played some unfair tricks on me on more than one occasion, as I could have sworn I saw Jason from behind the car's tinted glass. He's been on my mind more than I want him to be, I admit. I see him in my dreams, and then it shifts to my waking hours. I've imagined him at the grocery store, this time inside, yet when I move closer, no one fitting his description is there. I've imagined him outside the bookstore, our apartment, and even the hospital where Shelly works. It's driving me crazy.

And right now my imagination is playing the worst trick yet, because that must be his twin that's walking in the door to After Life with a tall blonde on his arm. The club's not usually packed on weeknights and tonight is no different. I have a perfectly clear view of his tall form wearing black slacks and a light blue dress shirt unbuttoned at the top, showcasing the familiar locket. His short beard under these dim lights makes the angles of his jaw seem more pronounced than usual, and blends to match the short hair on his head. My God, he looks even better than I remember. My eyes fix their sight on his strong hand resting on the back of his blonde, and my stomach clenches. He may as well have punched me in the gut. It would have hurt less.

I watch transfixed as he leads her to a corner booth, helping her sit on one side, before taking the other. She has to be at least ten years his junior. I may need to ask Joey to card her just for my own enjoyment. The strobe lights flash every other second in blues and red, making his expression hard to read from my vantage point behind the bar top. I must have been standing in shock for longer than I'd thought, as I hear shouts for more beer and Joey calling my name. Le sigh. I set my misery aside and get back to work.

***

About an hour later, I'm so busy I don't see Angelo standing to my left until I bump into him on my way to the ice machine. I've been successful at avoiding him on my nights here so far, but my luck has obviously just run out. I move to the left to step around him, but he blocks my way with a quick move of his arm, trapping me in place. I stop mid motion, causing the half filled drink in my hand to splash out the side of the glass and onto his shoes. Mouthing a curse, I look up to apologize, but his face is suddenly lowered close to mine, and it doesn't look thrilled to be there. "Office." One word. That's all he deemed worthy of his time. Asshole. I stare at his retreating back, dreading the next several minutes. Catching Joey's attention I motion with a hand, I'll be right back, and point to the hall that occupies Angelo's office. With my big girl panties on, I ignore the shaking of his head, and duck under the bar to make my way through the gyrating bodies on the dance floor. Right before I enter the dark hallway that leads to the door to his office, something forces my head to shift left and I connect with Jason's penetrating gaze. He's standing in a corner near the booth, I'd watched him and his friend occupy earlier. Solid arms held rigid at his side, with his hands curled into fists, he's looking directly at *me*. His blonde friend is dancing next to him, oblivious to our silent connection. She makes me want to puke right here, where I'm positive others have done the same. She's the perfect trifecta. Beautiful, blonde, tall, *and* she can dance. Like *dance,* not just move her hips and pretend to. Gah, is that jealously waving her green flag from behind my back? Of course he would want someone like that. I must look like a little girl to him. And not only that, I come as a package deal. Who would want that? I don't know how to process this incredibly vulnerable feeling. I must have seemed so naive to him. Before he can see the hurt he's caused flash across my face, I run back to the office, leaving them to their night.

It takes me a minute to shake off the gloom, and lean away from the wall I'd been sulking against. But as I've chosen to be brave tonight, I suck it up and move to stand before the office of my nightmares. The last time I was called to the principal's office, I was given a verbal dress down for not flirting enough with my customers. I wish I'd have knocked his teeth out. I snort. Yeesh, I'm glad my inner diva is at least a badass. I should take notes from her. I've just knocked on the office door when it flies open and I'm unceremoniously dragged into the dark room.

My healing leg is bounced against the doorjamb, producing white stars to flash against the dark backdrop of the room. It happens so fast my head is spinning before my body follows the motion. Invisible arms spin me around, causing my spine to bow backwards, and my shoulder blades dig into the desk. It's too dark to see who has ahold of me but the rich cologne puts a name to the smell. I try using the only self-defense move I know, and shove my knee upward, connecting with an upper thigh. Cursing myself for not nailing my intended target, I continue to thrash on his desk, trying to gain leverage against his hold. Pinning me firm against the desk, his gross hand covers my mouth, and I hold my breath through the stench of his fingers. It only takes a split second more to react. I bite the bottom of his finger forcing him to let go, generating enough space between us to throw my hands on his chest to push. My size, plus the laid out position aren't enough to budge him.

The scream pushing itself out of my mouth breaks off at the sharp object colliding with my throat. I silently congratulate myself, as he struggles to catch his own breath. I may not have the upper hand, but at least I'm making him work for it. Although I might be breathing just as hard, if my lungs weren't frozen from fear. This is an all time low for him. Normally he likes to use harsh words, not physical force. Who knew it was possible for him to hate me more then he already did.

"Bruja." Yup. There it is. Ugly words from him are becoming second nature. If he'd get off me it'd be just like old times. Ok, enough down memory lane. I need to find a way out of this. "Do you think you can fool me?" Another riddle. I'm quickly learning that I loath riddles. "Do you think I don't see you with him? Trying to take what is ours. He will never win. I will give you one week to give *joya-azul* to me or I will make a phone call to someone, I'm sure, your roommate would be unhappy to hear from." To emphasize the seriousness of his threat, the object keeping me motionless is pressed harder into my neck. I can't believe what I'm hearing. I must be hallucinating. There is no way anyone knows. "Ah, you need more proof." He mutters under his breath in Spanish too fast for me to catch the meaning, then switches back to English. "You must remember the name Nicholas Tegard."

I'm shocked. Speechless. My choice has been stripped from me with one sentence, and he knows he has me. You'd have to be stupid not to know I'd do anything for Shell. Lifting himself off me, I stay laid out, watching him remove the letter opener and slide it into his pocket. I didn't know they still made those. I've just decided I'm adding one to my self-defense items list. Blending with the shadows I lose sight of the direction he's moved, but I hear the latch on the door click, telling me it's safe to get up and leave. Sliding my shaking body off the desk, I take the time alone to calm my nerves. Blinking takes effort, as I'm afraid of closing my eyes too long for fear he may be hiding nearby. It's too dark in here - not calming at all. I tell myself I need to get back out there. So why aren't I sprinting full speed for the door? It takes seven steps to make it over to the exit - I should know, I counted them - but I falter at the door, clutching the door handle in a death grip. What am I going to do? I know I have to hand it over to him to save Shell. I know this, but the problem with this plan is that Shell hid it somewhere is her office to remove it from our home. At the time we thought we were so smart. Arming ourselves with false security and stupid classes. Did I really think that would work? I can't let her find out someone dug into her past. She's worked so hard to overcome all the crap she's gone through. And has the scars as a memento, which she hides even from me.

Finding my courage takes longer than I'd like, but I know if I don't get out there *pronto,* Joey will send the troops to find me. It takes two tries to turn the handle due to the nervous sweat coating my hands, but I make it through the doorway, leaving the dark office behind. Once in the hall I shrink back against the wall and use my hands to guide me back to the main area of the club. Once I make it, my eyes flit over to where I last saw Jason and his date, but the space is empty now. I have never felt more alone than I do right at this moment. My options buzz through my brain like lightning. I can't tell Shell, for obvious reasons. Drew doesn't *ever* need to know. And the person I am supposed to feel like I can go to because he's got the law on his side, I feel alienated from. Of course, I have other friends, good friends, but why draw them into this craptastic dilemma?

The walk to the bar is a blur. Stumbling under the bar top, I get right back to work to block out the rest. If I check on Joey, I will see worry or remorse on his handsome face and I can't deal with that right now. Thankfully my section of the bar stays busy for the rest of the night, and my tips have added up, bringing me close to what I make on a busy Friday. We work in tandem filling, restocking and flirting our way through the last hour. Finally, after another two hours of pretending to go through the happy motions, the bar is closed and the last of the patrons have exited. Joey graciously offers to take the trash out for me while I restock our section, which works for me. It may have been several weeks since the trash bin incident occurred, but it's still pretty fresh in my subconscious. He hasn't mentioned earlier, and I'm playing dumb until he does. As he walks back in from trash duty, he swings his hips in an exaggerated swagger, making his way across our provisional dance floor. I let a laugh out when he spins around, then finishing the last line of my favorite Stabbing Westward song playing through the speakers. I'd plugged his iPod into the sound system for our nightly ritual, something that's become habit when we work together. "…To forget about you." The sudden rock star, throws his arms up as he belts the last word. The goof.

He cracks me up. Definitely my type of crazy. The iPod shuffles to "Me Roar" by Halle Saale, and I start to groove with him this time. With a sore leg it's not as easy as it should be, but I make it work. Joey is moving his body in ways I wish I were capable of, reminding me of the jealousy I'd felt earlier. I shut that thought down by doing a bobbing, shuffle, sexy butt move thing that I'm positive looked better in my imagination. But I'm having too much fun pretending, to care. This man in front of me was born to dance, so I give him room to shake it like his mama made it. He moves closer to my bland moves and takes my arm, gently spinning me in to his arms and then back out again. It feels so good to laugh. The perfect remedy to cure my maudlin mood. I didn't know how much I needed this until now.

I already have a light coat of perspiration on my skin, so I step away from our mini dance party to finish cleaning so we're not here till six in the morning. Joey stays out in the room, tackling the heavy job of raising chairs, dancing as he goes. It's a nice show to help the hum-drum routine. The boy has a body on him that is lickable. Too bad the only tongue he would want anywhere near his body is attached to someone with less boobs and more body hair. Alas, that someone is not me. We are soul mates of a different sort, which works for us. While I wipe the counters and Netsky's "Love is Gone" plays in the background, Joey sets the chairs up on the tables for our amazing cleaning crew to take care of later. Those guys rock. I don't clean my room let alone random people's used napkins or chewed straws. Gag.

An hour later, we've finished with our chores and are ready to head home. He checks and locks both back doors, then we alternate turning lights off along the way to the front. As much as I love Joey, I'm glad to be walking to my car having escaped his interrogation. One less person to drag down the rabbit hole with me. If I tell Joey…no. Not gonna even go there. I'd parked my car under a light and can make out a man leaning against my passenger door from across the lot. I turn to Joey, who hasn't left my side since we left the front door, and try to explain I'm safe to go on from here alone without raising suspicion. I shouldn't have even tried. Throwing me a peace sign, he turns and heads to his own car, but not before I get a *'we'll talk later'* look. Yes, my friend, we will. Just, not yet.

Walking closer, I cram the feeling of relief that he's alone with no blondie in sight down deep into my box labeled 'things I wish not to admit'. Standing a few feet away, so my neck doesn't need to crane up an awkward angle, I look up at him. My hormones and my brain need to have a meeting of the minds and agree for once. Just once, that's all I'm asking for. My body wants him, yet my brain and heart know this will only lead to heartache. Before I can finish mentally chastising myself, he uncrosses his legs at the ankles, adding even more distance in our heights, and takes the keys I have clutched in my hand. And I just allow this to happen. All of my many pep talks about this exact thing, and they fly to the wind when he's near. The arm not holding my keys settles at my back to maneuver me around to the driver's side of my car. Not one word has been uttered, just glances and light touches. It quickly runs through my mind that this same arm holding me was just settled against a different back a few hours earlier. Another feeling that I cram down with the others that I'm not ready to handle. I'm sure that box is overflowing by now. Spring-cleaning will be a bitch this year.

My car is unlocked and the door is gently opened for me. I don't wait for him, just sit myself inside and turn the ignition, blasting the A/C I'd had cranked to max when I'd pulled in. I'm fiddling with the knobs to keep my hands busy but stop when I see him place his hands against my car frame and bend in. "Neva, look at me." I *am* looking at him. And he's looking at me, but I don't know if he's really seeing me. His eyes flit over my face and his mouth opens to say more, prompting me to wait for more. Closing his mouth he straightens and grabs my door. "I'll follow till you get inside." Then he adds "I'm not in my truck so don't be alarmed if you see an unrecognizable car tailing you." And then he's gone. He may have only said a handful of syllables, but if a look contained words he'd have written a novel.

Sure enough, during my ride, there is a sleek black car on my tail the whole ride home. I make it into our apartment, check on Drew and fall into bed. As I lay here, alone in my bed, I smile into my pillow. I know I shouldn't be. I have a crazy boss, unanswered questions, and another unknown group threatening me. Yet I lay here thinking only of a man who made sure I drove home safe.

CHAPTER 16

"So why am I here?"

Looking up from the drawing on my lap, I turn to Matt and give him a sheepish grin. "Moral support?" His look says it all. He's not buying my excuse.

"I'm not buying it." Called it. "You've had this session planned for weeks. You may have just recently nailed down what you are getting, but you've gone through *hours* of pain before on your own."

I mutter my reply.

"What?" He barks.

I keep my head down when I answer. "I said, *I don't want to be alone*. Happy now? Besides, it's not like you had anything better to do. Neither of us have work today. Plus you have no one to chase and make breakfast for, with Lizzie at your parents. You may as well sit here and keep me company."

"You are so right." His tone is dry as bone. He rolls his eyes then fastens them back on me. "I could have slept past 6am for the first time in a month, and read the paper. Instead I'm sitting *here*, *way* too early I might add, drinking crap coffee with some scary looking people. I didn't even know these places were open this early." He yawns to emphasize his point.

"First of all, this is Miami. I'm pretty sure they are always open. Second of all, you see that man over there?" I nod my head in the direction of the bald man leaning over the computer at the reception desk. "That's Manuel. I've known him for years." I stop to point to the mermaids on my lower arm. "He designed and drew it free hand. I only had to explain what I wanted and this was what he created. Took him six weeks to finish the drawing, but I love that it's one of a kind. He went to Florida State, graduated *summa cum laude* with a Bachelor's in Psychology, met his beautiful wife there, and now they have two boys under five…and a hundred pound Bernese Mountain dog. Don't let the neck tattoos and the devil horns fool you. He's a big softy."

"Yea, ok. Whatever you say." He replies dubiously.

He leans back against the hard plastic chair and sips his coffee. I laugh at the look of disgust on his face. I've never been brave enough to try it. I think I'll pass. I notice he's still casting doubtful looks around the room. "You don't sound very convincing."

He takes another sip and I silently gag with him. "I would need a gallon more of this sludge to attempt convincing." He offers me a taste and I shake my head no. "I'll never understand why you or Shelly put yourself through this much pain. A tiny needle jabbing you repeatedly for hours doesn't sound like fun to me. Although I admit they look good on you."

I answer with complete honesty. "I like them. Every one of mine has meaning and a story. And Shell only has one…"

"On her inner thigh, yes I know." He says.

My mouth gapes open. "How do you know that?" He keeps his eyes closed but rubs his forehead with the hand not holding the sludge. "OmeeGod. What? When? How?" He better start spillin'.

He lets out a tired sigh before answering me. "It was a year ago. One time. We regretted it immediately and decided not to tell anyone.

Just pretend it didn't happen. She didn't tell you so it wouldn't get weird when we were all together."

"So, why are you telling me now?" He snorts. "Don't waste your snorts. Save those for when Lizzie's a teenager. You'll need some in reserve." He groans. Ha. I love messing with him. He's going to be such a mess when she's older.

"I couldn't help picturing that horseshoe tattoo. It's a fond memory." Oh, that smile he's wearing is laced with some naughty things I don't need to know about.

I throw my hands up between us in a 'stopping' gesture. "Euw. Stop right there. No more." We sit in silence, watching the shop take on a life all of it's own. There are three other people in the uncomfortable chairs, sitting a few seats down from us, while the two artists working this morning are busy setting up for their first clients.

After he's had time to digest his coffee, the questions begin. "Ok, spill it. I know something's on your mind. What's going on?" I grab my purse searching for my chap-stick to stall. That job completed, I look back down at the drawing I have faced up in my lap. It's not what I'm getting today, but I wanted Manuel to have a look at it for next time. Today's session will be a fast one. Just a tiny addition to my wrist. "Hello? Earth to Neva..."

"Sorry, ok. So..." Stalling again I look back up at him. I can't tell him everything. But I can tell him some. And I need to get it off my B-sized chest. Since Shelly's working today, and yesterday she was gone, I'm using Matt as my surrogate best friend. He can hate me later. I still have two more days to figure out where Shell hid the stone, so I'm not mentioning that till I absolutely have to. "Ya know how when you're attracted to someone?" He opens his eyes at my question. "Please." I hold my hand up. "No talk of attraction and Shelly. I can't take anymore disturbing visuals." I sit and think for a second. "Let's play hypothetical. So you are attracted to someone. And even though you're not sure you're capable of love again, your body doesn't agree and you are hot for him. Like, on fire hot." I pause to check he's not sleeping during this. Sure enough, his face is grimaced. I'll take that as my cue to move on.

"Anyway, there's groping, kissing…twice, or maybe threes times, and heated looks. There's dinner with your son and damsel saving. Just go with me here. I promise I'm getting there. So, there's all that. Then he throws on the brakes, there's a warning from his work partner, and a blondie on his arm. I'm not really sure why I'm hurt so much about that. It's not like there were any declarations on either end. We didn't even pass third base. More like where Derek Jeter stands. That position."

"Short stop?" He asks.

"Yea, that. So with all of those things combined, I should move on and never look back right? Except last week he shows up, after sending blondie to who knows where, and makes sure I get home safe. And I would bet my last five dollars he wanted to kiss me. At least I think so. Anyway, since Wednesday night he's shown up magically wherever I'm at. He's there when I pick up Drew from school. He walks me to my car and follows me home from the club. He showed up Saturday with coffee and cop stuff to share with Drew. This started a morning full of male bonding while I sat there watching. He even helped Drew study. *Study*. On a *Saturday*. With Saturday morning cartoons *forgotten*. When this guy has time to actually work is beyond me."

I pause to bite my lip before continuing. "I told myself, firmly, it was for the best when he told me it wasn't going to work between us. I was okay with it. Or I could have been with more time. But now I'm more confused than ever. I don't know what he wants. But he's weaseling his way into somewhere I don't want him to be. I can't fall in love again. Like, ever. At least that's what I'm telling myself. But the more time I spend with him, even though we aren't sharing heart and flower moments, I fall a little further. What am I supposed to do?"

"Neva?" I look up at Manuel when he says my name. He's waiting for me to walk to his work-station.

I look back at Matt with a hopeful expression. "Crap. I wanted your advice. Or in the very least, your commiseration. Don't leave. I promise to buy you better coffee when I'm done." I wait long enough for his promise and walk back to the small room hidden behind strings of beads hanging from the door frame. They rattle together as we slip by them. His work-station has already been prepped for my turn in the chair, with tiny clear cups of blues and white ink. Today the chair has been propped up so my back can rest against it, and hang my legs over the front. Unlike the last time when I had to contort my body for three hours, today should be an easy one. We'd already discussed what was being done today, plus he'd had me in this chair a few times already, so there was no need for the beforehand speech. He props my left arm on the rest, wrist facing up towards his face, and cleans my arm before he speaks.

"New man?" At first I think he somehow knows about all the drama as of late and my run-ins with Jason. But then it dawns on me that he thinks *Matt* is my new man.

"Ha! No. That's Matt from the bookstore." I stop to listen as he starts the tattoo gun. I've always loved that sound. The first touch has me sucking in a breath before I can continue. "He's Liz's dad. Remember when Shell and I had the little girl with us at Josh's birthday party?" He doesn't answer; he's in his zone. "Anyway, that's her dad. *Just* a friend." The first small circle has started to become visible. It's a shade darker than the real image, but close enough. "What about you? How're Lydia and the boys?" Conversation continues through the next half an hour. This is how it goes with us. General questions about our day-to-day lives. Thankfully, no more questions about new men have been asked, and I'm staring down at my new work of art in its completion. "It's perfect. Thank you." And it is. Exactly what I'd needed. "It always amazes me that you can take an explanation of something I've said, and turn it into something beautiful and real." He places the healing goo on first, then the bandage over it, taping it on my wrist.

I head back out to pay and glance at Matt who's fallen asleep in the plastic chair. He must have really needed to sleep. There's no way I could sleep after a cup of coffee, not to mention that chair has to be uncomfortable to sleep in. Payment made, Manuel sends me off with a hug and I sit back next to Matt. I should let him sleep as payment for spending time with me, but I need his opinion too much to waste time on a few Z's. "Hey, Sleeping Beauty, you comin' with me for real coffee and food?" He smiles at my name for him. I really hope that's not some pet name he's used for Shell. "I'm finished. You ready?"

"Hmm, yes. Did it turn out ok?" He at least has his eyes open now. That's one step closer to food.

I'm giddy thinking about it. I beam at him. "It turned out perfectly. Exactly what I needed."

"You going to show me? Or is it still a secret?" He looks down at my newly bandaged wrist.

"Not yet. But soon." I say.

***

124

Hot cup of freshly brewed coffee in hand, I watch as our server asks Matt, for the fifth time, if he needs a refill. We've been here less than ten minutes, and unless he likes his mouth taste-bud free, there is no way he's slurped down that hot coffee fast enough to need this many refills. And I'm ninety-nine percent sure it's not my sweat pant and tank top combo that's bringing her over here. I bat my eyes at Matt and pucker my lips. "Hey honey bunny. I think I can feel our baby kick. Do you want to feel?" Two sets of eyes flash to me. One bugging out of his head, the other focused on my hand, lying against my flat stomach, with disgust mixed with obvious doubt. She looks back to Matt before heading back to the kitchen. Hopefully not spitting in my omelet.

"Unnecessary." He's using his snooty voice on me.

I give him a look over the rim of my coffee mug. "Oh *so* necessary. I selfishly need your advice here and I don't want to bring this coffee back up, with all the pheromones flying around here suffocating me." See? I can give *snooty* right back.

Moving his rolled silverware to the side he rests his hands on the table in front of him, giving me his full attention. "Ok, you gave me quite a bit of information back there. Some of which I think you conveniently glossed over. And some I could have lived happily, for the rest of my days, never knowing. But let me see if I can understand what you were saying. You never said his *name*, but by process of elimination I figure you're talking about the detective. Jason?" He waits for my affirmation and continues. "I'm not sure how good advice coming from me will be. It's not like I won the lottery on women so I have much to base this on. But, I will say, if he's making an effort, why not see where it leads? I'm not telling you to buy a white dress or, God forbid, advising you in the sex department. That's Shelly's job. But I *am* saying, it wouldn't hurt if you gave him a chance. My biggest advice is to ask him why he put a stop to more between you two in the first place. The male species isn't too complicated. But his reason might be. I'm not sure. I don't know him and my mind reading skills are limited to a hyper three-year-old. And even then I get it wrong half the time." He runs a hand through his black hair, making it stand up funny. I lean over and fix it before he carries on. "All I'm saying is that talking to him may clear everything up and you won't need to drag unsuspecting friends, male friends..." he points to his chest "...into things they have no business being in. I'm not saying I don't love our time together. Just...let's stick to the usual next time...no more girl chats." He shakes his head as he finishes his request.

"Gotcha, and thank you. I really appreciate that. I promise, from now on I'll stick to sports and beer. No more girl time. Although you need all the practice you can get for a future fifteen-year-old." I offer back.

"No. I won't. I lay that firmly in your hands. Or, if I'm lucky, my future wife will be there. But be prepared, because I don't see that happening." He counters my view pretty quickly.

When it's my turn again, I use the same tone as when I'm speaking to an unreasonable Shelly. "All things happen for a reason. I'm a true believer in that. Don't be so hard on yourself. Your Mrs. Right is out there, somewhere, waiting for you to find her."

He shrugs unconcerned. "We'll see. You wanna tell me now, what you left out, that had you chewing your thumb and your eye twitching? I think that's something I am more qualified to deal with. Is it Drew? He says school's going really great so far. And his friend Geoff seems to be good for him."

"No." I finish the rest of my answer in my head. Nope, nope, nope.

"No? No to Drew? No you don't want to tell me? What?" Our previously flirty server drops my omelet in front of me before placing Matt's bagel in front of him. We both ignore the napkin sticking out from underneath, showcasing a clearly written phone number.

I wait till she's far enough away to shut this convo down. "All of the above. Drew's fine. I spoke with his teacher via email last week, and she had nothing but positive things to say. And Geoff's been over twice after school and, you're right, he seems like a great kid and perfect for Drew. But, I can't tell you the rest. I'm sorry."

"Can't or won't?" He asks.

I shrug before answering. "Either, neither, both? I'm sorry. I need to fix this on my own. The less people involved, the less chance of anyone I love getting hurt." The fire in his eyes shines bright. "I'm serious. I can't lose anyone else. I have a plan. Not a perfect plan, but I'll be fine."

"I do *not* like this. I want you to swear to me. And I mean Swear. To. Me. If you get, even the slightest bit worried, you call me. And if you don't call me, you call Jason." He pauses. "Do you want me to have Drew stay with us this week? I don't get Liz back till tomorrow night, but we could have a guy's night tonight and I'd take him to school in the morning. Liz would love having him there this week, and it will keep him out of the way from whatever's going on."

I think over his offer. It might be just what I need. Keep my son safe, and give me time to play detective on my own. "I hate that its come to this. I think he might like that. But only if you really don't mind. And I swear to call if it gets bad." I hope he can forgive me for my lie.

CHAPTER 17

C hecking my rear view mirror for the ninth time, I'm awarded with the same view of the black Dodge Charger I'd noticed when I pulled out of the cafe. If I didn't know who was driving it, I'd be a little freaked out. They must like Dodge at his precinct. So far that's all I've seen him drive. This sight has become the norm over the past few days. Stopping at the red light, I grab my phone and scroll to Shelly's office number. Putting it to speakerphone, I balance it on my lap, just in time for the light to turn green and I merge with the heavy traffic. After some awful piano interlude I'm connected through to Shell. "Hey, you too busy to talk?" I can hear her typing as I ask.

"No it's ok. I have a few seconds. What's up?" I skip the why and tell her about Drew spending the rest of the week at Matt's. After explaining that Matt and I discussed keeping him, for safety reasons, the conversation goes smoothly. I make the suggestion we use this time tonight to fit in one of the self-defense classes she'd mentioned. With Shell's connections at the hospital, they might be able to squeeze us in tonight. She explains that twice a month there is a co-ed defense course in the basement where her office is, and suggests that's our best option. Neither of us has ever been, but she's heard good things about it, so I'm all in. Or as *in* as I'm gonna get when it comes to physical exertion. With a promise to get back to me on what time it starts, we hang up just as I am pulling into our apartment.

The black charger stops close enough to give the sense of security, but far enough away to keep a low profile. At least that's what I'm thinking. One mention of a self-defense class and I already act like I know what I'm talking about. They need to give me a badge. The windows are too dark to get a good peek inside, but the heat I feel on my skin isn't related to the sun. I *know* he's in that car watching me. As I get out of my car, I make sure to look at him so he knows I'm on to him. I may not be skilled in the act of flirting, but my inner diva makes herself walk slowly up the steps swinging her hips. At the top step I turn and blow him a kiss, then unlock my apartment door. After disengaging our alarm, I lean back against the door and smile. That was fun. Unproductive, but fun.

I walk to my bathroom and peel the bandage from my wrist. Taking the soap, I lather it up and wash the dried goop and blood away. Patting it dry I look down at my new art. It's perfect. Woven in between the words at my wrist, is a blue and white stone atop a gold ring. The colors are muted, helping it blend nicely with the black and grey words, but it's close enough in appearance I'm able to keep my memory, as well as save Shell by giving it away. Covering it with the protective gel I look up at my reflection. Time to put on a brave face and get ready for our class, then put my plan in place for after.

***

"What do you mean I have to change? I'm gonna be sweating my butt off in an hour. I think sweats and an old t-shirt should work fine." I glance down at the ratty grey sweats like they'll help me convince her. It may not be the sexiest outfit but I'm not going there to get a date.

She points at my 'offensive' choice in clothes. "You should always look your best. I don't complain during the week because nine times out of ten you're wearing work clothes and can't help it. But this is a co-ed course. Co. Ed. You never know when you might meet a potential hook-up."

I look at her choice in attire. She's wearing black stretchy yoga pants that contour to her toned legs, making them appear miles long. With her eight extra inches in height, she can make those pants look good. Her flat stomach is bare. The only thing holding up her jubblies is the band of spandex at her chest. She's like workout Barbie, but with short brown pigtails instead of the normal mass of blonde. "I see. I love what you're trying to do here but I will never feel comfortable kicking and jabbing in stretchy pants and bandeau bra. And how do you not knock yourself out with so little support?" I cup the air around my small boobs to emphasize the point. She most definitely has more padding in the upper-cupper department than me.

"Oh, I'm only there to watch and cheer from the sidelines. If I happen to catch someone's attention with my get-up, then yay me." This is stated with a finger twirl I haven't seen her do since high school. Great, she's breaking out old school tonight. I'm stunned I'm going at this alone.

"What?" I ask.

She cocks her head to the side and puts a hand on her hip. This stance does not bode well for me. "I told you we'd do this, but you haven't even *tried* to look into a gun safety course. That was the deal. But I will practice punching you after school tonight if it'll help?" Turning me around by my shoulders she smacks me on the butt to get me to move. "Go forth and dress thyself in something less homeless and more badass please. If I had time to wash clothes I'd shrink something of mine to your size, but time's a-wasting."

Rolling my eyes, I walk into my bedroom and open every drawer, searching for something that will appease her. At least enough to get us there on time. Finding an old pink sports bra, I exchange my current top for that. The only pants that I can find, that aren't sweats or jeans, are a black loose capri pants with a lime green drawstring. She's just going to have to get over it. Running back out, I wrap my braid into a thick bun at the base of my neck and grab my keys. "Ready." Not allowing her to critique my new outfit I walk right by her out the door.

***

We arrive at the hospital in just under twenty minutes, a record for this time of night. The guest parking is packed, but I find a spot close enough to Shell so that we can walk together inside. Walking in the double doors, I try to make mental notes without drawing attention to the fact. Shelly's office is in wing A, which enters at my left. If I'm going to sneak back in there later, I need to somehow nab the key off her key ring before she leaves. There just wasn't a time that I could do it before we left, making this class my only option. It's a good thing she has a date after this, forcing us to drive separate cars, and she won't suspect anything when I try to stay later. I am going to have to go all 'Neva the Ninja' tonight. I take one more covert peek at the hall to her office, before we turn the corner, spotting the elevators ahead.

I'm bouncing on the balls of my feet, giving away my nervousness. It's not a fun combination of nerves to have. I've been on edge since all of this began, and I'm not sure if it's a good thing I haven't been contacted by that gang *El Carlos* again or not. Such a stupid name. If I ever do meet them I may bring that up. No. That's even stupider. I don't ever want to meet them. I shiver, alerting Shell to my state.

"You cold? I have a sweater in my car. I should have warned you they keep the hospital to freezing." She says as we walk inside the elevator.

I don't want to lie. I hadn't even felt the cold. "I'm okay. What button? B or B1?" Hitting B for me, we start our descent. I lean my head against her arm as she hugs me to her. "I've missed our girl chats." The doors open and we're greeted with double doors at the end of the hall. "Wish me luck." Pushing through the door I find it opens into one large room. Blue mats line the floor, and roughly fifteen men and women of differing ages turn to watch us enter. Some are big and some smaller. Unfortunately, I'll take gold for smallest female.

Shelly walks over to find her cheering corner, and I follow to throw my keys and phone next to her. The doors we had just entered make a loud bang as someone comes in, causing me to jump. I look up at Shell and her mouth is gapping open in obvious surprise. Turning my head it takes a minute for my brain to catch up with what I'm seeing. In the bright florescent light, his eyes are a mix of brown and green. And they are locked right on me. There's surprise there on his face. An emotion I'm intimately familiar with right now. Well, this should be a fun night.

He walks to the front of the room, removes the bag hanging from his thick shoulders and throws it to the floor. I'm not going to lie; my eyes fly south as he bends to set it down. Black track pants ride low on his hips, lying over a pair of white Addidas shoes. As he stands tall once more, I watch the muscles constrict in his back through the white T-shirt, so tight it could be a second skin. Every valley and hill are defined through it perfectly. I have the urge to fish out a few dollar bills to thank him for the show. I know exactly where I'd stick them. He motions behind our group to where the double doors are, and I reluctantly turn, immediately wishing I hadn't. 'Blondie' is standing there, in clothes that rival Shelly's, and her hair is in a tight high ponytail, eyes on Jason. I'm already regretting my choice in clothes. Why couldn't I have been born with a few extra inches? Or bigger boobs? I'm not picky. His deep baritone snaps me out of my wishful thinking.

"Good evening. I'm your instructor this evening. My name is Grant. Behind you is Helea. She'll be assisting tonight. For some of you, this is a refresher course and I may ask those of you who are willing to be my spotters. Now, if you can come closer and stand facing me we can begin." He says.

I look back to make sure Shelly hasn't decided to abandon me, and she sends me off with a thumbs up. Walking to the line formed in the center of the mats, I stand at the end next to an older gentleman. He's in great shape and has a good ten inches on me. I look up and give him a small smile to which he bows slightly in return. I'm not sure what the protocol for my response should be. Do I bow back? I thought this was going to be a class on how to throw my knee in a crotch or shove my palm up a nose. I'm so out of my league here. Thankfully I'm saved from making a fool of myself, at least so far, by Jason walking up to the line. 'Blondie' (I refuse to call her by her name), stands behind him with her legs spread shoulder width apart and has her hands clasped behind her back, making her seem official. I knew I hated her. Jason surveys our line with a keen intensity and finally lands at my end. I'm positive my eyes are too big on my face while I gaze back at him, but he has me rooted to the floor by that hot look.

After he'd broken us off into couples, I'm standing with my teammate on the opposite side of the room from where I'd originally started. I have Shell in my sight, which is the only thing keeping me here. I know if I left she'd just drag me back by my thumbs, so I won't bother trying. I'm already breathing hard from my second fall to the floor, which I guess is the freaking purpose of this drill, but humiliation has crept into me. Crept? Ha. More like slammed into me with a baseball bat. Which is a pretty good description for what it feels like sparring with this chick in front of me. My face has to be giving away my distress, but she doesn't seem to care. Hopefully I can pretend it's due to how out of shape I am and not from how easily she's knocked me down…again.

"Again." He says from the front of the room.

Oh good. He wants us to do it again. We've only been at this for twenty minutes and I'm already bruised. Taking my stance again she comes at me fast. I may be new, but I'm a quick learner. I duck at the jab she intended to connect at my chest and spin, dragging my leg out to sweep her feet from underneath her. This time I stand over her instead of the other way around. That's a great feeling, even if it was probably done with a shit load of luck.

I lean over my sparring partner to help her stand and sense heat against my back once I'm upright. It's my only warning he's right behind me. Well, that, and the seductive look the girl I just knocked down is throwing up about a foot over my head. Gripping my elbows held down by my sides, he runs his hands down till they end at my wrists. Bending at the waist, he positions himself so the hair at the nape of my neck tickles my ear when he speaks, spiraling my body into a state of mass confusion. Chills battle with heat. My body wants to lean back into him prolonging the sensation, but instead I take one large gulp of air, causing my back to brush with the front of his shirt. When he speaks, I can feel the vibration against my back.

"Good. Let me see you try this." He says.

Pulling my wrists back towards my body, my arms are raised up over my head with my hands bent to an awkward angle. I'm staring straight ahead at the white concrete wall in front of me trying to control my reaction to his closeness. My body has become an addict to his touch, craving him like a drug. The flex of his grip advances to an almost painful level, dragging a whimper from the back of my throat. His body stiffens behind me and I'm released quickly, propelling me into a forward motion, almost stepping on my sparring partners toes. I look over to see his retreating back, before searching around me, trying to decipher what caused his sudden departure. I shake my arms in an attempt to release the tingles spiraling out of control. It's not helping. I need more of him. My partner sends me a look telling me I'm not hiding the fact. I should have just stepped on her when I could have, and blamed it on *him*.

Helea is suddenly in charge, demonstrating hand and feet placements. With my attention diverted, I lose track of Jason as I try to keep up the appearance of an attentive student. Thirty more agonizing minutes later, and she's informing us the time has ended. I walk over to Shelly's deserted seat and plop ungracefully onto the floor. Resting my head against my knees, it takes a minute to realize I've been awarded the perfect opportunity to steal her key. I search through the dispersing crowd and not finding her in the room I slide her purse closer to my butt. I know I shouldn't do this, but it's the only way. It takes looking through three zippered pockets to find them, but I grab the keys and make quick work removing the one I need. I hear Shelly laugh somewhere to my left so I stuff the stolen loot into my sports bra and drop the rest of her keys back into her bag, then blank my features when I see her feet standing next to me.

"Hey. Nice moves out there. That was definitely worth the price of admission. I'm uploading that kick combo you pulled off onto YouTube when I get home." She says.

Confused, I look up at her. "What kick combo? I didn't pull off anything of the sort."

She pulls the corner of her lips to the side. "Yes. I know. Which is why I'm sharing it with the world." She cackles as she says this. "So, where'd the hulk go? With the way he concentrated at your end of the room I thought I'd see you burst into flames from the heat of it. Here…" She reaches down, searching through her purse, and I hold my breath hoping she doesn't notice her keys have been moved. Retrieving her phone she scrolls through looking for something then faces the phone so I can see the screen. I'm staring down at myself being held immobile by Jason. From her position I have a clear view of our faces, and wow, she's right. His expression burns the metal in my hands. But it's what he's focusing on that stops me cold. I glance at the wrist he's studying and my eyes latch onto the newly inked tattoo. Of course. His interest has nothing to do with me, but what I can give him. Well, step in line buddy.

***

The lack of light inside the empty office has my extremely active imagination on overdrive. It just needs eerie music to achieve nightmare quality. I'm using my maternal ninja skills to find my way to Shelly's desk. Who knew all those times I had to sneak out of Drew's room at bedtime would pay off? Locating her workspace takes me more time than I'd planned, as everything looks different in the dark. Footsteps in the hall have me diving under her desk, smacking the side of my head on its edge. Ouch. It'd be nice if I could accomplish this without knocking myself out. Is it too much to ask for just one day without a new bruise? I hold my breath, along with my aching head, to hear if I'm still alone. There's no sound except my heart thumping in my ears. I let the breath out slowly and crawl on my hands and knees from my hiding spot, looking back at the door. Once I'm confident I'm alone, I open the drawer closest to me and reach inside using my sense of touch to assist me. Nothing in there. *Shit.* I check every other drawer thoroughly, leaving nothing missed.

The hand clamped against my mouth muffles my scream and my hands automatically grab the fingers holding it in. I twist and turn trying to dislodge my much smaller body from the tight embrace, but nothing seems to dislodge it. The arm at my stomach contracts, forcing me into submission, forcing me to stay still. He leans in and whispers, and I'm at odds with either relaxing into his hold, or maintaining my struggle to be free. "What do you think you're doing Neva?"

Removing his hand from my mouth, he keeps the other arm locked tight under my breasts. I slump against him, into his embrace, too relieved to carry on struggling to get free, and feel the evidence of his arousal at my back. I don't know what I was expecting, but confirming his desire for me was not what I'd envisioned. Images flash through my mind like a fast moving train. Our bodies moving as one. Sliding. Biting. Gripping. Exploding. It's so tangible I arch my back with a *please* leaving my lips. Digging my nails into his thighs, the hand cupping my chin moves down to apply pressure against my throat, which ignites the blaze between us even more. Before I can take back control, I'm flipped to lie on my back as his solid body pins me down. Grabbing my wrists with one of his hands, he pulls them over my head, while his other hand grabs at my bare waist. His hands are so large I feel his thumb next to my navel. My hips rise as if being pulled upward, but he holds me down underneath him with his weight, then our lips collide in a fierce assault that exceeds the workings of my imagination. This is so much…. *more*.

With my hands held above me I can't touch him. I want to touch him. Breaking the kiss I tell him so, and he stops to look down at me. All I can see is his chiseled face above me, looking fiercer that I've ever seen him. Letting my wrists go slowly, he trails his fingers down my arms, leaving tingles along the way. We just look at one another. He's granted my request, but I can see the strain it's caused him. I bring my released hand up to his face, running it against his coarse hair. I've never been a fan of beards, though I wouldn't call this a beard exactly. It's too short, and looks so damn good on him. I wonder what it'd feel like on my...

"...de esa forma. Aqui podras comprobar." The accented voice pulls us from our trance.

Jason slides off me and pulls me up by my shoulders, then he's shoving me under Shelly's desk, as if it's just another afternoon at the office. He's not even breathing harsh. I hunch as far back as the cubbyhole allows, waiting for him to join me, but instead he leans under part way and whispers something about me staying under here. Is he nuts? Part of me is frozen still with fear, while the other part of me wants to grab ahold of him and keep him safe. Which is ludicrous. What could I do to keep him safe? He's gone before I can make up my mind. I don't hear anything for the first several seconds. I can't tell if that's a good thing or a bad thing. He moved so fast it's like he vanished in front of me. I also don't hear the men that sounded so close to us while we'd lain on the hard ground. My Spanish is rusty, but I got the drift of what they wanted. Me. I've never wished for being wrong so much as I do right now. I try to scoot my body further under the desk, pushing my weight back by using my hands, when my palm bumps over something sticking out of the wood. I don't think about what I'm doing; just snatch it in my hand. I should have known she'd put it there.

I let out a tiny yelp as Jason puts his finger to my lips. I had been so distracted with my discovery I didn't see him until he was right in front of me. He keeps his finger planted in place, but guides me out from my hiding spot and begins to pull me behind him. Our feet are silent on the carpeted floor as we weave between the other desks and chairs and I'm starting to worry he's forgotten my short legs have a disadvantage to his longer stride, because I know I have to be slowing him down. Looking to my left I think I see someone move by the wall. Jason must have seen the same thing, for he crouches down low to the ground. Being the smart girl that I claim to be, I follow suit, and fall down next to him.

Leaning my head back onto the hard wall, I close my eyes, attempting to bring air back into my lungs. Not. Working. Fast. Enough. Jason's strong hand takes my chin, directing it towards him, but I stay closed off from him. I need to get it together. He finally gets my attention by squeezing me, making my eyes open to his silhouette. The little bit of light reflecting through the window shines on just his face, allowing me to read his lips when he tells me where we're moving to next. Be brave. Be brave. Be brave. I silently repeat this as we begin to crawl to the corner, and hopefully somewhere that's hidden. This office isn't huge but when low to the ground, we're camouflaged enough, our movements aren't visible. Or so I hope. I have no idea how we're making it out of here unnoticed, but in this moment, I know I trust him to get us out.

Once we clear the corner, Jason stands us up. Finger pressed back at my lips, I give him my best *what the hell* look. I think by now I've figured out how to be quiet. It happens so quick I almost forget I need to stay silent, but bite my lip to smother the sound. My arms hold tight around his neck as he tucks me into his body and up into the air. If we make it out of this, I'll replay this moment and remember how good it felt to be carried by this man, damsel style. I only get to enjoy my ride for a few moments, until my feet touch the floor of the bathroom he's hidden us in, but I don't have time to stay in one place for long. Moving me backwards with a push, he waits until I'm as far in the corner as possible before he cages me in with his arms. One thick bicep on either side of me, sheltering me like a human barricade. As he waits for sounds out in the hall, we lock eyes with one another, listening together. Reaching up, I use his bicep to anchor me, as he tilts his head slightly, right before

I feel the feather kiss on my forehead. That's the only warning I have before he backs out into the darkened doorway and away from me.

I was doing fine keeping my head straight until now. But as I stand here alone, my gasps have become too loud in my ears, and I can't find a focal point to center my sight in the pitch-blackness. Clenching my hands into fists, I suddenly remember the item I discovered. I should leave it here and let them find it. But which foe is this? If this isn't related to Angelo, I may as well hand Shelly over to Nicholas on a silver platter tied in a bow. This can't be connected with him though. I still have until Wednesday to bring it to him. Making my decision, I shove it down between my breasts, next to the pilfered key. Hearing a thump outside the bathroom, I run to the doorway and flatten myself against the wall to peek around the edge, trying to find the cause. I watch as Jason steps out from behind another door and walks over a bumpy shadow on the floor, holding his gun in both hands while aiming it down at the shadow. I'm either cured of my gun phobia, or I'm too scared to care it's next to me. Whichever it is, I'll gladly take it over losing my shit right now. He motions for me to come out and I do. Slowly.

Together we walk hand in hand back to the exit and our freedom from this hell. The pinch in my arm is so acute I can't keep from voicing my distress. "Ouch!" He pulls me behind him while firing the gun, one, two, three times at darkness. Hearing the subsequent thump, I understand that he can actually *see* right now. The sting in my arm has turned ice cold, and I see white spots floating in front of us, as we move to the door. What? I try making us stop but he pulls harder on my arm. I feel sick. And hot. He says something to me and I nod because, isn't that what I'm supposed to do? My eyes close to dark and…

CHAPTER 18

JASON

Neva starts pulling me to stop but I need to get us out of here. Hearing gunshots at a hospital is a surefire way to bring law enforcement right to the door. It will be hard enough explaining why I incapacitated two of Carlos' men. There are only three people who know I was here tonight. This is a fucking mess. If we move quickly enough, I may be able to smuggle her back to my house without anyone becoming the wiser. I turn to pick her up again and watch the life leave her eyes as she goes limp in my arms. "Fuck." Picking her up again, her head hangs over my arm blocking my view of her face. If time wasn't our enemy I'd stop to check her pupils but we need to go. And now. Whatever they shot her with worked fast.

Using one arm to hold her to me, I tuck the 9mm behind my back to free my hand and move us out into the hall. Checking first to see if my way is clear, I walk to the back exit using the shadows as cover. It's been four to five minutes, tops, since I put three bullets in that fuckers head. I give us two more before we're discovered. Looking back down at her throat, I'm relieved to see the pulse flutter slowly. I will deal with that emotion when this is over. For now I have one goal, and that's getting her to safety. I'd parked at the side lot, facing the highway, offering me a panorama of North and Southbound lanes. All clear as of now. I'd brought the truck tonight, which works for now, as the black blends enough not to stand out. I can hear the sirens as I step over the curb nearest to it. I need to move if I want to make it out of here. The back seat is tall enough so I only need to lean in to place her on it, but the belt is at the wrong angle. Split decision made, I opt for buckling the middle belt around her midsection.

I've lived thirty of my thirty-six years in this town. I know every back and side street to anywhere I need to go, keeping us off I-95 on the drive home. The motion lights flick on as the car pulls up to the garage, granting me an unobscured view, as I glance back to the woman laid across the backseat. She could easily pass for a child in my car. Running hands over my face I wonder how I could have deviated from my mission and not thought twice about its repercussions. I release the locket around my neck to slam both my hands against the steering wheel and get out of the car. Opening the back door I bend to pick her up, checking her vitals as I do. I have the tranq dart he shot her with in the front seat, but that will be dealt with when Val gets here. I'd imagined too many times what she'd think of my home, but never thought she'd be comatose the first time I brought her here.

I'd left a light on in the entry, helping guide me around the corner to my room. As I use the guest room as my workout area, it leaves my bedroom as the only viable option. She'll sleep like the dead for twelve or more hours, if I've calculated it right. I've already checked the dart and don't recognize the brand they used. If I had to guess, I'd say it's another homegrown concoction. There have been twenty-four of these discovered already by my crew, each originating from the same source. We've been trying to keep up with every new brand they formulate, but we always seem to be one step behind. Laying her on top of the comforter she barely takes up any space on my king size bed. In a perfect world I'd make her mine and never look back. The lines have started to blur with me. Running my finger down her cheek I tell myself it's to feel her heart beat. But I know I'm lying. She has an angelic look about her in sleep and her hair came out of it's confines sometime during our ordeal, and it now fans against my dark pillowcase, producing images of what she'd look like spread out beneath me. I only had a small taste of her, but I want more.

I'd almost ruined everything I've been working for, twice in one night. I can count on one hand the amount of people I can say I've been proud of. But I'd watched her tonight as she put her heart into training, and then with her bravery later hiding in the dark bathroom, I'd felt it once again. She has a fire inside that I want to capture for my own. Picking up her limp arm, I turn her hand palm up and stare down at the ink decorating her wrist, rubbing my thumb softly over the raised healing skin. She's made her body into a beautiful canvas. I trace the words circling her wrist that cloak the item that brought us together. I wish I could be more for her.

Kissing the wrist I'd been holding, I lay it down and position it along her body. I'll need to dig out a blanket from the guest room to lay over her, as I'd not turned the comforter on the bed down beforehand. After locating a blanket thick enough to keep her warm, I walk back through the house locking doors and turning off the entry light. After the search for the blanket I'd turned the master bath light on, giving me a view of her still form as I enter back into my room. I stand in the doorway to brand the image of her there into my mind. Realizing I've been staring at her for long enough, I walk to her and drape the beige, thick blanket around her. I know I don't have much time to be near her, but I still toe off my shoes and lie down next to her, gently pulling her into my arms. Just as my head hits the pillow, my phone alerts me of an incoming call. It's one I knew to expect, but thought I'd have more time to hold her. I don't have to be psychic to know who's on the other end, or what he wants. Kissing her forehead one last time, I head back into the hall to deal with him.

CHAPTER 19

NEVA

Cracking my eyes open, I lie as still as possible listening for clues as to where I am. The pounding in my skull makes me want to shut them again, but I leave them as slits to look around. I'm in a room. A big room from what I can gather, and I'm lying on my side facing a closed door that has a dark wood dresser - too masculine for it to belong to a woman - right next to it. The mirror attached to the top thankfully affords me a glimpse at what's behind me without the need to turn my neck. I can see blue curtains hung from a rod at the ceiling, in front of glass doors leading to a balcony. The curtains are pulled half way granting enough light to filter inside. Braving movement, I push through the fogginess and bring my right arm up closer to my face, dragging it against dark blue sheets, causing dust particles to float over me like I've hit the slow motion button. I should probably get up and out of this room to start solving this mystery, but the warm soft blanket I'm wrapped in has me cocooned inside its warmth. Enough, I tell my lazy self.

Giving the blanket a pat goodbye, I grab the sheet to give me leverage, pushing myself up on shaky arms to sit upright. Oh, ugh. I breathe slowly through the nausea. If Joey got me drunk again I'm going to hang him by his toes. He promised the last night of *crazy Cuervo* would never be repeated. But something tells me that's not the case here. My eyes seem to be working better when upright, not perfect, but it's an improvement. I realize the reason I'm having trouble taking in air, is because my pink sports bra is suffocating me. Grabbing the straps I pull up the top to peel it from my skin. Ow. *What the...?* Nestled between my boobs is something wrapped in tape, and a key. Huh…I'm getting warmer on solving this mystery. The key is imbedded into my chest and takes me a few pain-filled seconds to peel it from my sensitive skin. How long was I wearing this? I might have a permanent impression now. Not exactly the look I'm going for. But it's funny if you think about it. Like a visual aid for the key to my heart. Yikes! Stop that thought please. The key and the tape thingy still aren't giving me any answers as to where I am though. My brain hurts. Actually, everything kinda hurts. My right arm feels like someone punched me. Hard. It's tough to see between the words written there, but it looks as if it's bruised up close to my shoulder. I stuff the key and my barbell back into place, just as the door opens, revealing a sexy Jason carrying a steaming mug in his hand which made him all the more sexy. That coffee mug better be for me. If I didn't feel like death warmed over, I may have wrestled him for it.

It's either a huge surprise finding me in his bed, or he wasn't expecting me to be awake. Damn. There went my hope that's my cup of joe. Maybe if I stare hard enough at it, he'll take the hint. Although then I couldn't enjoy the visual feast standing before me this morning. At least I think it's morning. The sun is shining, he has coffee in his hands, so morning seems like a logical conclusion. Yet, it's not like I haven't had myself some caffeinated goodness in the afternoon before. It's always seven a.m. somewhere. Looking back up at Jason I realize this is the most casual I've yet to see him. I've witnessed his work attire, yum and a jeans/t-shirt combo, double yum. And let's not forget the track pants accompanied by a painted on shirt. That was a double yummy of epic proportions. But cargo shorts and a wife beater? I think I might either be dead or dreaming. He looks almost as delicious as that coffee. Maybe I could convince him to dribble it down his front and then I can enjoy both. At the same time.

"You have the oddest expression on your face. Do you feel alright?" He asks.

I drag my eyes back up to his, a little unnerved he'd caught me fantasizing. "What? Oh yeah. Peachy. Is that coffee?"

He looks down to the treasure in his hand. "It is. I wasn't expecting you to be awake so soon. I'll fix you a fresh cup when you're ready."

"Mmm – yes." Huh. I hope he understood that.

"I'll go now and get you one then." Proving he really *is* an amazing detective. Or it could be my glazed look that hasn't strayed from his cup since he arrived. Instead of heading directly to the kitchen like I'd been hoping, he points to his right at the door beside the dresser. "Bathroom is right there. I've set out an extra toothbrush, and a washcloth for you to clean up if you want it. Make yourself at home." He looks like he swallowed glass as he says it.

I make quick work cleaning myself up, skipping over looking at myself in the mirror. No sense in making matters worse, with having a visual to what death actually looks like, but the rest of the room is fair game. He has a really nice bathroom. You can obviously tell a man decorated, as the accessories are minimal, but the space itself is gorgeous. Cream and brown swirled tiles line the floor and continue up the walls all the way to the ceiling...I didn't know you could do that. It gives the room an elegant appearance. Never seen an elegant bathroom before. I can cross that off my bucket list now. Against the far wall is a big window, I mean *big*, and it's covered by another blue curtain. I'd love to move them aside to see the view, but vampire syndrome is in effect, and thinking of the sun makes my head hurt, so scratch that thought. The shower and tub are separated by a frosted glass wall, giving them the guise of privacy, which is positioned next to a door for the toilet. The tub is as large as its owner. In fact, we could both fit in there comfortably. And the glass walled shower comes equipped with waterfall showerhead. I could have a hay-day in there. As a whole, this is a beautiful bathroom. If I weren't so excited about that coffee, I may take more time to snoop. There are so many drawers my fingers itch to explore. But I'm not going to risk falling on my face just for more information on him.

Jason is sitting on the edge of his bed when I open the door, my borrowed blanket folded next to him. He's bent at the waist, with his empty hands bracketed by his knees. It looks as though his facial hair has grown since I've seen him last, giving him a rugged appearance. I prop my hip against the dresser my coffee is sitting on, and take my first sip back to the land of the living. Oh, I needed this. Now to ferret out some answers. Bits and pieces have come slowly back to me, but the end is still hazy. My cloudy brain wants to stay on a repeated loop of our face sucking session. Not good. Not needing to advertise the blush I know is there, I hold my cup up in both hands, in front of my face to keep that embarrassing fact to myself. Besides, I can always replay it later in privacy. "So, I'm here, why? And I'll assume *here* is your home?" I use my hand to demonstrate which *here* I'm talking about.

He keeps the same relaxed position as he answers. "Yes. I brought you to my home. I thought it best after the two men tried to kidnap you."

I nod like what he said is fine, and I deal with this craziness everyday. Lately that actually seems to be the case. "I'm having some trouble remembering past seeing the body on the floor. I remember running." I pause to see if more pops up. Nope. "Yea, that's it."

"Let's start at why you were breaking and entering an office, that was clearly closed, and crawling around in the dark I might add." He says.

"No, let's not." Nope. Not gonna happen. There's just too much I can't explain.

He doesn't appear to be affected by my refusal. "Did you at least find what you were looking for?"

"Nope." I lie. I stare at his forehead, instead of his eyes, trying to hide the fact. I have until tomorrow to hand this piece of jewelry over. One more day till it's out of my hands, literally, and into someone else's. If the other group coveting it discovers I no longer have it, I have no problem pointing a finger straight at Angelo. Let him be on the *underdog* side for once. I wish I could care why Jason wants it. But Shelly is innocent in this and I'm making it my mission to keep her out of it.

"So, how did we make it out of there last night?" I ask.

"I carried you." A grunted response it is then.

Okay. "Why am I a blank slate after hiding in the bathroom? I have no memory as to how I got here. And why were you carrying me? Not that I don't appreciate your manly prowess, but why couldn't I walk on my own?"

"You were shot…" I gasp and start searching my body for holes. "… by a tranquilizer gun." Phew. I let my arms fall back down. That explains the pain in my arm. And the lack of memory. And why I needed to be carried. Damn.

I scrunch my face in confusion. "Who does that? Shooting people with tranquilizers? Why not just use a gun if you're a bad guy? Isn't that their usual M.O?" I'm Alice in the rabbit hole. I keep sinking deeper and deeper. What happened to my normal life before crazy showed up?

"I would imagine it would be to abduct you without a fight. Not to mention they are nearly soundless when used and don't leave a mess behind to follow." He answers.

Yeesh, I'm getting hot again. This coffee was a bad idea. Then a thought occurs to me. I hold the gasp in, barely, before asking in a calm-ish manner. "Do you know where my phone went? I need to check in on Drew."

He straightens his back and pushes himself to stand. "Yes, I left it in the kitchen. It's rung several times since you passed out last night. If you're ready, we can continue this conversation out there while you return your calls."

Walking out of his bedroom, I am able to see his home for the first time. He lives in a single family home that still looks pretty new, either that, or he gutted it and started fresh. The carpet down the hallway still has that springy feeling while you walk on it, keeping our steps muffled as we walk. I'm glad he removed my shoes at some point, for I'd hate to ruin it. He allows me to walk first to the main living area, but it's killing me not to look behind us and see what I've missed in the other direction. I've always been a fan of the color green, so when we walk into his living room and I see the pale green walls, I get a little giddy. They are exactly the color I'd have picked for our home if we weren't renting. The room itself is exactly what I would have pictured for his bachelor pad. One whole wall is dedicated to every toy a man could possibly want for entertainment. To my electronically challenged mind, it's very intimidating. A large TV is mounted to the wall, surrounded by speakers of every size, and below that what looks to be several gaming systems. We've never had the money to own one, so I wouldn't even know what it is exactly that he has, but it looks pretty extensive. Drew would have an absolute cow if he saw this.

To my left, he has a tan leather couch, formed in an 'L' shape, and a matching recliner sitting next to a dark brown side table and lamp. The area definitely has a homey feeling, even without anything decorating the walls. His office was the same. I'm thinking he's not much of a decorator. I do see one lonely picture frame faced down on the side table. It's the only thing in the room that has a personal feel to it. My nosiness gets the better of me and I head over to pick it up, just as Jason walks back in from the kitchen carrying my phone. As much as I'd love to see who has the honor of being displayed in a house clearly absent of pictures, I need to call Drew. Our fingers brush when he hands it over, and I remind my eager body to calm down.

"Thanks." I say.

Walking closer to the kitchen I lean against the entry to make my call. The clock on the wall says it's four thirty, which means I'd slept for a long ass time. Ten minutes later and I've checked in on a happy boy. It makes my heart soar to hear him laughing. I'll never be able to repay Matt for this, but I can try. I just need to get through this and out the other side. Pocketing my phone, I turn to see Jason finishing his own call, probably to give me some privacy. The silence in the room might seem uncomfortable to some, but I'm enjoying being in the same room with him free of my usual drama. He's looking down as he talks, but I can still make out the line formed between his eyes, indicating this isn't a pleasant conversation. I wonder if it's about last night. Shooting someone in a hospital is bad enough, but he has the added stress of being a detective. The phone call ends and he stands still a moment, before he notices me in the archway. I can see the turmoil in his unfocused eyes, before he speaks directly to me.

"I need to head into the station soon. I don't think it's a good idea for you to be alone today. Is your roommate working?"

"She should be home soon. Tuesdays are her late day, while I take the morning shift at the bookstore. But Matt said you called him last night to let him know I might not make it - thanks for that. I'd have felt pretty bad if I'd just not shown up. Shelly should be home around six, so don't worry, I won't be home alone for long. I'll be fine." I smile to let him see I'm being honest. I may not have packed my big girl panties for my overnight stay, but I will find them when I get home. "Plus, I took this *awesome* self defense course last night." Teasing aside, I really did enjoy the class. Well, until it got weird, that is. I only have another night to get through and I'm confident this will get better. I wish I could tell him that. "So, thanks for last night. I'd not have done nearly as well keeping my butt alive without you. And ya know…the kissing was nice too." Shut up. Shut up. Shut up. I'm still smiling but I bet it looks pretty crazy. I think it's time I go before I make an even bigger fool of myself.

Grabbing my keys from his counter, I walk by him and open the door. I refuse to stick around and wait for his reply to my ridiculous comment. I stop cold on his porch. This would have been a great '*get the last word in and leave*' kind of occasion…if I'd remembered I didn't drive here last night. I turn back around and see him trying to hold in a laugh. Ha. Funny guy. Sure, laugh at the recently sedated chick. See if I care. I scrunch my face up and walk back past him to his entry and wait for his cue. He doesn't make me wait long, thankfully.

"You planning on walking?" He teases.

Ignoring his question, partly because I feel pretty stupid right now, I plop myself down on his couch instead. I know I have time to at least sit; I doubt he'll go into work in shorts and a wife-beater. More's the pity. But I probably have a suit-clad Jason to look forward to, so there *is* that. He laughs as he walks towards his room, cheeky bastard, so I just rest my head back against the cushion to wait for him. I'm startled awake by his deep voice and his hand brushing my hair off my forehead. Looking up I see I was right to hope; he's decked out in a black suit, white shirt and a solid red tie. The jacket is draped over his arm, and I want to reach for it to keep it from wrinkling. Yes, this is the same girl who leaves her wet clothes in the washer for days, only to end up rewashing them. But it would be a shame for his usual crisp look to be ruined by a wrinkle. Holding his hand out for me, I place mine in his and am pulled to standing. Vertigo takes a spin, literally, and I have to hold on to him so I don't end up on the ground. Mmm, he smells like man, with a hint of cologne. I take one more look around to memorize it and notice the picture frame I'd been sitting next to. Grr. I had all that time and I didn't use it to appease my curiosity. I don't have any more time to mourn my lost opportunity, as we head out to his truck.

As I'd predicted Shelly isn't home when we get here, but I won't be alone for long. Our alarm is still armed when we arrive, but Jason is adamant about checking every room before he lets me walk past the entry. He comes out from the back room and seems to be satisfied that no one has been here, or worse, is *still* here. I'm confident Angelo will be expecting me to deliver by tomorrow, so I'm not too worried that he'd show up today. In fact, he never showed Friday or Saturday this past weekend, which was strange, and I haven't heard from him since Wednesday of last week. It's this other set of goons that has me on pins and needles until I can get rid of this thing. And if I take down Angelo in the process? So be it.

Jason walks to our counter and places his hands at the edge, bowing his head. His shoulders slump forward and he squeezes his eyes shut. It's such a vulnerable stance. I'm shocked that he'd expose this weakness to me. One that screams unguarded, letting me witness the man inside - even if just a glimpse – rather than what he shows to the world. My mouth hangs open, as I stay frozen near the door, allowing him to have this time to deal with what he needs to. But it's hard keeping the shock off my face. Does he mean for me to witness this? My heart bleeds for him. I wish I could tell him what I feel. That if things were different, I'd admit how strong I see him. I'd tell him what it felt like to watch my son bond with him, and how much that means to both of us. I'd tell him that every time he shows up, I lose another piece of myself to him. I'd admit that somewhere between my anger for feeling used by him, to now that he's protected me with his life, I've fallen for him. And it's not just the protection he offers, or the safety he affords us, it the man beneath it that I love. He may only want me for a material object. I've had time to reflect on it and if things hadn't changed, I'd lay the stone at his feet. In fact, I'd lay myself at his feet. Because I love him. God help me, I do. Mind, body and soul. I guess when your heart decides on something, the rest of you is just along for the ride. And what a ride it has been. One minute I'm pissed as hell at him, the next I melt in his arms. And now? Now I want to claim him, and vice versa. But I know he'd not welcome these things, so I stay mute and just watch him. Five minutes go by, without either of us moving.

Finally, he seems to collect himself and walks over to me. As I step out of the way, preparing to watch him walk right out the door, he instead waits for me to stop moving before bending to kiss me. After his break-down in the kitchen I wasn't expecting this. It isn't the kiss we shared on the floor of Shelly's office, or the other times we've shared one, but a soft and slow touch of lips. He takes his time teasing my mouth, almost as if I'm a sip of his favorite wine and he's savoring the taste. It only lasts for a minute and then he's out the door leaving me flushed and heart-broken.

I don't know what to make of this, or how to stop it. My emotions are bouncing all over and all I want to do is run out there and bring him back. Instead, I set the alarm for staying in and text Shell to let me know when she's on her way, so I can disarm it. I'm not taking any chances right now and I'd like to be able to enjoy a long, overdue shower, without worrying about the door. And then I need to make a phone call.

***

I'm sitting on my bed with my phone in one hand and the jeweled barbell in the other. The phone call went just as I'd hoped. Unfortunately, this means tomorrow is going to be a long day for me. Trixie was more than happy to trade my Friday for her Wednesday, as she'll probably double her tips with my shift. I still have to work at the bookstore tomorrow morning and there is no way I'm calling out on Matt again. All I know is I plan to sleep all day Thursday, then I'll hopefully be able to spend some quality time with Drew after school. I hear my phone chime and know Shell is almost home. Looking back at the piercing in my hand, I try to figure out a place to hide it until tomorrow. The four spaced hits on the door alert me to the secret knock Shell and I came up with for when the alarm is still set. We're like adult girl scouts. With not much else in the way of choices, I shove the jewelry in between my mattress and box-spring, checking it twice that I've hidden it in there tight, then run to turn off our alarm.

Shelly practically knocks me over when I unlock it. I'm about to give her hell for running me over, when I catch the look on her face. My dormant panic comes quickly back to the surface. "What! What's wrong? Is it Drew?"

"No." She pauses like I'm not freaking out over here. "Ok, so don't freak out." Too late for that. I think whatever they knocked me out with last night has messed with my body temperature, because I'm starting to sweat again. "Ya know when I hid your jewelry?" Oh no.

"I stuck it under my desk at work. I mean, no one *ever* goes under my desk. Why would they, right? So anyway, every day since I've put it there, I check to make sure it's still stuck secure enough. Ya know, to see if I need more tape, but today, we had this meeting that lasted forever so I couldn't check till an hour ago. OmeeGod Nev, I'm so sorry, but it's gone." She has tears running down her face. I can't tell her it was me. Not that I think she'd be mad at me for stealing it. Or taking it back, seeing as it's mine. But if I tell her it was me, I'll have to explain that my boss knows about her past and can act on it, and then I'll lose her again. As much as she loves us, she'd have to run. And I wouldn't blame her. But if I can solve her problem and keep her from ever knowing about this, it's worth it. I make it my rule never to lie to those I love. Sure, I've told a white lie here or there. But never one as big as I am about to. And I hate myself for it. I need to remember it's for the best.

"It's okay Shell. We'll figure it out. I doubt they're even looking for me anymore. I haven't heard anything from them in a while. And I have my tattoo now, so I still have the memory. It's fine." My voice cracks with the last lie and my sore arm throbs, reminding me of last night. It takes another half an hour to calm her down enough so she's not sniffling anymore. She'd gone to the bathroom to wash her face a minute ago and I'm waiting to hear the water turn on before I make my next move. I hear the toilet flush, and the faucet turn on, so I take this time to run into the kitchen and quickly find her keys stuffed inside her purse, then put the stolen key back in it's place.

To keep myself busy, I dig out the gallon of ice cream she enjoys when we splurge on one her cakes, and set it on the counter. Turning from the fridge I see a new addition just begging to be devoured. She must have been busy while I was out getting tranquilized, if the double chocolate concoction on our counter is any thing to go by. My mouth waters in anticipation.

By the time she joins me back in the kitchen I have the plates out, loaded with enough sweets to make the Easter Bunny jealous. She takes hers out of my hand and we walk to our table. It seems like a lifetime since we've been together. Has it only been since yesterday, when we went to the self-defense class? That reminds me of her date. "And how did the date go last night? Keep it PG please." She proceeds to tell me her PG version of the date, and how she might see him again. Or not (her words). It's too mellow an account compared to what I'm used to from her. I only hope she's not still dwelling on her earlier discovery. I need to get her to think of something else. And so do I. Guilt and chocolate are blending in my stomach, and it's not as great a combo as I'd thought. Chocolate is supposed to be my cure-all.

With a mouthful of chocolate I try to change the subject. "I checked on Drew. He's having a blast helping Matt put together that swing for Lizzie. I think by this weekend it'll be safe enough for him to come home. But I'm glad he's in good hands if I can't be with him." I realize I'm veering back to dangerous waters with the jewel, so I blurt the first thing that comes to mind. "So how was Matt in bed?" The spoon she's holding crashes against her plate, splattering ice cream all over her scrubs. Whoops. Maybe I should have gone with something a little more subtle.

She clears her throat. With her eyes on her spoon she relents. "Hmm. Well, it was good. Uh, he's definitely thorough." Oh I am *so* regretting this. "He will make some lucky lady very happy. But it will not be me. Let's move on please. It was a long time ago." Wow, a flustered Shell. I need to write this down in my diary. I don't have one yet, but that's numero uno on the *to do* list as soon as all this crap is done.

"Anyway did you ever find out where your hulk went after the "Dirty Dancing" stunt he pulled last night?"

I can feel my forehead bunch trying to understand her terminology. "Dirty Dancing" stunt? I have no clue what that means."

"Yes you do. You remember when Johnny has to teach Baby the dance moves because Penny can't do it? And in one of the moves, she has to put her arm way up, and Johnny has her by the wrist and then he tickles her armpit? That's what it looked like last night when he was holding you. Or it could have been. You needed to laugh when he let go of your arm." She ends her fantasy by clucking her tongue at me. "It was almost perfect." She must have been watching someone else in that room. That never happened. But it's fun to think about. I wish I could keep her distracted with movie scenes, but she'll just ask the question again later. I am sure there is a special place in hell for lying to my best friend. This is getting out of hand.

"Nope. No clue. Did you see him leave?" I respond.

"I did, and girl, you should have seen him. He was on a mission to get out the door, but stopped anyways and just stood there. It was pretty hot. And I saw the exact moment he turned at the door and, I kid you not, stood there for a solid minute. Guess what he was looking at?" I'm not guessing. I know what she's getting at and I don't believe her. Not that I think she's lying to me. But she has a penchant for only seeing things she wants to see. "No? Fine. He was locked on *you* chicka. All in your mix-matched glory. Which brings me to my next thing. I am buying you workout clothes from your birthday. I should have just left you to your own devices in the first place, instead of making you change. Even if your boobs looked great in that top, you were still a hot mess."

"I'll keep that in mind for next time. And by next time I mean with you getting knocked on the floor right beside me. Down and dirty Shell."

"Does this mean you're ready to conquer your fear of guns and make an appointment with me? Don't get me wrong here, I understand where the fear is coming from. But hon, you'll never get over it if you don't face it head on." She has a point. I hate that she has a point.

I try and reason with her. "I just don't see why I have to conquer it at *all*. Let's pretend, for just a moment, that I actually need to use one. Do you really think, even with the knowledge of how to use it, that'd I'd be able to take another life? It's just not in my makeup to try."

She thinks first before answering me. But I can already tell she's going to trump my response with what she says. "I think, that if it was in response to keeping you or someone you love safe, than yes, yes I do. All I'm sayin' is that it would be a good idea for us to just have the know-how for a worst-case scenario. And I'll leave it at that."

Another solid point. I knew it. "True. Okay. I'll make the call, seeing as you took care of the self-defense course." I look back at our empty plates. "And with that happy thought, should I make dinner? I know we just ate our weight in chocolate, but I feel like we should at least try for something healthy."

"That *was* healthy. Eggs? Check. Milk? Check. Flour? Okay, I'm reaching here, but I'm sure flour is good for you somehow. But I wouldn't mind your veggie stir-fry. I will forever have room for that." She licks the last drop off her spoon and helps me clear the table.

"Done. Just help me cut the veggies and we can watch a movie while we eat." I say.

Walking back to the kitchen, we set our dishes in the dishwasher and begin pulling out ingredients. I'm so blessed to have her. Now, on to more food.

***

Lying in bed, I let myself replay last night and today. I avoid the scary parts and focus on the parts that make me wish he were here with me. Closing my eyes only seems to amplify the images of being under him and what it felt like to have his weight on top of me. My phone chimes on my dresser, distracting me from naughty images, and I reach for it through the dark. Jason's name flashes on the screen with a text attached. I read it three times before it sinks in. He misses me? Me? My hands shake as the text I'm staring at is replaced by a call coming through. It's a blocked number. I smile. Could he be calling to *tell* me he misses me too?

"Hello?" There's silence on the other end. "Jason?" I pull the phone away to see if I disconnected by accident. The numbers at the top scrolls slowly, telling me the call is still active. Huh…trying his name again, I think I hear something. Is that breathing? I'm not sure, but the call drops before I get the chance to confirm it. What? Lying back, it takes me several minutes to feel like I can respond to the text and not sound too eager. I fall asleep with the phone in my hand without ever figuring it out. I should probably be more concerned about the call, but the words *misses me* are all I can think about.

CHAPTER 20

"I can't believe you won't be working with me on Friday. You can't do this to me. And for the second week in a row? Dammit. How are Char and I going to get through it without you? I *depend* on you and your sassy mouth on Fridays."

I look over at Joey while he whines, repeating himself for the fifth time. "Careful Joey. You are border-line whining right now. I'm pretty sure only dogs could understand most of that." Joey has decided to join Matt and I at the bookstore this morning, hogging all the coffee from what I can tell. I reach around him trying to restock the napkins while he complains about Friday. Again. His rambling is helping me keep the jittering at bay for the time being though. I woke up this morning without my alarm's help. Odd feeling - that just doesn't usually happen with me. I had laid in bed, running everything I need to do tonight, over and over to exhaustion. To say I'm nervous is the understatement of the year. But, I'm going through with it. I will stay strong with this decision. I can always call myself foolish later. For now, I just need to get through Joey's meltdown.

"Is he still here?" Matt's question has us both turning to him, as he peeks around from the storage room, eying the man-boy eating the rest of my bagel. The guy can eat all day and still look like an Abercrombie model. So not fair. Joey just waves back causing Matt to disappear back through the door.

Joey looks back at me and smirks. "You know he really loves me. He's just mad that I'm so beautiful and he got that rugged look instead. Yum."

I laugh at his dreamy expression. "Down boy. Now, I need to finish the front. Are you happy here drinking your forty cups of coffee or do you want to move up there with me?" I ask.

Without response he takes the box I have balanced in my arms and walks with me to the front. The store seems lighter than the outside right now with the storm. These storms will start to become more and more infrequent as we move further into Fall, so I savor each one. This makes me wish I was home with a good book, and not working beside a bunch of them. I treasure these types of days. As I make room on the front shelf, Joey sets the box down and makes himself comfy on the love seat, throwing his legs over the edge and resting his head back. He's left his hair loose today so it hangs over the other side, making it look long and shiny. I admit it; I have hair envy.

Surveying the dusted shelf, I hope Matt decides to come back out to help with this. These books won't magically fly to the shelves, and I'm too short to get them up high enough for what we've been asked to do. As I contemplate my next move, Joey keeps the conversation flowing behind me.

"So, a birdie has told me about your Italian stud. What I'd love to know is, why I, yes, *me*..." He stabs his chest for clarification - like I don't know whom he's referring to - but I let him finish. "...your number one supporter, didn't hear about it from you? I heard there was some pretty hot looks and a few tongue twisters that went down." I'm gonna kill her.

With an innocent look directed back at him, I try to keep the guilt from my voice. "I have no idea what you're talking about. And what do y'all do when I'm not there? Talk about me and what I may or may not be doing? She has such a big mouth."

"Yes, she does." Joey and I turn to look at Matt as he states this. That's it. I'm never drinking coffee again. The taste of it coming back up is not worth having any at all. There are some things even a best friend does not need to know.

I stick both index fingers in my ears. "I'm ignoring that. La la la." Dropping my hands, I walk back to the shelves to finish the display of new releases the owner has decided to add to his store, letting Matt finish the tall shelf by himself. I'm still close enough though to hear Joey say he'd be more than happy to hear all about big mouths. Ugh. I need new friends.

An hour of manual labor later, I have my section exactly how I'd envisioned it. I may hate to clean, but give me new books to play with and I'm all over it. Joey left sometime after Matt kicked him out for, as he put it, fondling the shirtless men on his books. We're now ready for the afternoon shift to begin and I can get out of here, squeeze in a quick nap, before beginning my night. Matt's already filled me in on all that is new with Drew, and we've exchanged dirty for clean clothes to complete his week at school. God, I miss him. As I head back over to the back shelves, I come to the section no one ever goes to. Matt and I like to refer to it as the make-out section. Not that either one of us have ever used it for that purpose, or seen anyone do it for that matter, but it'd be perfect nonetheless. It's secluded enough that you are almost completely enclosed on all sides. I stand there a minute, as I argue with myself, over the idea starting to form in my brain. What if...no. But, yes. What if I hid the jewelry here until I had Angelo's promise to never mention anything to Shelly? It's a long shot, I know, but what if he plans to out her anyways, once he has it? This would be my insurance plan.

I realize I'm making this harder than it needs to be. Just hand it over and be done. Then, if that gang of goons comes for it, tell them who has it. That's solid. Right? I rub the tension that is stabbing my forehead. Can I do it though? He never said he'd drop it once I gave it over to him, just that if I *didn't*, he'd inform that bastard Nicholas where he can find Shell. Before I can talk myself out of it, I'm pulling the bottom set of books off the shelf as quietly as I can. Reaching my hand behind, I feel for the grooves that are etched into the wood, from where the records used to sit when these shelves were in the back room. The barbell is stuffed into my bra, and digging it out takes longer than I need it to. Once I feel that it fits inside the groove, without rolling to either side, I start stuffing the books back into their dusty home. I'm out of breath when I sit back on my heels. It's done, and I have goose bumps along my arms to prove it. This might be the brightest move I've ever made, or I am royally fucked.

I've just served my fifth "Sex on the Beach." I am *so* over these college kids who drink too much and end up being sloppy drunks. If you're going to end your night puking, at least make your trip getting there worth it. But as I never went to college, and missed out on that experience, it will remain a mystery why these kids act the way they do. It's just past midnight, and I have yet to see Angelo. Usually I'd be jumping for joy at that, but tonight I *need* to see him. This waiting game has to end. I'm working with two other bartenders that I don't know as well as I do Joey and Char, but so far we've managed to get our groove moving smoothly, and I won't be too far behind with my tips when tonight is done. I motion down to Josh that the Crown Royale is getting low, and he let's me know my side is covered till I get back. It's amazing you can communicate with just a few hand gestures, but it served its purpose.

It's not as crowded as Friday or Saturday nights, but I still have to weave between sweaty bodies to get to the back of the club. There are definite advantages to being height deprived. Wednesdays are usually more subdued than tonight, but I was told a friend of a friend wanted to play live music here for exposure. Whatever that means. It's a completely different vibe in here, with more standing and less dancing. The singer, and I use that term loosely, is screaming into his mic about 'girl parts' and 'fast cars' making him roar. It's not something I'll be buying when he hits it big, but more power to him.

The hall that leads to our liquor vault is the same hall that holds the office. I seem to be stuck at the entry, not moving in either direction. Forward sends me to the unknown, backwards sends me to a cowardly act. My legs refuse to take another step down the hall. The screaming music blocks all other sound and the beat of the drums seems in sync with the strobe light bouncing off the walls. I remind myself why I'm doing this. It helps my feet do their thing and now I'm a few steps closer to my intended target. I feel ridiculous tip-toeing down the hall, I snort, as if anyone can hear me. I could set fireworks off back here and the guy screaming would still be the loudest thing heard.

Turning the corner I stop cold. If I move even an inch I'll be discovered and right now I think that'd be very bad. The man I need to see has another man I've never seen before up against the wall with a gun, yup a gun, against his head. Well… shit. This can't be good. The exit sign provides enough light to make out their faces, and let's not forget *the friggin gun*. I watch horrified as Angelo leans closer, yelling into the terrified man's face, probably spitting as he does. I can't hear it, but I absolutely see it. It makes my knees weak, and I hit the floor, hard, covering my mouth as I go. He shot him. In the *head*! I'm at the same level as the vacant stare of the dead body, once he's slid down the wall. I can't stop looking. A pair of legs cut off my view and it's then it happens. Shit. I knew this night was going to be bad. I throw up all over the shoes in front of me. Yup, that's right. My dinner gone, displayed on top of brown leather loafers. There's no time to catch my breath before his fist hits me in the side of the head, and I land on my side. I'm so stunned nothing really hurts, until my arm starts being pulled so hard I almost black out. My legs try to find traction on the ground to relieve the pressure in its socket, yet there's nothing to give me leverage as he quickly hauls me further from the dead guy.

His office is more lit than the last time he'd dragged me in here. I look quickly for anything I can use to fight him off as we clear the door, but he shuts it behind me before I can find something of use. I'm beginning to think my plan to negotiate wasn't a winner and I pray hard that I make it out of this alive. Taking my shoulders in a grip sure to leave me with bruises, I'm pushed down in the chair by the door. He pins my arms so hard to the armrests that my fingers immediately go numb. He leans in close, breathing in my face, and I can smell the alcohol on his breath. I think I might be sick again.

"Ah, my lovely snow princessa…have you brought me what is mine?" Oh, I screwed up. I can't lie to him, or talk my way out of this now. He'll only search for it. Or just shoot *me* too. I need to convince him I can get it.

"No. But I have it. I left it somewhere. We can go right now and get it." The weight is removed from one of my arms so fast I don't see it move, only feel the grip as it latches onto my throat. He's talking to me but I can't hear him through my need to breathe. He loosens his hand enough for air to burn down my throat as I suck it in.

This time when he leans in close I can see the calculated decisions being made, right in front of me. "Yes, we will get it. I'm counting on you to do the right thing. The life of your friend means something to you doesn't it?" He shakes me for emphasis. "I have her somewhere safe until it's in my hands. Don't make me change my mind and do something that is so simple to stop with your cooperation. All I want is a small token, and she'll remain unharmed." His voice is deceivingly bland.

I have to be hearing him wrong. Am I hallucinating with lack of oxygen to the brain? What does he mean he has her? I did this so she'd be left out of harms way and it may all be for nothing? She doesn't deserve this. And neither do I. The anger hits me like a sledgehammer. He. Will. Not. Hurt. Her. The tingle of my fingers sends awareness to that part of my body, and my swift reaction surprises both of us. My unattended hand flashes out, and I know I hit him where it counts, by the redness on his face. He falls back against his big desk, bending at the waist from my blow to his manhood, and I'm up out of the chair pushing him back with all the strength that my smaller body affords me. I must have distracted him by my move, as he just looks at me, giving me the opportunity to grab the first thing I see off his desk and bash it into his skull.

The door to his office is pushed open with so much force it gets stuck against the wall by its knob. The first one to enter is an enraged Jason, gun out, pointed right at the stupid man who dared threaten my best friend. I feel vindicated that it was *me* that knocked his ass out, and not someone bigger, or with more experience. Others filter in as Jason deems the room 'clear', but all I can focus on is the pride I see in his eyes looking back at me. I drop the weight from my hand and it falls to the floor with a thump. I don't even care what I hit him with. I need to save Shelly.

"Shell... He has Shell." I gasp.

CHAPTER 21

Jason doesn't react to my distress, just stands there, poised in the same position as when he entered. Can't he see I *need* him to help me? My best friend is out there somewhere, probably hurt, or at the very least scared. Shifting my eyes behind him I notice the other men dressed in padded black uniforms fanning themselves throughout the small office. The one closest to me is tying a zip-tie around an unconscious Angelo, so I step to the side to make room for him. I'm suddenly wrapped in strong arms and my head is cocooned against his abdomen. He holds me so tight, I feel dizzy, but I let him help me keep it together for just a second longer. I feel his body shift us towards someone to my right and I turn my head to look over his arm and see a face that looks familiar. I can't place it at first. Then it hits me. I saw him at the station, briefly, after I'd received the second note. Feels like a lifetime ago now. He looks so out of place in a room full of burly men in SWAT gear, wearing jeans and a loose shirt. His hair is longer too and he keeps brushing it out of the way of his glasses. Dark brown eyes survey the chaos like he can't understand how he got here.

His voice has a soothing quality to it when he speaks. "Okay boss. I'll get what we came for. But if you could get the D.B. out of the hall before I exit I'd be grateful." He disappears behind me so I can't see what he's referring to. But I don't care anymore. The thought of Shelly alone has me burrowing into Jason's embrace, and digging my nails so hard they have to be hurting him. This is all my fault. I should have ended this at the beginning and not been so selfish. I may never forgive myself if she's hurt. I'm not sure he hears my plea, from the foot below him, until I feel his arms tighten around me telling me he did. He yells behind him to someone, throwing out phrases like 'ATL's' and 'missing persons.' Please let him be talking about Shell.

"We need to go find her!" I yell up at him. He looks down at me and I can see it in his eyes. He thinks we're too late. "No, no, no, no. Please!" I don't recognize the wail that comes from my throat. My arms fling out, beating his chest, and he allows me to use him for my outlet to release the debilitating agony I feel. The pain consumes my whole body. I can't do this without her. She's my sister in every way but blood. He crushes me to him, halting my fists, and I try to sink to the floor, but I don't make it far, as I realize I'm being raised high as he picks me up. Throwing my arms around his neck, I tuck my head as close to him as possible and block out the rest of the room, and sob uncontrollably. It isn't a conscious action, just a release of the torment destroying me. We sit down in the chair I'd just been threatened in and he rocks me slightly while I let out the misery eating me from the insides.

For the next hour I sit held by him in his lap, as two police officers question me about the events leading me here. I sit here in his lap looking at the wall, not answering. I'm so mad they aren't using everyone in this room to search for Shell. I know I'm frustrating them, but I just don't have the energy to care. I hear loud voices in the hall and the two inquisitive men move to intercept the mayhem. Jason is talking to me, I think. I hear the tone of his words but not the meaning. He takes my chin and brings my attention upward and he says it again.

"She's fine, Neva. She's been at home this whole time." He whispers close to my face.

I cry out so loud he jolts us in the seat. She's okay. She's okay. She's okay. My best friend is okay. I try to move but he's not letting me. I *need* to move.

"I need to go to her. *Please.* I need to see her." I beg.

He's still holding me tight, rocking me. "Soon. I promise you."

I pull back far enough to see that the sincerity in his voice matches his expression and tell him thank you. It's difficult to make out his features through the tears, but I do notice the tender expression he wears. His face moves closer, and I feel the lightest brush of his lips on the crown of my head. I decide, as I lay my head back down, that this is right where I need to be.

***

My reunion with Shelly is bittersweet. I have never been so happy about being lied to than I am at this moment, but now Shell knows something is up. Angelo used my love for my best friend to attain my compliance and I have to give him credit. His performance was Oscar worthy. I fell for it…hard. Shelly was never in any trouble. In fact, she'd been asleep the whole time, blissfully unaware. But it backfired on him in a big way. His lie gave me the boost I needed to fight back. But even with the threat to Shelly gone, I still need to explain what I know. I'm done lying.

We're sitting in our living room, facing each other on the couch. I had grabbed the quilt from Shell's room to drape over us, and we've snuggled under it. Work attire has been replaced by my comfy pajama pants and tank. Shell has her short hair braided on either side, and is still in her own pajamas, as she was woken up from sleep to cops entering our apartment. I should feel awful for her being woken on a work night, but that doesn't even register right now. I'm just ecstatic to have her here with me. We both yawn simultaneously, bringing a short laugh to the surface. Shell looks tired when she talks. "Now that you see I'm alright, can we start some coffee for the rest of story time? I have a feeling I'll need my wits about me for whatever you're about to say."

"Yes please, I could definitely use it. If you don't mind setting it up, I'll see Jason to the door." I say.

Looking over toward where Jason is sitting, I get up and walk over to him while Shell heads to our coffee maker. Once I'm a foot or so from him, he reaches for me and I gladly allow him to pull me in close to his warm body. My face is once again in the crook of his neck and I whisper a thank you into his ear. With a squeeze he lets me go and pushes me back so our faces can be seen. He has shadows under his eyes. Even after a full day on the job, he still makes my heart beat faster. He's utterly gorgeous.

"Do you want to stay for coffee? You've got to be exhausted. *I* at least get to sleep today." I offer.

"I appreciate the offer, but no. I have paperwork that needs my time and effort. Will you be alright on your own today?" I can only nod in response. I don't want to see him go, and the tears I hold back are tickling my throat. "I have two marked cars stationed on either entrance of your building, and several under-covers that you won't even notice. You should be able to get some rest without having to worry." He takes his hand and places it against my raw cheek. I'd almost forgotten about it with all that has gone on. I must remember to dig out my heavy-duty concealer to hide the bruise from Drew when I see him, for sure. For now though, I can just be thankful it isn't closer to my eye. He studies the scrape with a clinical expression. "This needs to be looked at. I'm sending over Carmine to check on you, so if someone knocks on your door, don't be concerned. I'll make sure he's aware to identify himself at your door. Do *not* answer that door unless it is him. Or me. I will come back if you need me. All you have to do is ask and I'll be here."

I'm quick to respond. "You don't have to do that. This will heal on it's own. Save your friend's time. He doesn't need to go out of his way for me."

He doesn't even pause. "It's not up for discussion. It will be as I say, and you will accept this." He waits for me to bring my eyes back up to his and I can see the turmoil he's attempting to conceal. Could this have been just as hard for him as it was for me? Up this close, the color surrounding his pupil melds together to create one color. There needs to be a name invented just for his eyes. "It's not in my nature to say please, but I will ask you to accept this, for me. This…" He motions between the both of us. "…Is not something I'm good at. I don't have the experience to know if what I'm doing is right or wrong in this. But I have always relied on my instincts to guide me. They've never steered me wrong before, and I will follow its lead for this as well." He moves his hands up until they frame my cheeks. "Let me help you. Let me take care of you. I *need* to do this for you Neva."

Holy smokes. I'm speechless. For once I hope Shelly is eavesdropping so she can relive that for me, from her point of view. I think my heart may explode from all the emotions swirling inside it. I want to scream to him how much I love him. Maybe I'll tattoo those words along my arm to solidify it. He must have taken my silence as acceptance, as he kisses my head and stands to leave. Instead of walking to the front door, as I'd expected, he walks around me to our kitchen. I wait where I'm at, watching him walk to Shelly and settle his hand on her shoulder. I can't see his face, as his back is to me, but I can see Shelly's tear filled eyes, gazing up at him. He bends to hug her and I hear him say, "I'm glad she hasn't lost you," before he's heading for our door. We connect eyes right as he disappears, and then he's gone.

I look back at Shell and her eyebrows have risen inches up her forehead. "Wow. That was hotter than this coffee. I think you may have found yourself a medal winner in the amazing guy category, and can I just say how jealous I am of the head kiss thing. I've always thought that to be super romantic." Done with the tirade, she becomes serious once more. "Now, come here my itty-bitty friend and give me a hug. I am in desperate need right now."

I practically jump at her and am immediately a sobbing mess. I don't know what I would have done if today had been as I'd predicted. Breaking apart from the hug, we decide to move back over to the couch and get comfortable for this. Quilt thrown back around us, and our hot mugs in hand, it's now or never that I get this off my chest. It may just break me to see her hurt by this, but I can't keep it to myself anymore. I start at the beginning and purge the bad from me. Everything. It just pours out. Her office fiasco, Angelo's threats, the heat between Jason and I, *all of it*. I've never been as proud of her as I am right now. She's always been strong, but as I disclose all the ugly, she proves once again what a rock she can be. I should have known better. Never again will I keep something from her. "I'm so sorry I kept this from you. But I thought it was best to not get you involved."

"I know." She lets me go from our fourth hug since I'd started. "I knew that someday my past would show itself again." Looking me in the eyes she adds. "But I *am* mad at you. Not for how you went about this, but that you thought you needed to do it alone. I will *always* be there for your tough times, as well as the good. Next time *please* let me help. Even if you think it's something I can't handle."

I swallow the emotions down. "You're right. I've made some bad choices lately. I thought I could take this on and solve it all by myself. I'm going to change that." I promise.

"What are you thinking? Please, please, please… tell me you're going to ask that gorgeous man for help. In the very least, let him keep you safe. Maybe handcuffed to the bed, ya know, just in case. Besides, Angelo is in custody therefore I don't need to be looking over my shoulder for Nicholas to find me. Well, not any more than I normally do. And as soon as they find the connection between Angelo and that stone, I'd love to hear it. How does he play into all of this?" I had asked the same question, but I'm too tired to go that path right now. "And Drew is with Matt. Having a wonderful time, I might add. You know Matt loves him and will guard him with his life if he has to. But who are you allowing to take care of you? Please, let Jason in to do that."

I sigh. "You're right. The first thing I plan to do is give him the stone, then I'm going to tell him how I've fallen in love with him." She doesn't even flinch as I say this. I guess I didn't hide it well. "Will you go with me to get it from the bookstore? I… I just don't want you out of my sight right now." I grab her hand, that's positioned between us, and give it a squeeze.

She squeezes me back and tips the corner of her mouth up, displaying the dimple in her right cheek. "Sure thing. How about you sleep while I'm at work today and we'll head over as soon as I'm home? Unless you think you need to be with me at work today too? You did tell me how much you enjoyed being beside my desk."

"Ha." I give her a sheepish look. "That was a good time though. But I think waiting till after work will be a better idea. And then I am going to surprise him at home." I throw the side of the blanket I'm under over onto her, then stand up. Setting my hand on my cocked hip I hold the other out to her. "Now, up you go. I'm finally going to let you play dress up, and help me pick the perfect thing to wear tonight."

She allows me to help her stand, then stares at me with a methodical eye. "Done. I have a trench coat that will cover your naked body completely till you get there, then you can leave it at his doorstep. That'll get the ball rolling perfectly. Oh! And you can accessorize with the piercing in your nipple as a surprise. See? Two birds… one blue and white stone…and most importantly, a nipple. Can I give you my phone so you can video this? I'd love to see his reaction."

Turning away from her, I head to my room. "You're crazy. But the last part isn't a bad idea. I can't think of a better way to give him the stone and offer myself at the same time." Sticking my head back around the doorframe, I try to act intimidating. "But I draw the line at the trench coat." The last thing I see, as I pull back to round the corner, is the smug look on her happy face.

CHAPTER 22

Standing in front of his wooden door, I start to doubt my sanity. This was a sound plan up until now, or so I'd convinced myself. I look down to check one more time, at the outfit Shell and I had finally agreed upon for me to wear tonight. And by 'agreed', I mean she threatened to cut off all my hair while I slept if I didn't wear this. And yet, I do agree with her. I feel beautiful. At Shelly's suggestion, I've left my hair down so it falls in waves on all sides of me, playing peek-a-boo with the strapless red dress that ends a few inches below my knees. The fitted top is tight enough to push up what little I'd been gifted so I can see my cleavage. And, I guess, it's fine that I can see it, as long as Jason can notice it as well. The skirt isn't what I'd usually refer to as sexy, but on the length swirls around my legs in a dramatic flair. Shelly commented that I look like a pin-up, but I'm not so sure about that, even if it was nice to hear. I had dug through my closet and found a pair of black stilettos I haven't worn since before I had Drew, but they match perfectly with their red heels, and give me four extra inches. I'll take all the help I can get, even if it's from the back of my messy closet. After we played the '*let's see how many dresses we can make Neva try on*' game, Shell helped me apply my makeup. I'm not used to wearing much so it was a change, and that's saying it mildly. After she'd finished prepping, poking, swiping, blotting, ooing, and ahhing, I was finally allowed to take a look at all she'd done. I sat there, looking at this new person, and was seconds away from asking who that was in the mirror. No wonder she took so long. She'd made my eyes appear darker, by lining them in dark blue and silver, and with my mascara done right, my lashes went on for miles. I stared at my reflection. I look like one of those anime characters, with eyes too big for my face. The light blush on my cheeks accentuated my cheekbones, which only left a pink coat of gloss on my lips to finish the transformation. Now, hours later, I should be feeling like a sex goddess, in complete control. Yet I'm still standing here, contemplating all the ways this can go wrong.

The door opens without my knock, and I suck in a mouthful of air as I survey what has been right on the other side of this door. I must have caught him unaware, but I'm damn sure glad I did. Shirtless. Hard pecs. Rippling abdomen. Thick arms. Jeans. Bare feet. I force my eyes upward. Oh. Sweet baby Eeyore - he's wearing his glasses. That's it, I am now a puddle on the floor.

The heated look on his handsome face has me eager to fall down on my knees in front of him, but instead I continue to admire all the muscled skin on display. He steps backward without a word and my feet follow him inside. Just as I step through the doorway, his long arm reaches over me to push the door closed, and I look up at him, hoping he gives me a hint at what he's thinking. I try to convey without words, how much I want this, and that I'm his to command, not caring if that's too forward. I'm willing to rip this dress over my head here in his entryway, if that's what it takes.

There's no warning besides the feeling of weightlessness, then his body's heat, as I'm bodily picked up, slamming my back into something behind me. My legs automatically crisscross around his waist, hiking the dress up to it's max, and baring my thighs as I lock my heels together. He finds leverage to hold me under my legs, digging his hands into me with a punishing grip, and moves his face close to mine. Gah... I love that. His whispered praise causes me to tighten my thighs, right before he kisses his way down along my shoulder, to the top of my dress. My weight is balanced with one thick arm, so he can use the other to pull down my top, exposing my chest. It's hard to breath right now with his eyes and mouth attacking me simultaneously. I want to rub myself against him, but don't have the room to move. He cups my right breast and stares at what he's unveiled. I may not have the biggest breasts, but I hope he enjoys what I'm offering. Running his finger along the outer curve he brings it inward and stops in the middle. I know what has captured his attention, but does he comprehend the two things I'm offering him? One item I know he covets, while the other I'm wishing he does.

The phone rings from his kitchen, snapping us from our heated moment. Digging my heels into his back I silently plead with him to ignore it, but I can tell he's made up his mind. I'm comforted by the fact he looks as miserable as I feel. "I'm sorry. I have to get that. If I'd known to expect you I would have made damn sure we'd been left alone tonight. But I know who that is and he'll continue to call if I don't answer. Do not leave." The last sentence is growled at me, inches from my face. Up this close, it's easy to see, and feel, the strain this is causing him. He slowly unhooks my legs, holding me steady as he does, and allows me to slide down his body. Once again I am at a disadvantage in height, but I only feel petite, not inferior to him. With one last look, he turns and heads to the phone. I realize I'm standing here, alone, with my boobs on display. While that was all fine and dandy while we'd been kissing, it's just too strange to continue this naked parade, all on my own. I remedy it by pulling up my dress, then checking to see if I'm presentable again. He'd made it look so easy to pull down, but pulling up is much harder with this tight top. Either that, or my boobs just want to stay out for playtime. Soon, I promise them. Dressed again, I try and calm my nervousness by shaking out my arms. If I thought I was nervous before, that was just a sneak peek for the opening credits. I'm practically terrified now that he's gone.

Looking past his archway leading to the kitchen, I can see him through the glass of his patio doors. He appears unapproachable, with his right arm bent on the railing and the muscles tight along his back, his left arm up holding the phone at his ear. The glasses are gone, and I honestly have no idea when that happened. Watching him is not helping me cool down, so I look back into the room for something to distract me. Slipping my shoes off by his door, I head further inside. Everything is exactly how I remember it, including the frame on the side table, that still lies face down beside the lamp. I head straight there before I can change my mind, but glance over to make sure he's still with his back to me. When it's solidly in my hands, I note how heavy it is, considering it's only wood and glass. Must be an expensive frame based on how intricate the woodwork along the edges is. I'm so used to buying things from second hand stores that I know what to look for in quality frames. The wood appears to have been braided, curving around the edges. And it's not some cheap wood either. This has to be teak, but I'm only guessing here. I realize I'm wasting time while I could be easing my curiosity, but I still pause, holding it face down.

I'm not sure why I'm so afraid to turn it over. I guess part of it is that I'm worried how incredibly intrusive this is. Shrugging to myself, I flip it around, to see the image of three faces. Two with a keen resemblance to each other, while the third is questionable. Running my hand over the dusty glass, to better my view of them, I summarize each character, starting with the boy on the right. He was tall, even in his youth, and is still just as handsome as he is right now, standing shirtless on his balcony. I can't tell how old he was at the time of the picture, but he has the lankiness, and youthful appearance, of a teenager. The other boy on the opposite side could almost be his twin, if their height difference weren't so pronounced. Yet, there is a sad expression on the shorter boys' face; he looks lost. We've never met, and yet my heart still hurts for him. He has much longer hair than his brother, but his facial features emulate that of his sibling almost to a tee. I'm confused when I see the boy on the left wearing the locket I've noticed countless times hanging around Jason's neck. Did he lose his brother? Does he wear it as a memorial?

That thought is just too sad to stay focused on, so I move to the third person inside the frame.

In the middle is a woman, probably mid thirties, with a huge smile on her face. The black hair reaches her shoulders in a blunt cut, and she is extremely thin, to the point of frail. Not anorexic though, but still thin enough you want to toss a cheeseburger her way and try and feed her. I try to make out any characteristics that could tie these three together, and only find the brothers to match. The skin tone is wrong, as are the features in general. I guess she could be a second cousin? A Great-Aunt? No, there are just too many differences.

I almost drop the frame when Jason reaches both arms around me and cups my hands. I had just settled my heart beat down to a reasonable level, but it's sprang back to it's fast pace with him near. I wait for him to say something. Will he be upset I intruded in his privacy? Taking the picture from me, he stares at it for a long time. Sighing he says. "My brother...and Ma-ma."

I glance up at the sadness I hear in his tone. I must have the question written in my expression, because he answers without me having to voice it. "She adopted us from foster care when I was 10 and Adrian was just 8." I run this new information over in my mind, and I'm struck by how much closer this makes me feel to him. We have that part of our history in common. "She lost her husband when they were both young. She decided never to remarry, but still wanted kids, and that's where Adrian and I came in." Setting the frame back on the table, so it's face down again, he says no more. I want to ask him what happened to his family, but can't formulate the right words. He leans forward, so he's over my body, and runs his hands down my arms, effectively erasing any previous questions. Our fingers interlock, then he crosses our linked hands in front of me, and tucks my back against his stomach.

I'm surrounded by him. His voice is strained, this time, when he speaks. "No more talking. I need you."

I melt back into him with a mixture of relief and heat. Finally. This is going to happen. Spinning me to face him, he begins to walk forward towards the hallway behind me. But with my steps notably smaller, and me moving in a backward motion, my feet lose their footing and my hands grab ahold of his thick biceps. Though I'd pictured myself on my knees at his feet in a few of my titillating daydreams, I hadn't planned on adding an ungraceful fall into the sexy mix. My plan had a more naughty bent to it, so when I feel myself starting to fall, his arm slips under my legs, pulling me high into the air. He's made his motive very clear.

Focusing on his sharp jaw, I'm unaware we've entered his bedroom until he lays me on top of his firm mattress and stands before me. My skin feels feverish lying here fully dressed, but not due to the dress I'm still wearing. *He* has caused this reaction just by the way he stands there unmoving, penetrating me with his stare. I drop my eyes from his, and follow the movement of his hand, as he reaches for the button on his jeans, and drags the zipper down, affording me a glimpse of dark hair leading down to black briefs. My fingers beg to touch him, but I won't relent from staying still, so I can watch him. When he bends to untangle the jean cuffs from his ankles, his left hand settles at my waist, and even though I can't see them, I sense his fingers run along my thigh. The involuntary goose bumps race along my arms, as if he's touched them as well. Jeans thrown to the floor, he brings his body back up to tower over me once more, but not before running those callused fingers down from my hip to above my knee, nudging me to spread my legs for him. I now get to take all of him in, as I lay with legs open, gazing at his almost nude body. From the close cropped hair on his head, to the hard pecs, his washboard abs, and finally down to his impressive cock, barely hidden by the black briefs. I want to explore him. I feel drunk as I lay here enjoying his strip tease. Hooking his thumbs into the band on his boxer briefs, I notice his erection poking over the top and I hold my breath wanting to see *more*. His size should scare me stupid, but it only makes my body more ready for him, as I witness what is only moments away from joining my body. I'd never understood the phrase '*liquid heat*' until this moment in time. It's like those words have been ripped straight from the dictionary and slammed head-on into my consciousness, not only mentally, but physically as well. I'm on fire for this beautiful man.

Rising up from my position on his bed, I reach for the zipper at the back of my dress and we start to disrobe together. His briefs take only a second to dispose of, and while I want this dress off, fast, I take my time to pull it from my breasts, slowly unveiling my body to him. Sitting on the edge of his bed, with my clothes pooled around my waist, I'm only inches from what I want inside of me. It's beautiful, just like the rest of him. Long, hard, thick. I lick my lips, anticipating his taste. He tolerates my hand extending closer, but just as I graze the burgundy head, he wraps his hand at my wrist, ceasing the motion. As I look back at what I want in my mouth, I'm torn between disobeying his command and simply submitting to him. But I'd promised myself I'd give him all of myself tonight, and that means giving up control, so I relax and give him back my attention. And if I hadn't glanced up, I may not have heard his whispered words. As it is, the whoosh, whoosh, whoosh of my heart inside my head, is blocking all other sound.

"Don't. I need you too badly. Lie back." He demands.

I do as commanded and lift my hips for him to pull my dress the rest of the way from my body. As he slides it slowly down my legs, and on to the floor, he turns his attention back to the scrap of satin still covering my core. His smile turns wicked when he uncovers what I'd hidden under my dress. "As gorgeous as these are, they will have to go." And then they are taken down the same path as before, only this time it turns me on to see his desire spiral further out of control. When he holds them up, close to his nose, I notice the tiny pink triangle is virtually see-through from how wet I am. Putting a knee on the bed he spreads my legs to lie between them. I feel so small under him. I'm surrounded by him. His weight. His smell. Him. He uses his legs to spread me further and bends to take my pierced nipple into his mouth and bites. *Hard.* I gasp as my back arches off the bed. The pleasure rolls through me while his other hand finds my center and pushes upward with pressure then circles his thumb. I am only sensation. Shaking my head against the comforter, my arms fly above me to grab the bedding and my body explodes. Crying out his name, I breathe through the thousand sensations running their course through me. It takes a while for the fog to clear, and my eyesight to focus after coming down, but he's still circling his fingers, prolonging my pleasure.

The pressure from his thumb stills, and then starts back to a soft rub, and my abused nipple is released. Once we're face to face again, he searches my eyes, looking for some reassurance that I'm back with him. My chest rises and falls, drawing his attention downward. I can physically feel the heat from his stare, as he drags his eyes from my face down to my rising breasts. I can't see what he sees, but I can watch the transformation on his face from desire to understanding. He recognizes my other gift to him, and the neglected nipple tingles in anticipation for its turn. The fire burning in his green irises only enhances my own, causing me to squirm under him for more. I'm seconds away from begging, when he brings his hand out from between us, and uses it to tilt my face closer, crashing his lips down onto mine. I can feel my wetness left on his fingers as he moves it up along my cheek and into my hair, then takes a tight grip and pulls our lips apart. Our breath is mixed together, with his mouth directly above mine. If I were to lick my lips I could taste him. I want to bring my hands down to pull his face back to mine, but he's pinned me with his weight, effectively holding me captive. He hasn't released me from his stare since the kiss ended.

I can only see directly above me as he shifts to lie more evenly on top of me, spreading my thighs to an almost painful level. I try to communicate with my eyes that I'm ready, that I can feel him *there* and I want him inside, but he speaks in a hushed tone asking for permission anyway. "Are you sure?" At the quick jerk of my head he continues. "I have never wanted anything more than I do at this moment. You are beautiful laid bare under me. You are *mine*." Sucking in air, I hold it, and the tears start to form. No, no, no, not now. "Say it. Say you're mine." I don't need to think about it. "Yes, I'm yours. Now please, I need you to take me." Then he's inside me, with a push of his hips. He is almost too big for me, but I revel in the sensation of being full, owned by him. He's tied every sensitive part of me into one tingly knot, ready to explode.

"Are you alright?" He asks.

Am I? Seems like such a silly question, but I can see the concern for me when he asks. I don't answer with words, only bring my legs up closer to my core, allowing him to slide further inside. At some point he had released my wrists, allowing me to bring my hands down to his hard back. I caress him, moving them from his shoulders to lower, so I can help guide him. He lets me have the illusion that I'm helping, but we both know who is in control right now. I bite his neck to tell him how good it feels to be owned by him, leaving small indentations at the column. The grip in my hair tightens and he begins to move, me underneath, him above. Nothing can fully describe how this feels. He takes his time building me up, then stops to play with the jewelry in my chest. The fullness at my center keeps the orgasm close to the surface, while he plays. "You bewitch me Neva. Every part of you." I don't want to ruin the moment by speaking, but if I did, I'd tell him he has it backwards. He has stolen my heart right out of its solitary existence, forever sealing it in his care.

His lips meet mine, this time punishing my mouth with bites and sucks, while his grip tightens at my side, branding me with finger-tips. His hips piston at my opening in a hurried rhythm, and I counter his moves upward, not able to back down. I'm moved into a new position, as if I weigh nothing, just pulled closer, or pushed further. Wherever he wants me, I comply with submission. My feet rest on his calves and bear down as my orgasm comes crashing down into me with so much force I can't help the sound from escaping from my throat. A wail, a cry, his name. It's all just a long drawn-out shout. My walls constrict along him and I can hear him grunt by my ear, telling me he felt that too. He pumps two more times, then empties himself into me, making my orgasm crescendo to its highest level yet. My hands that had been digging into his back, move to cup his cheeks, and I lean up to kiss his jaw with a whispered thank you. Neither of us move, just lay exactly how we'd ended, with me spread underneath him, still connected. When he rolls to the side, he takes me with him, keeping our bodies touching from head to toe, and I curl up next to his warmth to let my body rest.

***

I'm facing away from him toward the closed bathroom door with my back spooned into his front, while he rubs his chin back and forth against the goose bumps on my shoulder. He's tracing the letters on my arm, tickling my skin as he goes.

"Tell me what this means. I know what it says, but I want to know what it means to *you*. To Neva, the woman with a heart of gold and the bravery of a million warriors? I want to know you in here." The hand that had been tracing my arm is now pressed against my heart. I look over at what he's referring to and try to find the words to explain.

"All my tattoos have a special meaning to me. I don't just think something is pretty and permanently mark my skin. There is a lot of thought to my process. Let's see." I bring my arm up to let him inspect it closer. "When I was a little girl I loved all things magical. I had a similar upbringing to you; bounced around in the foster system until I was fourteen. Before I was finally adopted, I only owned two possessions that were mine and mine alone. The first was the blanket I was swaddled in when I was found on the steps of the church. No one knew where I came from, or if I was even going to make it through the week, but that didn't stop the couple that took me in, from caring for me. The blanket was blue and green, not pink, like you would usually find around a newborn girl, but…well, it went everywhere with me before it fell apart. Unfortunately I don't have it anymore, but the colors down *here…*" I pull my left arm from under me to show him,"…Are the same as I remember the blanket to look like. Anyway, the other possession was given to me when I was five. I'd already been separated from the couple and moved to a home that cared for orphaned kids, and that Christmas they took us to see, hmm, it was kind of like a Santa's workshop. But not what you'd see today. It was very small. I don't know, the memory is fuzzy but what I do remember is my first Christmas present. It was a stuffed unicorn, with pink and blue hair." I smile as I see the image in my mind. "I loved that thing. Took it everywhere with me. Some days all I had was that animal and my imagination. I would spin tales in my head of magical kingdoms and knights saving the princess. I'm sure that's born into a girls nature, but for me it's what got me through the toughest times." Turning so I can move onto my stomach I prop my elbows on the bed to free both arms. "This is my unicorn." Pointing to my upper left arm. "It's more what I'd picture one to look like, but the coloring is the same as the one I'd carried around for so long. This…" I point lower. "…is my band of mermaids. Another of my imaginations' creation."

I look over at him. He's watching me like I'm telling his favorite bedtime story. I should probably feel self-conscious lying naked in bed with him, but he makes it comfortable to open up the memories from my childhood. He seems genuinely interested in what I'm telling him, so I switch to my right arm.

"Most of what's written on this arm follows things from those childhood dreams. When I met Shelly, we became fast friends. We created this list one night while I stayed at her house, of the places we wanted to visit when we got out of the hell we were both living in. Her mom had this book of places from all over the world. One night we snuck down and brought it back up to her room. We sat for hours looking through the pictures and writing down where we'd go. My favorite place was a small village in France, and I'd butcher the pronunciation if I tried to say it, but it had this castle that was almost exactly the one from my dreams. It was high on a mountain, overlooking the village below. It was beautiful, magical I guess is the best term. This sparked my fascination with France and it's culture. That is why you'll notice every saying, word, or phrase is in French. Some are simple words like *heart, butterfly* and *star,* or this phrase that basically says *to love me for me.* It's a reminder to always be happy with who I've become. The rest are all pretty similar to that theme."

He takes my arm to look closer and traces the words at my wrist. The ring is camouflaged inside them, locking the meaning tight. "And this?" I knew he'd ask. This is the hardest for me to talk about, yet I answer honestly. "It says *to love and be loved.* That was my biggest fear as a child. Never being loved or wanted. I found it for a very short time. That's why it's where I can see it at all times."

He keeps his face blank but continues to trace his fingers along the letters on my arm. I'm suddenly pulled up and on top of him, with his hands against my lower back. As he guides me down pushing himself back inside me, he takes my lips against his in a searing kiss, locking us together. This time he takes it slow. Neither of us is in a hurry; we just enjoy the ride getting there. After we both come back from the peak of orgasm, I lie very still as I listen his breathing even out. Once I'm certain he's asleep I whisper to him *thank you for helping me find love again.* I know he can't hear me, but I needed to say it.

CHAPTER 23

I'm awoken by a sound. Glancing over to the sliding glass doors, I see the darkness through the split in the curtains, confirming I haven't slept through the night. Turning onto my back I reach for Jason and find an empty space next to me, but with nature calling, I decide to tackle that problem first. If I didn't have to pee so bad I don't think I'd ever leave this warm cocoon. I don't remember if the fan was on earlier or not, but I'm cursing the fact I have to get up naked while I'm freezing. I rip the blanket off like you would a Band-Aid, and get up to take care of business.

The last time I'd stood in this bathroom, I had avoided the mirror. But now, I use it to stare at my reflection in utter horror. I'm sure sex hair has to look good on some people, but *clearly* I am not one of them. I contemplate rummaging through his drawers, but I'd bet my last paycheck the man doesn't own a brush. After finger combing through my hair, and washing my mouth out with water, I feel half way back to normal. My body has already darkened in patches around my hips and thighs from how rough we were. I place my hand on my abdomen, running it smoothly over the marks from his fingers. I have this insane urge to tattoo them permanently on my skin as a reminder of tonight. With a final look at the mirror, I decide it's time to find the man responsible for the smile etched into my cheeks. Walking back into his bedroom, I look down at the crumpled sheets, and the discarded blanket. Biting my lip, I flush from the memory of us together. The warmth of that blanket looks inviting, but as much as I'm tempted to crawl back into his big bed, I make the choice to search for Jason. At the doorway to his room, I pause to listen for him, and then ask myself a very serious question. Right or left? Hmmm. The right side of the hall would take me back to his darkened living room, but to my left is unchartered territory. As the living room is dark, I choose the side of the hall that contains the sliver of light. There are three other doors down that way so I make my way to the only light visible through the crack from under the furthest door. I pass one door that has been left open, and can't help myself; I peek inside. Not sure what I was expecting, his bat cave? But I only find a guest bathroom and it's too dark too see any details. As I get a few feet more down the hall, I can hear Jason's mumbled voice coming from the door with the light. Maybe it's later than I thought. Who could he be talking to in the middle of the night? The closer I get, the more I can hear. Not the words exactly, but his tone; it's sounds as if he's angry. I should turn and leave him to his business, on some level I know this, but the craving to see him overshadows that thought, as I raise my hand to knock. With my hand merely inches from touching it, the motion stills at what I hear.

"…no of course not…do you think I don't *know* what I'm doing?… Yes dammit, you think I would risk *everything* for *her*?" My hand lowers and I move closer so my ear can press lightly at the door. My body is chilled standing here naked, and it's not because of my lack of clothes. This doesn't sound like the same man who had worshiped my body only hours before. My mind screams for me to leave, but can't, or won't. Something keeps me from walking away, as if I've suddenly been glued to his carpet. "It's none of your business what we were doing. What… you need me to clarify I wanted to get laid? No…she was just a nice distraction that was delivered last night… Yes. You *know* this. She won't stop me from finishing this." There's silence and I think he's done talking, but I still can't open the door to ask him what he means. I need him to finish this first. "Yes, she has the jewel…when was I supposed to do that?….mmm….once I have it she will disappear, have some trust in me, man. This was always the plan."

Backing away slowly, the floor tilts sideways, and I use the wall to steady me as the hallway blurs behind unshed tears. Could I have heard wrong? I was just a lay to him? And *disappear*? The words tonight don't match the moments we've shared. In fact, if his voice weren't so familiar, I'd have thought someone else had said those words. How could I have got it so completely wrong? There's an acute pain stabbing my chest and causing my body to bend as I apply pressure to ease it. It doesn't help. I want to walk in there and demand he say it to my face. *All of it.* Why? Why would he do this to me? I was giving him what he wanted anyway. If that was all he wanted why not just say so? Why lie to me about needing me and use words like beautiful, or worse, making me admit that I was *his*? Last night meant something to me and I thought he'd felt the same. Maybe not *love*, but how presumptuous of me to think he cared. I am so humiliated. I knew he wanted the jewel, he made that clear, but I was offering myself as well. How *stupid* I am. I should have known someone like him wouldn't want someone like me anyway.

I have to get out of here and *fast*. I turn to walk back to his room searching for my clothes in the darkened room and find my dress in a heap by his jeans. Stepping into it, I hear it rip somewhere in the seam, not even caring that I may have ruined it. An agonizing moan from deep inside me resonates from the back of my throat and sounds loud in the empty room. I. will. not. start. crying. right. now. My mind races as I run my hands along the floor, trying to locate my underwear. What am I doing? Who cares if I'm wearing underwear? I'm taking too long. Giving up the search, I head to the door as quietly as I can, making sure to check that he's not standing in the hall waiting for me, before I move out of his room. The hall is dark, but that doesn't stop me from hurrying, and I make it to the front door without making a sound. My purse lies next to my shoes where I'd removed them hours ago, and I grab both while trying to conceal the rustle of the bag. Before moving again, I stop to listen. Has he heard me? Nothing. As I grip the handle, my sadness at his betrayal is transformed into anger. How dare he use me like this. I'm not one to give of myself without my heart being involved, and I thought I was offering it to someone who deserved it. Shame on me. I make it outside and to my car, not caring at this point if he hears me leave, I just rush to get away from the cause of my heartbreak. The rumble of the engine vibrates my body as I start it, but it could also be from my heart cracking into pieces. Damn him.

The ride home is a blurry image of roads, and a few other cars out this late that fly by my window. I should call Shell so she can turn off the alarm, but if I call now I may wreck from losing my shit. All I'd have to do is hear her voice and it would be all over. I have to keep myself from crying until I can do it without being behind the wheel. I remind myself to breathe. It only helps a little. The light ahead of me turns red and I slam on my brakes, coming to stop a few feet from the middle of the intersection. Oh my God… I need to pay attention and get my mind out of this funk. While continuing to berate myself for my careless driving, I sink back into the seat and attempt to calm my nerves. Gripping my steering wheel with shaky hands, I wait for the green light to signal so that I can complete this miserable journey home. Come on, come on.

Bright lights shine through my driver's side window, making me squint up at the traffic lights to check if it's green yet. The sound of breaking glass and crushed metal are all I hear as my body is propelled sideways. Gravity is keeping me from lifting my head to see what is causing the screech of tires and the grinding of metal.

The whirling motion finally stops, and my car rocks once more, like it's as confused as I am as to which direction is up. Breathing takes effort with the cloud of smoke coming off the airbags. I don't even remember them coming out. I can't seem to push them away from my face fast enough. God, please get me out of this. I can't get any air. The driver's side door is wrenched open, making the cloud of white worsen the sting of my eyes. I feel a tug on my arm, and I'm hauled out into the night, breathing for the first time since I was hit. But my relief is short-lived, as my knees slam against the pavement, jarring my pain-filled torso. There is a split second where the gratitude for my working lungs outweighs the pain, but it's gone when I notice a body lying next to my legs that's not moving. The panic that I've hurt someone mutes my own agony, and I reach to check if he's okay. My fingers glance off his arm just as a glove-covered hand grabs me and hauls my shaky body upwards. The '*wait*' is on the tip of my tongue, until I realize the masked person holding me up must be the reason for the accident. Call it intuition, premonition, gut reaction… whatever makes the most sense. But I *know* this person means to harm me. Using the small amount of knowledge from my one and only defense class, I shove my knee upward, only to be met with another knee. The resonating pain stuns me in place, causing my ears to ring from it. I can't seem to move, even when I watch him bring something out from his pocket, and worse, when he jams it into my injured arm.

I throw my arms up to remove the hands that are around them, but he's too strong to budge. My eyes start to feel too heavy and it takes too much effort to keep them open, so I close them for good, but not before I hear him laugh.

CHAPTER 24

JASON

It takes all my concentration not to throw the phone across the room. I sit at my desk and look at the clutter I'm responsible for, and consider using my arm to clear it onto the floor. That little bit of destruction would emulate my emotions right now. But as I contemplate my next course of action, my eyes zero in on the package that was delivered yesterday, stopping my madness. The chain at my neck serves as an admonition, as the light from my desk glances off the gold and reflects tiny orbs against the wall. I am enraged. There are few things I'm capable of as outlets to relieve my inner demon, yet none of them are as enticing as the thought of bending Neva over this desk. I've sat at this desk, numerous times, since I first saw her, envisioning what she would look like bared to me. But the reality of her, the unleashed passion she offered without hesitation, was so much sweeter than I could have dreamed. She has a radiance that shows itself within every part of her, making me yearn to be near her. And yes, making me *love* her. I can't define the exact moment that pinpoints when that happened. It just *is*. I've only known familial love, never this all-consuming love for another that steals all reasoning. It's a treasure and a curse wrapped in a gorgeous tiny package. I should be dealing with this new complication, but her soft words spoken in the dark, filter through my brain like an incantation.

I place my phone beside the box on my desk, and lean forward, letting my head fall into my hands while using my thumbs to push the tension, building in my skull, back to a reasonable level. This just keeps spiraling further out of my control, and control is all I strive for. In life, and now I can add love to that tally. The purpose for my deception is down the hall, ready for me to take, and I sit here like the bastard I've been programmed to be, dreaming of a life I'll never possess. What would it be like to keep her for myself? I can't say. I have nothing to base this on. Who am I to wish for happiness? My past has not educated me on how to make her happy, so what am I thinking, going down this absurd path? I want to tell her who I am, and what that means, but I have been trained better than that. She may feel she's found something in me to love, but she will realize soon enough I am not worth her devotion. As much as it pains me, I see no happy future for us. Only heartbreak and misery all of my own making. I understood the risk, but took it anyway. Fucking asshole, that's who I am. When this is over I have no doubt she will detest me, but not as much as I will despise myself for hurting her. As soon as I take the jewel away, I will have to say goodbye to her, but in all my extensive plans I'd never predicted her to keep something with her when I disappear. She won't know she takes *my heart* with her, but I will.

I look up at the box on my desk. This was the final nail hammered into my proverbial coffin. I have to complete this or I won't be able to live with myself. The little amount of family I have left depends on me. Getting up from my desk I head back towards my room and the sleeping woman I long for. Shutting the door to my office behind me, I slip silently back inside my room to a hollow feeling. I already know she's gone the second I step inside, but I won't be convinced until I can see for myself. I click the switch by the door, illuminating the room, and stare at the vacant bed. The sheets are pushed to the bottom of the mattress and the comforter, we'd thrown earlier, is neglected on the floor, giving me proof of what I'd feared. The only thing left in its place is the blanket I'd wrapped her in before I left the room. Feeling the sheets for warmth, I find them as I thought they'd be; cold. She's gone. At least from here. I still have a tiny blip of hope she may have wandered to the other part of my house. I don't want to believe she'd walk out after what we'd shared, but I can't blame her for retreating. I *know* I heard her right though.

Making my way into the dark living room, my hope dies a quick and painful death as I notice her shoes and bag are gone. Slamming my fist into the wall beside me, I watch the drywall crumble around my fist just like this fucking night, it turns out. The sting on my knuckles isn't enough not to punch it again, causing the newly painted wall to become ruined and torn. I know how it feels. Leaning my head onto my arms, I feel the blood trickle out from my injured hand. I was already amped from Val's phone-call; I did *not* need this too. What the *hell* am I going to do now? And *why* isn't she here? My mind is at war with itself deciding what pisses me off more. She took the damn stone. That's enough to have me pounding the wall again. But what has me livid is that she's gone. She's *gone*. I'm one contradiction after another. I knew she couldn't be mine, but I wasn't ready to let her go. She was never supposed to be a fixture in my life after we'd accomplished our goal. So why does the thought of her and Drew not being in my life rip me to shreds?

I don't bother getting dressed, just head to the couch and slump down onto the leather, letting my head fall back to look up at the ceiling. I replay the phone call I had with Val one more time, dissecting every remark and my response. He and I both know what will happen if I don't pull through, this much we are in agreement. Months of preparing have just been for nothing. *Fuck.* I was our only hope. He knows I have done *everything* to gain the upper hand. Our method was faultless until now. The plan to keep my distance and my heart closed was not. He read my lies over the phone like the human lie detector he is. I've never brought a woman here whether she's my mark or not, and he called me on it. The pain in my chest gets heavy at the conclusion

I've come to. If she'd eavesdropped on my call, no...there is no way. I've been trained to locate a pin dropping on a busy street. A civilian woman, getting the better of me, in my own home, is ludicrous. The possibility of her sneaking up on me without my knowledge? Is plain impossible. I replay the last thirty-eight minutes back again, and don't find any clue she could've made it past my bedroom door without me picking up the sound. But why else would she have gone? When I left the bed she was sleeping off the rapid release of endorphins, blissfully unaware of my exit. I begin to play the 'what if' scenarios, and continue to drive myself insane.

Would she still have been naked while hiding in the hall? I'm hard just picturing it. My mind flashes to what it felt like to be inside her. She was so tight I was actually afraid I'd split her in two. Her usually pale skin flushed to a dark pink, drawing my attention down to the perfect tits, offered up to me like candied apples. Legs spread like white butterfly wings fit around my waist, like she was created just for me to be there. I mourn the loss of seeing her thighs marked by my fingers.

My eyes fly open at the ringing of the phone, and it takes me a minute to erase the disorientation of heavy sleep. Cracking my neck to relieve the ache from sleeping upright, I stand, and hear my legs crack in the joints as I peel my body from the leather couch. I am too young to feel this old. My kitchen is too bright for my tired eyes as I pass the ringing irritation on the counter and turn the coffee pot to fill. Ignoring the phone, I walk back to my room, to throw pants and a t-shirt on. I can't face this discussion unclothed. The ringing ends and begins again, while I wait for the coffee to do its thing. I'm anticipating more bullshit this morning, and I will delay it till I'm good and ready. Hitting talk, I set it to speaker to keep my hands free, and doctor my coffee just how I prefer it. "Hello?" My voice sounds like my coffee grounds had contained rocks instead of beans.

"Hey, we have a problem." He's talking to me? *WE* have a problem? Last night the fault was firmly placed at my door. What could be worse than losing the stone, *again?* I haven't even dropped that grenade on his blonde head yet. Let's see how much worse he's going to fuck up my morning before I release that info.

"Yeah?" I grunt.

"Got a call from Shayla Keenan this morning." He says. I sense something off in his voice.

"Fine, who the hell is Shayla Keenan and why do I need to know? Unless she can produce the stone, I don't have any reason to talk about her." My irritation is plain in the tone I use, and he knows it.

"You would know her by the name of Shelly. Couldn't figure out why I never found anything on her in my investigation, but Angelo Morretti has seen the light this morning and is singing a fine tune. Does the name Nicholas Tegard ring any bells?" He pauses for me to respond, but I only grunt my answer. "Fine. Anyway, evidently our fine US congressman has a stalking problem. Started years ago and ended with the roommate being pretty bad off. Changed her name and moved states. Had been living with Neva and her son about a year when the husband died. His involvement also confirms our suspicions in regards to how Morretti knew about the stone." I'm not liking where this is going. "She called this morning. I guess your little lady never made it home by the assigned time and she's not answering her phone, so the roommate began to worry, and called me. And as I have been ringing your fucking phone for hours, I'll take a guess that you didn't answer yours either when she tried you. Hence the phone call to me. But don't worry, I'm not calling to bust your balls again about who you choose as a temporary bedmate. I've been informed we have movement over at the Riverside compound. Had Greer hack in to their surveillance tapes on the east and south quadrants pulling as much as we could while they were visible." I'm fitting the pieces together and I'm not happy with the outcome. I will *not* lose my shit until he says it. "The footage shows an unconscious woman fitting Neva's description being carried inside." I hear the cover on the phone crack from my grip, but relax my hand as to not break it before he finishes destroying me. "They must have known there was a chance we had eyes on them, because faces were covered, hers included. But we got a match with hair color and body type. Reports this morning have been pouring in about a hit and run with a Honda Civic 2008 model, at the corner of 24th and Sunset, at approximately 0400 hours. When MPD arrived they found a civilian next to the vehicle and ran the plates; they match. Nothing else at the scene. Another onlooker said the SUV was dark, couldn't tell what color or type we're pursuing, so that's out. John Doe is at Jackson Memorial in ICU, so we won't know what happened from him till he's awake. No wallet on him for identification either. Conveniently, all traffic cameras were shut down in that area. My guess is they'd been following her from your house."

I can't think straight. The bellow is pulled from inside me so loud it echoes through the phone. *"YOU SWORE SHE'D NEVER BE HURT."* The ice in my veins has turned to an inferno ready to explode. She was never supposed to be a victim in this, just a tool we used to fix this fucking situation. I'd already grabbed my cell and keys while he'd been talking, but I wait for him to finish before I walk out the door.

"I know man, I'm sorry. This was not supposed to be how it played out. But you and I both know the two of you never had a chance. And I'm guessing she left with *Le Joya-Azul* still on her person, am I correct? I think that should be our biggest concern, not the girl. Without that, we are fucked. And from what was told to me this morning, it isn't the congressman that has her. Which means this could be exactly the lead we've been looking for." His voice cracks at the end of this, but it doesn't stop my thoughts from deciding to beat him bloody when this is over. *Fuck* the jewel and *fuck him*. I don't care anymore. I will get her back. And God help them if they've hurt her.

"I'm walking out. I'll call you from the car." I hang up without waiting for his bitchy reply. At the door I check my 9mm and stuff the other into my boot, then dial him back from my cell. My mission just changed and I will not fail this time. The call connects as soon as my car's in motion. "I need Shelly and Neva's son brought in. Ask Greer to pull satellite video from 0100 to 0430 starting at my block to Neva's address. I want extra security on her friend Matt as well. You know this needs to be done. I am not asking you, I'm ordering you, as your commander, to get this done. I'll be there in twenty to view what he's found from the recordings." Once again I get the last word in, slamming my phone on the center console. Driving back streets, at maximum speed, I make it to the station in just under fifteen. I will find her. Even if I die trying, I will find her. And this time I won't let her go, *ever*.

CHAPTER 25

NEVA

The dripping sound has been my only companion since I've woken up. I have no reference of time, as there are no windows in my dark cell, just the bare light bulb hanging above me. Looking around the room won't give me any more clues than it did the first several times, but I'll try it again anyway. Besides, I have nothing better to do. Concrete walls and a locked wooden door. That's it. At least they were kind enough to give me a chair to sit on, even if I *am* tied to it. I have yet to figure out where the dripping sound is coming from. As I look around me, the walls are dry, and the ground has dirt covering it, and it's sticking to the bottom of my feet. Of all the issues to pick from here, this should probably be the least of my worries, but I really wish I'd found my underwear.

My nose itches, and as my arms are tied behind me; this poses a serious problem. Turning my head, I attempt to pull my shoulder up enough to rub the itch away. Gah that hurts. I'd almost forgotten about my parting gift from *Captain Jackass*. There was zilch in the sympathy department on that one. My body already ached from my car being rammed at the side; I'm pretty sure it caused my broken ankle and I didn't need a bruised cheekbone to add to it. Thankfully I can't feel the pain in my ankle, only numbness. But the pretty purple color I'm sporting is a nice side effect. I'll have to keep that in mind for picking out clothes in the future. If I have one. It's time I turned away from those thoughts or I'll go insane in here.

I try to arch my neck from the prone position I've been sitting in, but that doesn't help the rest of my aches. I'm happy to have mobility in my neck again, even if it does hurt the rest of me. My head throbs because, *lucky me*, the jackass hit me on the opposite side from where my face was bashed against the car window, leaving me with matching headaches. To add to my maddening issues, my fingers tingle from lack of blood supply and no matter how many times I curl them it just seems to get worse. I'm afraid if I sit here much longer I may just pee in this chair. If that didn't completely gross me out, I'd consider doing it just to piss them off. Ha. See what I did there? I need to stop thinking about pissing. It's becoming too close to a reality. That's it; I've lost my mind. Can you go crazy from being hit on the head?

I try again to shift in the chair and change to a position that's more comfortable, but that's not helping either. How long have I been in here? I was obviously unconscious when they brought me in. That much I've put together. But the time between then and the punch to the face, things get fuzzy. The only memories I *do* have consist of covered faces and pain. Now I'm worried they've forgotten me and I'll die alone in a chair full of piss. I've at least figured out *why* I'm here. I can pat myself on the back for my riddle-solving skills. Well, I guess I can't really, as my arms are tied, but I do it mentally anyways. I'm just not sure *who* they are that took me, although I have a strong suspicion. I sigh. This could only be due to one thing. This damn stone has become such a nuisance. And the icing on the chocolate-covered cupcake? I really miss my boy. I'm scared as hell and all I want to do is see him one more time. I'm comforted by the fact he will always have Shell on his side for everything, but *dammit*, I am his *mom* and it should be *me* that stands by his side. I look up trying to keep the tears from falling and it doesn't help, they fall anyway. If I do die, I know I'm leaving this world having done something right. I am so proud to be his mom. He's the strongest person I know, always seeing the good in our dark world with mean people. It will hurt not to be there to see him grow into a man and witness who he becomes. I'm so thankful he'll have good male role models to look up to with Joey and Matt in his corner. For a short time I thought Jason would be by his side as well, maybe not as part of our family, but still a part of our lives. Stupid, stupid heart...

It amazes me that the emotional pain from his deception hurts worse than the physical pain I've endured since the accident. I have no doubt that I love him. I never stood a chance against falling down that rabbit hole. But, was that what he was aiming for all along? I knew from almost the beginning he was in search of the stone, just not why, and yet I continued down that path like a kitten chasing a string. And I'm kicking myself for not questioning it more. Was I just so ready to be loved again that I couldn't see past my own agenda? Well, he fooled me. And I can get over that. I can...I will. It's not like my heart hasn't broken before, yet this time I got to watch it happen like a slow motion movie accompanied with live action and sound effects. Snap, crackle, pop. Broken heart. What I can't look past is hurting Drew. Jason will forever be nothing but a dark stained memory in my *once upon a lonely time* column. I've learned a valuable lesson in all this. *Never* fall in love again.

The footsteps echoing beyond the door stop me mid rant. I hear the jingle of keys touch the door, and I watch the old brass knob start to turn. I'm not ready to die. Please God, let me see my baby again. From the force they'd set me down in the chair my hair has fallen forward and into my eyes, causing my line of sight to be like looking through a waterfall. I try to blow it out of my way, but the strands are too heavy to have much effect. Through the strands I watch as the door cracks open enough for a pair of black boots to fit through the opening. I remember hearing somewhere that if you can identify your captor then you're as good as dead. This thought keeps my eyes downcast to just his shoes walking closer. I will do everything I can to stay alive. Even if that means I won't ever know who is responsible for this mess.

I'm not ashamed to admit how terrified I am. The panic is starting to set in when the boots stand directly in front of my chair. I can't place the reason why they look wrong, or why that thought even entered my terror-filled brain over the more obvious distress I need to focus on. I let out a shriek as my hair is pulled from behind me, snapping my head back, and my plan to never look is forgotten. Midnight black hair atop a scowling face greets me and confusion has now taken first place over my hysteria. Am I seeing what's really in front of me or has my brain finally decided it's had enough and gone crazy? The voice used sounds too charming to be attached to that black look.

"Surprised?"

CHAPTER 26

SHELLY

I've paced our apartment approximately twenty-three times. Twelve feet to door. Sixteen feet to table. Fifteen feet, and three side steps around corner of couch, to window. Check window. Repeat. I'm a piping hot mess. This is so unlike her. I mean, I'm happy for her if this is nookie-related. That girl needed something other than her BOB for TLC, but I would never have thought she'd not at least *call* me. If nothing more than to say, *'yeehaw, Shell, I got me some'*. The drama lately has put both of us on alert, so she knows I'll worry. The phone in my hand has dialed Matt's number, then hit end, so many times it's pathetic. I just don't know what to say to Drew if I get through. *I'm sorry my little man, but your mom is missing after a night of some bump and grind action. By the way have you seen her this morning? Maybe walking funny?* Nope. That won't work.

Shamefully thinking about said bump and grind, I have high hopes for her and that sexy beast. But I'm not just referring to their intimate playtime between the sheets, although, that man looks like he knows how to play a serious game of naked Twister like he'd majored in it in school. Okay, maybe not Twister, he's too big for that, maybe horizontal Zumba? I bet he's hard as a brick, and can choose to either snap you in two, or slide into you gently. I walk over and check our thermostat. Hmmm. Still 76 degrees in here. Must be a hot flash. The knock at my door seems loud as it interrupts my smut-dream. Fanning my face to dissolve the blush on my hot cheeks, I check the hole through the door first to see who it is. It's been over an hour since I called the blond detective. Maybe he's here to give me news that my worry is for nothing and we're invited to the elopement of the two Zumba dancing love-birds.

The image shows something blue, with shaggy dark hair sticking out. Well, that tells me nothing. I err on the side of *if you're here to kill me, ain't no way I'm opening this door* side, and ask who it is, while checking that the lock is securely bolted. The voice that answers is deep. Like Johnny Cash deep. Yum. Well, *hello* me *lover*.

"Uh, my name is David. David Greer. I'm from the Miami Police Department. Detective Valdez said he spoke with you? I'm here to pick you up and bring you into the station with me. I was kinda their only person. So, if you don't mind, uh…we need to get back there." He says.

Oh. Kay. I need more information than that stilted excuse, but this door isn't making this easy. Unlocking, then opening the front door I stand and stare. Wow. He's probably a good six inches taller than me and has that nerdy/masculine thing going on. He looks like Orlando Bloom's stunt double, with more muscle mass in the chest and arms. If I had to guess I'd say he's close to my age, if not a tad older, which only intensifies my attraction. Scanning the rest of his sexy playground, I start at the bottom and work my way up. You know, for research purposes. He's wearing loose Levi's that make his legs look uber long and amp my curiosity for a peek underneath them. I send out a silent wish he doesn't have chicken legs, then move on, but I'm so tempted to ask him to turn and let me see what the back view has to offer before I do. Keep yourself together chick. But an idea forms before I can stop it. Maybe I'll make him walk down the stairs first instead. Saves me from asking and I get to find out if the tush is as excellent as the rest of him. His white t-shirt is so old it's kinda see-through. And thank you, thank you, thank you for that. What a nice package he has displayed on the underside of that shirt. I could play a naughty game of tit-tat-ho, on there. Even with a baseball hat on I can tell his hair is the perfect length to let my smallish hands grab a hold and pull. I wish I could get a better glimpse at his eyes, but then he'd have to take off those seductive glasses. I don't want to throw the universe into the spin cycle. Not sure I could handle it if he had beautiful eyes too. I close my mouth and peek through the glass over his eyes.

"I'm staring, aren't I? Sorry about that. It's my bad habit to look at hot guys and categorize all their attributes. Anyway, do I have time to grab my purse before we go? And how long are we going for? Is Neva there waiting for me? She will hear a piece of my mind about this. So not cool to scare me." Aaaand I'm rambling. I've turned stupid around this geeky Adonis. It makes me feel slightly less stupid to see a blush on his cheeks. That really is cute. Okay. Time to act like the sane grown up that I try pretending I am. I don't wait for his yay or nay, just run back into the kitchen to grab my purse. A quick check in the glass of our microwave to make sure my hair isn't in crazy mode, and just as I'm about to pull away, I catch the reflection of David watching me. Whoops. Caught me. Oh well. Note to self, act like a sane grown up from here on out. Starting… now. "I'm ready. I was…uh…checking to see if I turned the microwave off." Much better Shell. I'm going for gold here in the dork department.

He looks unconvinced but doesn't call me on my shit. Another point in his favor. "That's ok, but we really need to get back there."

"Can you at least tell me where Neva has been? What's going on?" I see him reaching behind him for something but I ignore it to check out his arms as they tighten while he stretches.

Looking back at me, the V between his eyes forms into two lines, indicating his discomfort. "I really can't say. Valdez will have all that information for you when we get there. Listen, I don't mean to sound rude but I'm supposed to be searching for a few things back at work and I need to get back. Do you mind if we get going? I don't mind, um, well the questions are fine. It's just, I really wish I could offer you more info, but I was told to come collect you and get back ASAP."

I can hear the anxiety and my heart goes out to him. Fine. I can take a hint. "Gotcha, let's roll sexy." He gestures, with his hand, for me to go ahead of him to the door. Damn. That plan's foiled. The walk down the stairs is quiet, except for my sandals flopping against my heels. I turn to ask him which car is his and notice he has a gun held rigid in his hands, aimed at the floor. I just stop and look at him. What am I missing here? "What...?" His eyes sweep over the parking lot checking for... what? "Uh, is Nev ok? I mean, should I be freaking out right now?" I'd stopped on the bottom stair as he moved past me, so when he turns we are almost eye level, and I can see the dark brown irises through the glass. He doesn't look nervous, but there is some emotion that makes my stomach sink and the hair raise on my arms. This is worse than I thought. I mean I had a pretty good idea that these guys looking for the piercing weren't Eagle Scouts, but she was just supposed to be having a night filled with the horizontal hula dance. What went wrong? Now. Now, I'm freaked out. My behavior before this was just a test run. "Which car are we headed to?" At least I sound calm. I cross my arms and stick them in my pits to cover the shaking. He takes one more look at the other cars and motions to the maroon car parked illegally on the sidewalk. Figures.

When we pull into the station, David asks for me to wait so he can walk beside me to the entrance. His paranoia is not helping me calm here. Once we are safely through the glass doors, that I'm hoping are bullet proof, he escorts me to a door just past the busy main area. It's crazy in here. It's like the police station is throwing a party. Not a very *fun* party seeing as there are no appetizers or streamers, but it's almost as if the room is wired for something *big*. The huge man on the far side of the room grabs my attention and I stop expecting to see Neva standing nearby, I only see the blonde detective scowling at him. Before I can question David where she might be, Jason has pushed the other man back into the wall with his hand at his throat. Holy shit that was hot. He's not yelling, as far as I can tell, but I can almost feel the animosity between them from here. If I thought the room was wired before, I hadn't been even close. Several of the men standing nearby are up out of their chairs and trying to pull Jason off, but they aren't even making a dent in moving him. What in the *freakin hell* is going on?

Jason pushes himself away from Valdez and walks to one of the desks, while my eyes follow his every move. The amount of guns and ammunition he's messing with on that desk could start a small war. I stand here, enthralled by this beast of a man, as he checks each compartment of the gun in his hands, then moves on to the next gun and repeats the process. It's like a choreographed dance for policemen. And sexy as hell. My dear Neva, you lucky bitch, which reminds me! I don't know if I'm asking anyone in particular or if the question is just a statement of my confusion. But I'd really like it if somebody started spilling the beans here. "Where's Neva?" I mumble.

"Aunt Shell!"

I turn to the tiny voice coming from inside the room I'm half in, to see Drew dragging a laughing Lizzie behind him. "Oh God little man. What are you doing here? Where's your mom?" He's almost out of breath when he reaches me, and I immediately bend to hug him before pulling Liz up into my arms.

"I don't know. I was helpin' Liz color and Uncle Matt answered the door. Then these guys in black shirts came in and told Uncle Matt we had to go. Where's my mom? Uncle Matt said she'd be here but I haven't seen her. They gave me a soda and told Liz and I we had to wait for you to get here." I wish I knew buddy. I can't tell him that though. I turn to David and notice he's watching our interaction with a strange expression, but I don't have time to figure it out.

"David. I'm going to get Drew and Liz settled in here and then I'm coming back to ask some questions. Be prepared to answer them." Walking in the door of the room with a kid on each arm I find the couch where they'd been keeping themselves occupied. Crayons and a few sheets of marked paper litter the coffee table, set next to three cans of diet pop. Yeesh. No wonder Drew was speaking in tongues a few minutes ago. It'll be a week before the sugar wears off. "Okie dokie bud, how 'bout we see if there's any water bottles in that fridge and then I can help find something for y'all to do while I check on your mom. Do you know where Matt went?"

"Yes."

I wait. "Can you tell me where that is?" Sometimes I forget this super smart boy is only ten.

He thinks for a second. "Oh. Umm. He went down that hall. Told me not to leave or let Lizzie leave. And to color something for mom when she gets here." Just as I thought. He's as much in the dark as much as I am.

I set Liz on the couch and focus on Drew. "Sounds like a plan. Can you keep Liz busy for just a few more minutes while I go talk to Mr. Greer outside the door? I won't be long."

"Ok." He says.

Two water bottles and two new blank sheets of paper later, I'm headed back to where I'd last seen David standing, although now I find an empty spot. Looking back across the room I don't see Jason or his partner either. Well, this sucks. Before I can throw the mother of all she-fits, I see Valdez walk around the corner with visible steam puffing out his ears. Ok, here goes nothing.

"Hey, can someone puh-leeze tell me what's going on?" I expect to get some flippant remark, not for him to rock me into the spin cycle of a roller coaster. I didn't want to accept this was bad. The clues were smacking me upside the head but that doesn't mean I want it to be real.

He pins me to my spot in the hall with his sneer. "Your roommate is in some serious shit. Worst of all she's smack in the middle of it with our only bargaining tool. This never would have happened if she'd just given us the damn stone when she knew what we were looking for. That bitch might just get what she deserves." I can't believe I'm hearing this. Who does he think he is? My fist flies out and hits him square in the nose. Ouch, that friggin' hurt. Shaking out my hand to bring it back to life, I'm about to give him what-for, when I catch the hatred on his face. Grabbing his nose in both hands, he gives me a look with so much hostility, that it has me backing away. He's pulled backward by an invisible force, knocked right to the ground, and I see Jason towering over him. Leaning down Jason threatens his partner, with a lot of colorful words I didn't even know existed then looks up at me when he's through. My body coils tight at the frightening look. He's like a panther before the kill, all sleek muscles and fierce expression.

"Shelly, look at me." I thought I was. But then I really look at him. He's beyond frightening. He's fucking pissed. My muscles relax and my mind calms. Whatever is going on, he means business. "I will get her back. I. Will. Get. Her. Back. I make this my vow to you." He emphasizes his commitment by beating his chest with each stuccoed word. I have no doubt that whatever is going on he'll move Heaven and Earth to fix it. I just need Nev to hang on till her knight gets there.

"Ok." And I believe him.

CHAPTER 27

JASON

I know I'm scaring her. I can smell it on her. I still have my boot atop of Val, holding him stationary. Pushing down slightly with my foot I hear his answering moan, validating my dominance over him, and his behavior towards *my* woman's friend. He should know by now that I mean what I say. And I'm done taking orders from this misinformed *idiota*. He may know the details we are dealing with, but he hasn't worked intimately with the person at the root of this problem. I *have* and know this is no joke. My plans have changed, for that I sorry, only because this affects more than just me. First on my agenda is retrieving the woman who has stolen my heart, and I won't accept anything less than a faultless execution. Second is to eliminate all of those who've caused her harm.

Looking down at Val's burning hatred for me, I come to the realization he has always been out for his own goal. And up until now, we were in accord. No more. I refuse to be the puppet for our demise. His answering leer speaks volumes about his thoughts for me. When he communicates his opinion, he uses my native language to keep his words hidden, reminding me of the mistakes I'm making. Like I don't know what's at risk. It's my blood that's out there waiting for me to make my move. I have no doubt of his feelings on the subject. He has explained them to me repeatedly since the inception of this tragedy. When I answer his statement I use English, informing the persons standing around me of my reply.

"You have a choice to make. You will either fight beside me in this battle, or against me. You have one minute to decide, as I'm walking out that door and finishing this for good. If you make the correct decision, we can work together with the rest. Adrian would not condone your actions. You know that as strongly as you believe in his love for you. He has always been the rock between us all and he's stronger than you give him credit for. We will find where they are keeping him and help him get his vengeance. But not while gambling with the life of someone who has become everything that is right in my world." I make sure he's focused enough for me to continue. "I will let you up, only after you apologize to Shelly for your callous remarks. *Only* then will we attempt to work together." Removing my heavy boot I move closer over to Shelly to demonstrate my accord with her, and watch as he rises off the ground. He still carries the irritation around his shoulders like an invisible cloak, but his expression has changed to one of acceptance. Good. I need him on board with this new purpose, not being an asshole. Reading between the lines of his apology, I detect humiliation at the forefront, but not enough for me to relent from pushing him into action. We've wasted enough time already.

"Good. Let's go." I turn back around so I'm facing Neva's family. "And Shelly? Hang tight. She may need you when I bring her back to you. Be prepared for the worst but have faith I'll get to her before that's a possibility. Matt is being brought up to date on this ordeal and should be back to help with Drew shortly. I think it's best we keep the seriousness from Drew as long as we can, don't you?" She looks back at the room holding my future son and agrees with a solid yes. I look each and every one of my men in their eye and ask them silently if they are joining me. Most of them only have an outline of knowledge on this case. Almost none of them understand that I'm not only leading this case, but am living in the center of it as well. These men may not have the particulars, but they prove with their agreement to help, that they are loyal to me regardless of the reason. It's a humbling experience to witness these strong men give me their allegiance. One I would never take for granted. With a nod to Shelly, and another to my men, we move as one unit, heading for the garage.

***

In the tree line just south of the Riverside compound, I wait and observe the activity surrounding the building. Reports have been filtering in through the earpiece, keeping me connected to my team including Greer at home base, who has his eyes glued to the satellite feed ready to inform us of any new threats. I watch my men fan out in a circular pattern, keeping themselves concealed, using trees and shrubs for shelter. The heavy breathing in my ear informs me Reed has moved into my asked position and I await his feedback on how many we are dealing with. Through my scope, I have Val in my range of vision as he moves behind the grey SUV parked a hundred feet from the entrance to the building. I'm trusting him to keep watch for any trouble as I enter through the side. There are seven of us total surrounding them, although I've made it clear I will be the one to enter alone, as this mission is personal and I may not walk out of here.

"South quad clear. Two up front but facing west. Ready for you to make the call." I hear a similar echo from Simmons and know now is my time to act. Approaching the window undetected takes too much wasted time, but I will just have to make up for it once I'm inside. Peering over the edge, I notice the room I'm below is empty, allowing my entrance to go as I'd hoped. I'm a big guy, so the slide of my body through the window needs to be flawless, or I'll make too much noise. As I climb over the edge and fit through the opening perfectly, I land quietly on the ground. Good. Neva's tortured wail bounces off the hollow walls, freezing me in place by the window. I wait several beats before I feel confident I'm not going to ruin this by acting like a fool and busting through the door. I take my time to silently walk over the concrete floor, rolling my feet to muffle the sound. The room I'm in is filled to the ceiling with boxes, making me weave around the piles. As I get closer to the final pile, I notice each of them is stamped with the letters CXD on the side. Well, gentlemen, when this is through, so is your operation. There is enough contraband and evidence to seal their fates nicely for the rest of their shitty lives. I hear a moan, and the answering laughter reverberating throughout the room only confirms my suspicion. She will regret hurting Neva and Adrian. If this is my last hoorah, I will make her pay.

CHAPTER 28

NEVA

Surprise is just one of many emotions I'm pulled between; confusion, angst and disgust are also vying for first place. This is clearly written all over my face, as she nods, like this was to be expected. I'm not sure if she believes my stunned reaction is due to her being a woman, or if she somehow has the knowledge that I've seen her before. Does she know that I'm aware of who she is? That I saw evidence that she has two adopted sons? Her black hair is longer than in the picture I held at Jason's house, before I was taken. Even two decades older than in the lone picture I saw on Jason's table, she still has the appearance of someone who knows how to take care of herself. The fine lines at the edges of her eyes are defined, showing her age, but the rest of her face is nearly wrinkle free. It's difficult to tell how tall she is with me seated below her, but I can tell that Jason would dwarf her if they stood side by side, and she still has the skinniness of someone afraid to eat. Twenty years younger she pulled that look off nicely. Now she just looks scary, with her bones on display and her face nothing but sharp ridges. I'm feeling very bold, as I glance at this waif, who had to have a jackass tie me up, so I ask the only question eating away at my brain. "So does crazy run in the family or does it end with you? Jason never told me his adoptive mother was a psychotic bitch." I see the slap coming but can't move out of its way. I breathe through the sting on my cheek, which still burns from its earlier punishment from *Captain Jackass,* but keep my eyes from closing so I can keep her in my sights. Note to self: be careful what I say while I don't have use of my arms. That slap *hurt,* like it was intended to, I'm sure. If there was ever

216

a face needed to describe the word evil, she could send in her photo and be offered the chance at immortality in the book of horrors. It's a face described to children at bedtime to keep them in theirs beds. Her cold blue eyes are filled with so much malice I'm shocked I haven't caught on fire where I sit. What does she have to do with this? She puts her face close enough for me to see her pores, causing my neck to bend back at an awkward angle to distance myself, as far away as I can. There is a slight accent as she puts me in my place.

"I see I'm going to have fun with you before you die. Tell me, was it fun fucking my son while he pretended to care for you? Couldn't you see he was just using you to get to me?" I shake my head. Not as an answer, but as a way to block her words. "Ah, I see. Did you fall for him? Stupid wench." She grabs my hair again in her fist and pulls her hand back, until I see nothing but the ceiling above me. This is more frightening than watching her. I gasp as something sharp pierces my side, and black spots float along the ceiling. I think I'm passing out. The sound ripped from the back of my throat is haunted, and somewhere in the back of my consciousness, I'm aware she's thriving on this. My head falls forward when let go from its hold, and I look down at a black and brown handle placed against my ribs. It doesn't look real. Isn't this supposed to hurt? Blinking doesn't help take away the image, only makes the one handle morph into two, then back into one. That is a freaky trick my eyes are playing on me. I want to close them for good, but know that'd be a stupid mistake. I need answers for my impending death before that happens.

"Why?" That's all I'm able to say because the moan that follows steals all other words from escaping. Opening my eyes I see she's now holding the knife I'd just had in my side, but she isn't where I remember her standing. The fact that I've lost time has me terrified, shaking me from the inside out. My body has become cold; at least I think it's cold.

Could I be numb? I only know I'm shaking, because the chair keeps rattling underneath me, but I can't feel myself moving.

"Your husband should never have been in possession of that ring." She walks behind me where I'm forced to do nothing but listen as she speaks. "Le Joya-Azul has been in my family for generations. Imagine my horror when I was informed it was taken by one of my sons and brought to the States to hide from me. I am still not sure how your husband plays into this mess, but by the time I figured out where to look, he was dead. Killed before I was able to meet out my own justice." I hear her clothes rustle as she moves closer and I tighten, expecting another blow or worse, but she stops to continue speaking. "Spoiled boy turned into a spoiled man. It's so cliché my teeth hurt saying it. Rebelled against my ruling. It was simple. Obey *me* and all I say, or be cast aside. He chose to disobey. Loving another man disgusted me and I forbid him from being with his lover. So he took it from me and gave it away. How I found two of the most stupid boys to adopt will remain my burden, until I can take their lives myself." I'm trying to follow along. Parts make sense, while others raise more questions. But the loss of blood is affecting me from asking what I need to know. I need her to keep talking. If nothing more than to help me stay lucid.

"I'll make you a deal." She pauses to laugh like she's just told the funniest joke. Her laugh could give nails on a chalkboard a run for their money. Obviously, I've missed the punchline somewhere. "You really have no choice. But as I'm feeling like the queen I was born to be, having you sit here, I will tell you a story." The prick of the knife startles me upright. I look over and can just make out the new gash on my upper arm leading down. Silly, but my first thought is the sadness I feel for the loss of my tatt. But she's got my attention again, that's for sure. Walking back in front of me I keep my eyes transfixed on the steel in her hands, as she cleans each side of the blade along her pant leg, then settles her body against the wall behind her to tell me her story.

"Mmmm, where to begin? Yes. There once was a girl who had everything. A father who doted on her, her father's men who adored her, and a husband who was everything she dreamed she would have one day. All that was missing was the child born between them to make her world complete, and to assure the legacy of the man who ruled South America. She put all her faith in her husband to make her dreams a reality. But it turns out all he was looking for was a place by her father's side. Not hers." She stops and smiles. "Do you understand what I'm telling you? He wanted my father's approval and not mine. That was the wrong decision to make against someone like me." Again with the creepy smile, like she's proud she is this way. "He was my first kill, and his slut was my second. She had the pleasure to watch me as I sliced his throat before I turned on her as well." Her accent has become dangerously close to unrecognizable in my ears. I have no idea how this fits into why I'm sitting here woozy and tired. "I swore to myself as I stood over their lifeless forms that I would never love again. Never again would I put myself in the position to feel betrayed. And so it was my mission to carry on my father's legacy on my own. I found two boys that…" If there were a word to describe a face that portrayed happy and sad at once, she'd have nailed it. It was a scary combo. "…lost their family. Oh, I may have killed them too, yet the details are immaterial now, and took the boys for my own. They were perfect for me. They might be American, but with their Italian bloodlines, their lineage was camouflaged in my Brazilian home. Groomed to be strong men from a young age, spoiled enough to know that money is power, and handsome enough to welcome into the fold that is my familia. And so it began. The family I had envisioned, minus one cheating bastard, of course.

Yet as they grew, their loyalty was not to me, but to each other. And when I cast one out, they both left me behind. And in their possession was the *joia de familia* - Le Joya-Azul. My father's prized jewel. His true joy. So when *it* left, he was not pleased. Do you know what's it's like to displease the most powerful drug lord south of Mexico? Hmmm?" She walks quickly over to me and gets back close to my face. I can feel her breath on my nose when she whispers her words. "It is not something I wish to sit in this dirty room and recap with you, as you bleed your filthy blood on the floor, but, I will tell you this much: I was forced to live as an outcast until I found it for him. This was his decree." The knife is place gently under my chin to raise it up. I don't know how much longer I can stay awake.

"Years passed as I searched, and grew my own army to conquer my fathers, when finally the time came for it. And as I learned more and more after moving to America, I find that one son became a man of the *law*." I hear her spit after saying the word, almost as if it caused saliva to collect just to utter it. I haven't had my eyes open since she dropped the knife from under my face. It's so much easier to relax into her story with my eyes closed. I'm not even cold anymore. My body is humming nicely with tingles shooting through my arms. I hope I'm able to hear the rest of this, but it's becoming harder and harder to comprehend her words. "And the other shacked up with another man, working as a private investigator. Such disappointments are my sons."

"But, I had great pleasure in reuniting with my Luis. And have kept him safe from that stupid detective that has corrupted his mind, and his brother. I knew taking him would start my plan flowing beautifully. It made my son Marcelo find the wife of the man who was given my heirloom and bring her right to me. Isn't it funny how I was such an amazing *detective* finding my boys who had new identities and both work as *detectives* themselves? And now that I have you, I plan to take back my throne as queen of *Le Carlos* just as soon as you hand it over."

Her voice has gone in and out of focus but sounds closer now. "Now, where would a *cadela* like you hide something like *Le Joya-Azul*? Could she have hidden it on her person? Or did she put it somewhere…?"

I hear banging. Is that banging? My body feels as though it's falling. Or floating. Am I dead? I hit the ground slamming my head against the floor and reviving the searing hot pain I'd forgotten about until now. I lie here alone not caring if I make it back up. I send out a prayer to keep my son safe, and for him to be able to live a happy life. He is my proudest accomplishment and my most treasured joy. I will miss him.

I'm floating again. My head feels funny leaning back and I slit my eyes. I never would have imagined seeing his face in death, but here he is. He's yelling to someone in the room, but nothing he says makes sense. Who is the person he's talking about? I wish I could tell him I'm sorry for the life he's had with that woman. It still hurts to think about his deception, but a part of me understands you do everything for those you love. Even deceive someone who loves you. And I include him in those few people I can say I've loved. Some I loved as the family I never had and some, like him, I let into my heart and loved as he was a part of my soul. I hate that my mouth won't work. I hate that he'll never know. I hate that we were both put into this position. I feel my body shift again against something hard. With my eyes still slit, I can watch his lips move, but I can't hear his voice. I hate that I can't hear him. I look at him and try to communicate everything, but all I say is 'I hate…'" before the room explodes in sound.

CHAPTER 29

NEVA

I try rolling to my side but something hard keeps me from turning. Moving my arm feels like too much work, so I opt to move my head instead. My eyes land on a mop of dark brown hair and I suck air though my nose to breathe in his scent. There is a heaviness on my hand that tells me he has a tight grip on it, so I squeeze it to let him know I'm here. I'm *here*. Alive. And lying next to the sweetest creation ever made. In answer to my squeeze he bolts up, jarring the bed to look down at me. His smile is the brightest thing in the room. "Mommy. I missed you." He lies back down and hugs me hard, pulling me close to him. I will never stop loving his hugs, even if this one is accompanied by a sharp ache in my side. He hears my gasp and relaxes his hold, but thankfully doesn't move far away.

The tears at seeing him move swiftly down my cheeks. "I've missed you too bud. I love you. Forever and ever and always. I'm sorry you were scared." My head turns slowly to look on the other side, as movement changes the shadows on the wall. Shelly is there with tears on her cheeks, holding an equally emotional Charlene's hand. She looks like she's slept here, in her scrubs all night. The dark circles under her red-rimmed eyes have me cringing in sympathy. Yikes, how long have I been here?

"Well, well, well. Look who decided to grace us with her magnificent presence. The queen has returned." Hearing Shell say the words trigger a memory out of nowhere, and I suck in a breath. I try to cover it by pretending I'm in pain. I must not have been as convincing as I'd hoped, if the look between those two is any indication. Attempting to lighten the mood I offer up sarcasm to release the tension.

"Your face is raining Shell. Turn that stuff off please." I can't keep the sob in completely, but the small laugh she lets out does its job. Char takes this time to walk over and place her hand against my shoulder. Her red hair has been unleashed from its tie, and flows around her pale face in beautiful waves. It's so good to see them. But, I want to know how I got here. I *need* to know. My eyes fly back and forth between them, hoping someone offers me the answers. Char reads my mind and looks down at Drew, which makes me turn as well, to see him curled at my side. Her voice is calm when she directs her question to him.

"Hey little man, how about we see if there is anything to eat down in the cafeteria?" He has panic written plainly for us to see, so she offers a compromise. "I promise, we won't be gone long. We will make sure to bring back something for your mom and Shell too. How does that sound?"

He looks at me like I may disappear from the room if he leaves, breaking the little of my heart still intact, to pieces. I don't want him to leave either, but I also don't want him to know the particulars of what I've been through. "It's ok, baby. I won't go anywhere. I wouldn't mind a bottled water if you can find one. And I bet Aunt Shell would love a soda." He's torn, but a desire to please has him gently rising from the bed and taking Charlene's outstretched palm. That's my boy. Again I'm struck by how proud of him I am. He makes it as far as the door, before turning back and running to my side of the bed. The kiss on my cheek is fleeting, but sweet.

They round the corner, and Shell walks over to shut the door behind them. I need to use this time wisely. Shell still has the tears, but seriousness has replaced the sadness, changing the mood once again in the room. "Hey, so break it down for me. What's happened since I've been out? How long have I been here? And I hate to say this, but keep it to the short version. We don't have much time."

She takes the chair she'd been in earlier, and pulls it close to the bed. Only after sitting does she begin. "Alright. Short version. But I can promise you there will be a long version at a later time. There is just too much to tell. First of all, you've been in here for two days. You've woken once, but this is the first time you are awake enough to talk back. You had us a little worried. Anyway, if you don't remember, Jason, or Marcelo, as his dear mother calls him, rescued you... again... this time from her evil clutches. And I mean evil. With a capital E V I L. Crazy. Loony bin crazy. Like..."

"Shell! Time." I don't mean to snap at her. But I need answers.

"Oh, sorry. Anyways, backtrack, when I was at the station, he and his partner got into it. I mean seriously, it was hot, then next thing I know, your man is going all *He-man* on him and swears to me he'll get you back." I don't even bother correcting her about the 'my man' part. "From what I got from Matt, I guess David..." She tips the corner of her lip in a small smile when she says his name. Huh...that's something we'll be talking about later too. "Yea, so David was monitoring where you'd been taken, and seeing as he's their, like, computer wizard or something, he knows how to do that. He told Matt, and of course Matt told me, that when Jason got to you, you were in pretty bad shape. He somehow apprehended his mom, whose real name is Iara-Abril Carlos, or something close to that, and took you out of there. She's equal to the devil. Or the daughter of one, evidently. Remember, I'm summarizing here. He didn't actually kill her, but I heard it was close. You were brought in after they rescued someone else that'd been a prisoner too, right down the hall from you. From the little I could gather, she'd been

224

holding her other son, Jason's brother, in a hole for six months. Would just move him from one hole to a different one so as to not be discovered. The poor guy was in awful shape, but she'd kept him alive to get the other brother's compliance. Get this, she would send things…" She stops and rubs her arms to ward off the shiver. "…And I say *things*, like a finger… a freaking finger Nev. She'd send Jason these things, informing him, *with a finger,* that his brother was still alive and he better get her the ring, or else. It's like some weird movie. This stuff just doesn't happen, or so you'd think, right? But here's the crazy part, and yes, it gets worse…"

Just then, Drew and Char walk back in. He lights the room back up from all the heavy Shell is telling me. I *so* want to hear the rest of her explanation, but now is not the time. He places my bottled water on the side table then walks Shelly's soda over to her. My pain level has been slowly increasing as she's talked, and I'm afraid what that means. I don't want to fall back to sleep and miss out on being with them, but the pain in my side is pretty bad. I try to raise the blanket up to get a look, but Shell stops my hand and looks down at me. I didn't even notice her stand up. "Let's not look right now. Even though you are lying down, why risk it. Huh? I'll gladly describe it to you. I am wearing scrubs, you know."

"Ha. I don't remember you completing med school recently, but thanks. Did I have to have surgery?" I'm not getting a very good vibe at her reaction. If I had to have surgery… so? I'm alive. That's all that matters.

"Yes, you did. I will let the doctor explain the particulars to you, but I can say you have a sprained ankle and a nice cut down your arm that they glued back together. Hate to break it to you, but your tatts will never be the same. The rest I'll have him tell you." She won't look me in the eye when she talks. What am I not grasping here? I'm being selfish, I know, but I don't want to wait for some random person to tell me. I need to hear it from her.

I check to see that Char has Drew occupied, then whisper up at Shelly. "Shell...please."

In the smallest of voices, she whispers back to me, but grabs my hand as she does. "They had to cut out a few things, the bleeding was just too bad Nev. I'm sorry, but they had to give you a hysterectomy." I hear her, but I'm not comprehending the words. She nods like she understands this. "Yes, hon. I'm sorry. There was nothing else they could do." She let's that statement hang in the air. I look over at Drew, and I take it all in. I guess...I guess there's nothing else I can do but accept it, even though a small part of me mourns the loss of not having more children, the thought that I'm alive trumps it all. Right? It'll probably hit me later, but for now there's just this numb feeling, accompanied with the growing pain in my side. And the kicker? I would have loved to give Jason a child. Even with all his 'mommy issues,' I still love him. Have I forgiven him? Not yet. But I do understand it, on some weird level.

Looking back at Shell, I try and smile through my water works. "Ok. Well, I'll have to deal with that later. Did the doctor say anything about pain meds? I really don't want to sleep again, but I'm feeling a little uncomfortable." At my remark, she leans over me and hits the call button next to me. Oh, I guess I could have done that, seeing as it's right next to me. "Thanks" As we wait for the nurse to come, Drew regales us with his week and the shenanigans he and Liz had gotten in to, lifting the dark cloud over my head for a brief time. By the time the nurse arrives to take my vitals and administer more meds through the IV, I'm feeling sleepy again. Before I pass out, I make Shell promise to get Drew home for some rest and a shower, then let my eyelids slide closed, but not before picturing Jason's face as he carried me out of that hell. I miss him. Where is he?

***

This time, upon waking, I'm alone in my hospital bed, but not alone in the room. I see a haggard-looking blond detective standing near the door to my room first then look over to see a familiar face I've never met before.

"Hello." His voice is clear, even though he must be in pain himself. He's sitting in a wheelchair, so I can't tell if he shares his brother's height, but the facial features are almost identical. He's clearly not as muscle-massed, with a thinner face and smaller arms, but there is no mistaking who he's related to. He's an incredibly handsome man. And with a quick peek at the detective behind him, he agrees with my silent opinion as well.

"Hi. You must be Adrian. It's nice to finally meet you." And it is. Nice I mean. Even under these strained circumstances. "It's looks as though she wasn't terribly nice to you either. I may not understand it, but I'm sorry you had to endure it."

He gives me a small smile then turns to his friend behind him. With a nod from Valdez, he looks back at me. When he shifts, I catch sight of the locket at his neck. It's the same locket I'd seen Jason wear ever since I'd met him. I don't have time to ask, before he speaks. "I wanted to meet you, and also explain a few things that you may be wondering about. Clear things up, per se, as you, unfortunately, were dropped into the middle of it. It's also none of my business, but I am hoping you will forgive my brother." He holds a shaky hand up, when I open my mouth to speak, halting my words. "I know, this is incredibly presumptuous of

227

me, but I've never seen him act this way towards anyone. He deserves to be happy, and you seem to do that for him. But he's battling his inner demons right now, blaming himself for things out of his control. He also is quite certain that you want nothing to do with him. This is not helping him heal. I may have physical scars, but his are worse; they are within him. When I mentioned I wanted to speak with you, there was a fire in his eyes I've never witnessed before. He mentioned your hatred for him, but I hope with what I tell you, that you may forgive him for his actions. Don't worry, I will let him do his own groveling, but I may be able to explain a few things before he does."

I don't want to interrupt, but I need to set the record straight before he continues. "I don't hate Jason. Why does he think that?"

He looks shocked by my remark, causing his eyes to widen. "Hmmm. I guess he was wrong then. I should let him explain that to you himself, but he clearly heard your words as he carried you out. I believe the word 'hate' was used. I guess that's what he gets for assuming." He smiles at this. "That explanation will need to come from you, I hope. He will not believe me if I were to tell him, but please, if you'd let me explain, then you may understand what he was up against." At my nod he starts. "After Jason and I escaped from our adoptive mother, we had a choice, make something of ourselves, or continue the path we'd been taught from a young age. After many years, moving from one job to the next, Jason went into law enforcement, and I started my own PI firm. This was an easy decision for us, as we both wanted to correct the wrongs we'd been forced to conduct when we were moved to Brazil with Iara (our adoptive mother). Unfortunately, our good deeds were halted by her discovering where we were, and I was taken to that compound we were both rescued from. But I'm getting ahead of myself. I won't get into the details of my time there, but it was an unpleasant experience, one I hope, in time, can be forgotten. This all started because

I took something of hers. A family heirloom, as it were. Passed down each generation to the firstborn child. The monetary value would be in the millions in American currency. But even as corrupt as their family is, the stone was priceless to them on a higher level. It represented a bloodline of evil, in my opinion. But to them…" He pauses in thought. "…To them the stone was a symbol, you could say, of a united force. And I took it from her in a selfish fit. A choice I regret, but at the time I was young, and wanted to act out against all that we had been put through. This is my burden that I carry, and will for a long time. I put myself, and more importantly, my brother in a dangerous position."

He shifts slightly in his chair, and I watch as Valdez visibly tenses by the door. The love between them is easy to see, and I'm happy for them, if not a tad envious. "During my time as a P.I., I met many people, and one of those people was your husband." What? "Don't worry, he was innocent in all this. But we'd met through a mutual friend of ours, who also worked at the high school. Between the two of them, they helped with an area of my life that I've dealt with since a very young age. Jeremy didn't know it at the time, but his son would be diagnosed with something very similar that same year. It was not something that was understood when I was Drew's age, and I've had to work on it through different avenues."

I blurt out the first thing that comes to mind. "Like medication? Did Jeremy give you drugs? How? He was a history teacher. Right?" I'm so confused.

He offers a kind smile. "No, no medication. Sometimes being around similar minds…it helps to talk things out. He may not have had a… what's the word?" He stops to collect his thoughts. "Jeremy didn't have a frame of reference, as he was not inflicted with the same challenges, but we had the love of history in common. It gave us a comfortable topic in which to start a friendship, and it grew from there. Haven't you ever had a friend that didn't judge? Just listened. Sometimes without a cure for your problems? That was what Jeremy was for me. Most days I felt I was burdening Jason with my issues. It was easier to talk to someone who hadn't grown up with me. I'm sure it was difficult having me for a younger sibling. School was never my strong suit." He ends with a deprecating expression. Wow. I had no clue. I smile to ease his discomfort. I understand this. I don't know what I'd do without Shelly.

"Again, he was not at fault in this. I asked him to give the stone to you. I thought, naively, that by getting rid of it, my problems would disappear. And who better to give it to than someone not connected to our past. I couldn't put the burden on Jason's shoulders, as I've said." Again he stops, to shift his weight. I feel bad he's not lying down somewhere. He obviously needs more time to get well. "The love Jeremy had for you was one of his most treasured possessions. I asked him not to inform you how he came about owning this..." He raises his right arm and shows me a clear bag. Inside sits my piercing, with the blue and white jewel on the end. It shines in the fluorescent light, with the blue twinkling as he twists it. I can't believe that tiny stone is responsible for so much drama. I keep my hands down at my side, barely, but I'm dying to reach up and verify it isn't on me anymore. "...or why he suddenly had something of such value. But as we were friends, he accepted my request and took it off my hands. I wanted to believe that he was none the wiser as to its origin, but your husband was an extremely smart man. The expression on his face, as I handed it to him, told me he knew I was not telling him the entire story. But I will never truly know the answer to that."

He closes his fingers, hiding the stone, and tucks it away in the pocket of his hospital gown. He appears worn out. This has clearly been too much for him. I'm about to tell him to rest when he continues. I close my mouth and listen.

"You probably don't remember, but I was at his funeral," he says. I hold my breath waiting for more.

"I wish I could have offered you my condolences, but I didn't want to draw any attention to myself, or show that I knew him. That would have been a red flag if someone were watching. As it was, I stayed far enough away in the background to stay unnoticed. Because, at this point, I already knew that Iara was looking for me, and I had to plan out how to keep the knowledge of the person I gave it to, a secret. It wasn't until I was locked away, after days of being tortured, that I learned our mutual friend was the catalyst for Iara discovering who had the ring. And in that, I'm sorry I ever gave it to Jeremy, for it's caused you this…" He gestures at my body in the hospital bed. "…result. Again, I am sorry. There are so many things I am sorry for. My apologies will never bring him back to you, but be at peace with the knowledge that his assailants were dealt with swiftly."

I gasp. How? What? Not one sound makes it past my lips, but he can clearly read my look of shock, for he finishes quickly. "I won't offer the specifics, but the two men who mugged and murdered Jeremy are no longer a threat, to anyone." I nod in answer, because what else is there to say to that?

He looks back at Valdez and smiles. It's a secret smile, full of promises and longing. I look away so at to not intrude. "My husband has his own apology to make. And no, we are not married in the traditional sense, but he is my husband in all ways that truly matter. I ask that you forgive him as well." With that I look back over to him. Forgive him for what? Thankfully he answers without my question being voiced. "He was the person behind the notes you found on your doorstep. Yes,

I know about those. He told me, after our reunion that he did what needed to be done, and that was to convince you to hand over the stone. I admit there were, maybe, better ways of accomplishing this, but he and Jason needed to be careful about who they trusted, and how they retrieved it. Neither of them knew what lengths Iara would go to if she knew exactly where to look. We've found out she knew from the beginning, and still played her sick game. Manipulation is her calling card, and revenge I think. Revenge at me for getting the better of her, and for the situation I put her in with her father. She was not happy, I suppose, to learn that her own flesh and blood could so carelessly cast her aside because of a material object. Especially after the betrayal from her husband, it was the final straw, you'd say. In my opinion, she lost her mind a long time ago. Living in the presence of a drug cartel could not have been a healthy upbringing. So, my point is that I apologize for my part in your pain, and I apologize for Val's as well. Maybe when he's had time to settle, he will offer his own to you."

You'd think that I'd have tons to say. But I'm utterly speechless at all that he's revealed. The tiny bit of anger I'd still be holding on to just vanishes. How can I fault him in this? I can't. Even bruised, and battered, and - dare I think of it now? - without the capability to conceive again, I still forgive him. And yes, love him *more*. I wish he were here to offer his own thoughts on this. Turning back to Adrian, I see that Val has moved closer, to offer support to his lover. It's heartwarming to see. Even if I still want to kick him in the shin for scaring the shit out of me with those notes. But, now isn't the time. Later. I owe him that much. Adrian has his hand pressed against the chain around his neck as if it's his lifeline, and he catches me looking.

"I see you keep looking at the locket. Yes, this was mine, from our biological mother. I was sick as a child, and when I spent many weeks in another hospital bed, she gave it to me with pictures of herself, our father, and Jason. This was the first item Iara sent Jason after I was taken. It was to seal the fact that, yes, it was me who she had hidden away. This began a long list of *items* she sent to him." He raises his left arm, which had been concealed from my view, by the edge of my bed. He has a newly wrapped bandage running from his pinky, up to his wrist. At least, it should be his where his pinky is, but that digit is blatantly missing. I suck in air as the realization hits me. This was what Shell was talking about. "This was the second. There were more, but I won't bore you with those details. As my brother, who has been my closest friend and ally for our whole lives, loves me beyond reason, he had no choice but to follow her orders and collect the stone. I don't think losing his heart in the process was planned, but he did, all the same. And for that, I wish him the best, and hope with all my heart, you forgive him." With that final sentence, he's guided out of my room. No goodbye. He came to say what needed to be said, and left. Left me alone, with my thoughts, and a new focus. I lay my head back and make a promise to myself. I will get my man, and together hopefully, we can be a family.

CHAPTER 30

I t's been three days. Three long, agonizing days I've been home and this is the first without my warden, a.k.a. Shelly, to keep me in my bed. Over the course of the three days I've been visited by everyone I love. Well, almost everyone. The one I want to see the most has been silent. I've held my phone, while lying in bed, willing it to ring. Or willing myself to have the guts to make the call myself. But, I'm being selfish again. I'd hoped he would make the decision to come see me, without being prompted to do it. What must he think? I hurt at the thought of him thinking I hate him. I don't. I can't. He's become someone incredibly special. Someone I want around, not only me, but my family as well.

Easing my sore body to the side of my mattress, I take it slow to stand and walk to the bathroom. I haven't allowed myself to look at my scars, not because of my penchant for fainting, although that's part of it, but because I'm not ready to come to terms with it. It isn't *real* until I see it. This has made bathing myself a little tricky. But sponge baths have been my mode of staying clean since I left the hospital, so it hasn't been too big a problem so far. I'm dressed in loose yoga pants, and a long T-shirt that hangs off one shoulder. Both are grey, like my mood, and I stand at the sink to brush my teeth, before I plan to head out to the kitchen for food. My hair looks like mice have taken up residence and thrown one hell of a party. That's just the tip of the iceberg in my many appearance problems. Oh well, no one here to see it anyways.

Drew left for school this morning, as usual, and Shelly had already taken enough days off work, so I have the apartment to myself for a few hours. Matt's at work, working overtime in my absence, and Joey is now the manager of Afterlife, so he's working during the day. This leaves Charlene as my only buddy who isn't busy today. But, as she's spent enough time with this cranky patient, I informed her she's not on babysitting duty today. I love my friends. They are amazing in their own way, but it's nice to sit alone and stew all on my lonesome for once. It feels like a year since I've not felt threatened, nervous, injured, pins and needles, scared…the list goes on. I can just take today and *be*. First things first; come to terms with this scar. Yes, that one. The one on my arm isn't as bad as it felt, when she used the knife to carve me up. I had this vision of it being a nasty, jagged line. But thankfully, the doctor is a miracle worker, and it will eventually be a faint scar cutting through my many words. And my face has started its healing process. I now look like the wicked witch from Wizard of Oz, with green around the eyes. It is not something I plan on imitating ever again. Hmm, maybe for Halloween, though. That'd be sure to scare the neighbors' kids. That thought makes a tiny laugh slip out, then fades again as I look back at my body in the mirror.

I place my hand at my abdomen and it's an instant reaction. Sinking to my knees, I cry out as the internal pain hits me hard. It's not a physical pain. It's of anger, and sadness and finally gratitude; that I'm still alive to mourn the loss of something that can never be. I let go of my stomach to cover my face, and let it all go. My body jolts as thick arms encircle my body. He holds me so tight I can feel his heart beat along my back. I'm rocked gently in his arms, as he allows me to have this time. Lightly moving my hair off my left shoulder, he whispers, *"I'm here,"* in my ear as I'm held by him. It feels so good to finally let this out. I know I'm crying ugly, unattractive tears, but that doesn't stop the cathartic release from deep within me.

After what feels like a lifetime, I lean my head back against his shoulder, and look up, through teary eyes to him. The tracks of his own tears are still wet on his face, and I reach up to rub them slowly away with my thumb. This giant, alpha male, is sitting here, on my bathroom floor, unashamed of showing me his sadness. It's both heart breaking and humbling, matted together in one big ball of emotion inside me. He reciprocates, by taking his much larger hand, and wiping away my tears, still evident, then leans in to gently kiss my temple. Closing my eyes, I realize I'm at a loss as what to say to him. I wish I'd written everything down these past few days, as to what I wanted to say, but the fact that he's simply *here* has me tongue tied. How did he get in here? I relax when he finally speaks, but his arms grow tighter around me, as if he fears I may fall. I have missed his deep voice more than I knew, up until now.

"I'm so sorry." He whispers.

Burying his face into my neck, I hear him gasp in air. His body vibrates with tremors, rocking us both. I think he needed this as much as I did. Reaching up I run my hand, starting at his forehead, over the crown, and guide it back to his face. I feel his large hand move, and he gently places it over my injured stomach. We sit here, holding each other; words aren't necessary, just his presence is soothing enough. And in this moment I fall a little further in love with him. He seems to compose himself, and the muscles soften around me. He raises his face and looks me dead in the eye. "I love you. It doesn't really matter to me that we haven't known each other long. I *know it in here.*" He beats three quick bumps over his heart with a fist. "You walk into the room and I want to fall at your feet, begging you to love me back. You should hate me. The things I've put you through, the things my *family* has put you through, is unforgivable. But, if you can find it in your heart to forgive me, I want to spend the rest of my life making it up to you. I will remind you, every morning when we wake, and every evening as I kiss you goodnight, that I love you. And Drew, he's become just as important, but in a different way. I never wanted children, but I can't not love him as my own. Please, I beg you to say something."

My response is instant. "Yes, yes I forgive you. Yes I love you too. There is nothing to forgive anymore. You have a brother that you've been looking out for, and loving, your whole life. Of course I don't blame you. If there's blame to cast, let it fall on the correct shoulders. Not yours, or your brother's." Turning in his arms, so I can rise to my knees in front of him, I cradle his face in my palms, and move my face closer, so only my eyes are in his line of sight. I want him to *see* it, to *feel* it, that I'm being sincere with him. "And *YES*, to spending the rest of my life with you. I can't imagine a more honorable and deserving man to spend it with, or to be a father to Drew." I rub the fresh tears away from my eyes to witness his reaction. He has a look of such profound joy that I get weak again and start to sit back on my heels. But I don't get far. Once again I'm crushed against him and he murmurs, "*thank you, thank you*" at my neck. I pull away and try to put a serious look back into my expression. There is another important matter I need to address. "Now, I need your help." He acts taken aback at my serious tone, so I smile to complete my request. "I need a shower, like in a *bad* way. I was wondering if you could offer me your sexy self to help me get squeaky again, although no funny business. Doctor's orders. But I could use a hand, or two."

It takes us a minute to untangle our limbs, and get vertical again, but we get there. He makes sure I'm steady, before turning to my tiny shower and starting the water to running. My disrobing is a careful act, full of docile touches that are mercifully pleasant. No pain so far. I keep my focus diverted upward, still not ready, but he takes my shoulders and turns me to the mirror behind me. I'm looking at this huge, sexy man, still fully clothed, with his tan hands against my bare, creamy shoulders. I glance down at my reflection, and see the bandage hiding the incision, and I jerk my chin up and away.

Gently directing my face back to my twin, he tries again. "It's ok, Neva. It will be ok. Look at this body. It is beautiful and I couldn't adore you anymore than I do now." He places his right arm under my chest and drags it down to just above the wound. He has to bend pretty far to reach my stomach, but he's not discouraged by our height differences. "You are still beautiful, no matter that something is missing on the inside. You do not need it to be whole. You have created life inside you, and I won't take away your right to grieve, but know this… you would make an amazing mother to others, not to mention you already *are* to your son; that is amazing. You did that. You've raised him to be a respectable, loving human being. You should be proud of that. And if you want it, we can make it happen again. You and I both know the feeling of being unwanted. To live your life without parents. True parents, ones that would sacrifice themselves and their happiness to secure that for their child. Unfortunately, you and I both have lived with that reality. Let's make a child's life worth living by giving them our love. There are other children out there, waiting for the right mother and father to come rescue them from their own hell. *We* can be those people. Just because he or she isn't created from our union, doesn't mean they won't be ours."

Oh this man. He has surprised me again with his thoughtfulness. It doesn't erase the sadness completely, but it has given me a new purpose, and hope. I think we can truly make a difference with someone. "Yes." My throat was too tight to get it out, so I try it again. "Yes. I want that. That's a beautiful thought. And I'm a little ashamed to be feeling this way. You're right, there are so many kids, waiting, and here I am, sad that I can't have any more children."

"Don't." He turns to guide me to the shower. It has started to fog the mirror and cloud the bathroom with steam. He checks the temperature, before undressing quietly beside me. It's a struggle, but I don't look over to ogle all that he exposes, barely. The heat from the water feels heavenly on my back, and he forces my head to fall under the spray. Oh good

God, please, that's it. More. His hands work in small circles, lathering the shampoo, then conditioning it before he speaks again. "I want you to understand something. You shouldn't ever feel ashamed in front of me. Never. I want you to know, I will always be on your side. In good times, in hard times, in troubled times, or just in times, period. You have a right to feel as you do. Take all the time you need to make sense of your grief. I will never judge or dishonor you, especially for your feelings." He finishes with my hair and sinks low, bending his knees. He's way too big to do it, but he makes it work somehow. Running the bar of soap up my legs, he cleanses my tired body, worshiping me as he goes.

When we are clean, I am wrapped into a towel then smoothly brought up into his arms and carried out to the bed. He tucks the blanket around me then releases the towel, throwing it on to the floor. I have a brief second to panic, thinking he's leaving, before he walks to the other side and climbs in next to me. He's better than the blanket, even slightly damp, but I wouldn't change this for the world. This is exactly where I want to be. I kiss his chest and raise my lips from him, to look him in the face. "I love you, forever and always." He smiles like I'd meant him to. "But if you're planning on being my husband, you should know... I'm a seriously messy person, so I may not have room to talk, but if you ever leave a wet towel on the floor again, there will be hell to pay."

I still have his laugh ringing in my ears, and a smile on my face as I fall into a restful sleep.

THE END

Epilogue

SHELLY

As I sit here, in my chocolate-colored *maid of honor* dress, I have my stockinged feet propped up on the white tablecloth, sipping some damn good champagne. I have a perfect view of the dancing couples, and I'm sitting next to the most handsome man in the room. He looks dapper in his mini suit, including the black bow tie currently sitting at an awkward angle. His hair has been cut recently, so he doesn't look as boyish as I'm used to, but he's still melting the hearts of quite a few women in the room, young and old alike. I look down and see his knee bouncing to the fast rhythm of the song his mom had the DJ play to get this tiny person's groove on. Nudging him with an elbow, I get his attention over to me, and point to the dance floor. Oh, that friggin' smile. Nev and Jason are in big trouble when he gets older. Few more years and he'll be breaking hearts all over school. He bobs his head and we are both up out of our seats to *shake it like my momma made it.*

The little guy can *move.* He takes my hand and spins me like he's channeling Casanova. On my second spin, I catch sight of the happy couple at the far side of the room stealing a private moment to themselves. I can't keep the silly smile from forming, and my cheeks burn from the strain. The little I saw, as I was moving, showed Jason staring down at his new wife with all the love in the world shining in his face. It reminds me of their engagement. That, ahem, *I* had a hand in. Another spin, oiy this kid is cracking me up. He slows us down, which helps me stay on memory lane. Where was I? Oh! Jason had picked up this Casanova from school, and had taken Drew with him to get ice cream, when he asked him permission to marry his mother. Melt. Heart. After they came to a happy agreement, Jason dropped him off with me and picked up Nev for a late 'dinner', where he surprised her with flowers, a walk on the beach at sunset, and a friggin' rock for a diamond. And, of course, dammit, Jason wouldn't let me hide in the bushes to film it. You know, for documentary purposes. Spoil sport. I had to live through it from Nev's detailed description. But, I'm so happy for them. I'll never forget the expression on her face when she retold the events of their night, and also the look of horror that she couldn't keep from me at the diamond engagement ring she held in her hand. Thankfully, for her, she picked the best of men to agree to marry, as he bought her a chain for it to rest around her neck, alleviating her weird ring phobia. And I was let in on the secret that before they head to Venice, and that's Venice *Italy* not Florida, Jason will be getting his first tattoo. Yup, that's right. The two will be getting matching wedding band tattoos. The freaks.

Maybe one day... Nope. Hell no. Not happening. As the song finishes, I bend and kiss Drew's head and thank him for his mighty fine dancing skills, then watch as he heads over to the table full of teenage girls. Yikes, I should stop that. Oh well, it's gonna happen some day anyways. Shrugging to myself, I head back to my lonely table, but the tall man I've had some naughty thoughts about moves in front of me, about ten feet away from where I'm standing. I haven't seen him since the trial. He definitely comes in second for most handsome man in the room. I usually see him wearing jeans and T's, but tonight, he's jaw-droppingly hot. Tonight, he's decked out in his own suit. Yet this is far from mini, with his long legs and torso. Longish dark hair is brushing his eyebrows, and he keeps pushing it out of his face. I think it may be too crass for me to yell across the room for him to leave it alone, so I stow that impulse for later. The last time he and I were in the same room, was at Jason's bitch of a mother's trial. I was there for moral support, of

course, for Nev, as she had to testify. Not an easy time for any of them, but thankfully we won't ever have to worry about seeing her outside of a barred cell ever again. Go team Justice.

David disappears around the corner and I watch like some kind of fanatic. All I need is a sign with his name, and twenty other girls behind me screaming *I love you*, to make it perfect. Le sigh. It's a dream that will never come true anyway, so why do I want to kick my own ass at letting him walk away? I complete my trek to the table that holds my forgotten champagne, with my high spirits effectively dampened. Stupid, stupid thoughts and dreams. Everywhere I look there is love bitch-slapping me in the face. I walk around Adrian and his man, who I just smile at rather than flick him off like I want to. Neva may have forgiven that blonde idiot for his actions, but I'm still holding onto that grudge like a toddler to his toy. I do give Adrian a genuine one though. He's growing on me, like fungus, but it's still better than his boy toy.

I finally reach my drink, I mean the table, and can hear a buzzing noise coming from my seat. I know good and well I didn't bring my vibrator, so the next logical device would be my phone. I look around to make sure I'm not needed, then sneak myself, and my purse, to the hallway, and out the side door. As I'd learned the hard way, a long time ago, never lock yourself out, so I take my shoe and shove it in the crack of the door, before fishing my phone out. Clicking the bottom button to light the screen up, I see I have three missed calls from a private number. Well, hello Miss Popular. I don't remember handing out calling cards, or making a banner. As I'm staring at the unknown number, it rings again, and I answer before the first ring has ended. "Hello?"

"Well, hello Shayla. You looked ravishing in that gown tonight. I have missed our dances. Have you missed me as well?"

The phone slips from my hand and cracks on the pavement. The champagne I had thought was such a grand idea makes an unwelcome return, landing next to the ruined phone. Leaning back against the brick wall, I wipe my chin, and say the first thing that comes to my mind. "Shit."